ASHLEY FARLEY

AFTER
THE
STORM

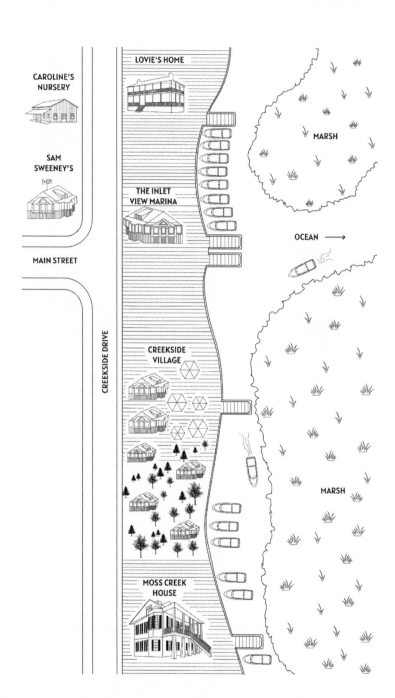

For my darling girls, Emmie and Willa

prologue

The storm systems slammed into the South Carolina coast as a Category 1 hurricane with 80 miles per hour winds. Driving rain pounded the window from which Sean watched pine trees sway and the tidal surge spill over the seawall into the yard. With dusk setting in, he could barely see the dock or the marsh beyond. The damage to the area would be widespread. Meteorologists really blew it by predicting the hurricane would be downgraded to a tropical storm. Most locals didn't consider it a threat and therefore didn't bother to prepare.

A loud banging sound startled Sean away from the window. At first, he thought a tree had fallen on the house, but hearing the noise a second time, he realized someone was pounding on a door. Who in their right mind was out in this weather? His parents' home on their ten-acre estate was secluded—the last house at the end of a winding inlet creek—and sometimes creepy, especially when he was here alone in a storm.

After checking the front door on the main level, Sean hurried down the stairs to the game room. The figure in the door's window stopped him dead in his tracks. He almost didn't recognize his own twin brother at first. Cooper looked like he'd been through hell.

Sean unlocked the bolt, swung the door open, and hauled his brother in out of the storm.

He engulfed Cooper's drenched body. "You scared the heck out of me, Coop. What're you doing here in the middle of a hurricane?"

"When I left Richmond, the forecast was only calling for rain and wind gusts. I didn't know it would be this bad. It's raining so hard, I had to drive ten miles an hour from Charleston."

"Thank goodness you made it safely." Sean helped Cooper out of his sodden raincoat and draped it over the back of a chair. "Come on up." He motioned him to the stairs. "I was getting ready to make some dinner."

Cooper cast an uncertain glance at the door. "I should get my stuff."

"Forget it, bro. You can get it tomorrow." Sean nudged him toward the stairs. "I stopped by Sweeney's and picked up some mussels on my way into town."

"I'm not hungry. But I could definitely use a drink," Cooper said as he traipsed up the stairs. He went straight to the bar in the family room and helped himself to their father's whiskey.

Sean watched him with curiosity. Cooper usually preferred beer.

"What're you looking at?" Cooper asked, filling the glass with ice and brown liquor.

"You! You look awful. When's the last time you showered and shaved? And since when do you drink the hard stuff?"

Cooper mumbled something Sean couldn't make out, but he didn't ask him to repeat it. Something was off about his twin, but Cooper would confess his problem in due time.

Sean went into the kitchen, removed a bowl of mussels from the refrigerator, and set it on the counter. He was melting a chunk of butter in a pan when his cell phone blared out a piercing alarm. An automated voice alerted them to a tornado sighting and directed them to an interior room on the lowest floor.

"So much for dinner," Sean said, returning the mussels to the refrigerator.

The lights blinked several times. "There goes the power." Sean grabbed a battery-operated lantern off the counter. "The downstairs bathroom doesn't have windows. It's probably the safest place for us."

The brothers were halfway down the stairs when the house went dark. Sean clicked the lantern's power button, but the light didn't come on. "Ugh. The batteries must be dead."

"And you call yourself an Eagle Scout." Cooper snatched the lantern from him and fiddled with it a minute. "Yep. Dead batteries."

"For the record, I got more Scout badges than you," Sean said, and used his phone's flashlight to guide them through the game room.

Closing the bathroom door behind them, the brothers sat side by side on the floor with their backs against the wall. Sean turned off his phone's flashlight to preserve his battery, and they were once again enveloped in darkness. "Why didn't you tell me you were coming home?"

"It was an impulse decision. I needed to get away from Richmond for a while," Cooper said with an unfamiliar edginess in his voice. The twins were close. Even though they lived in two different cities, two states away, one rarely made a move without letting the other know.

"How long are you staying?"

"Indefinitely. My boss gave me approval to work from home."

Sean's suspicion mounted. "Indefinitely doesn't sound like an impulse trip to me, bro."

"Stop with the inquisition already," Cooper grumbled. "Why are you here anyway? I thought I'd have the place to myself."

"Good to see you too," Sean said, sending an elbow to his brother's ribs.

"Where are Mom and Dad?"

"In Charleston. They were invited to a big engagement party tonight. Since I was coming down for the weekend, they asked me to secure the house. I took the boats out, but since the storm wasn't supposed to be bad, I didn't bother with the hurricane shutters."

"You've been down here a lot lately," Cooper said. "How are you managing so much time off work from your busy restaurant?"

Sean sighed. "Believe me, my boss isn't thrilled with me at the moment. But that job is getting old. I've been thinking about moving back to Prospect. Competition for restaurant management jobs is steep in Charleston. I have a better chance of finding something here."

"I couldn't wait to leave South Carolina when I went away to college. I was eager to spread my wings and set the world on fire. But lately, I've been homesick for the Lowcountry. I miss my family and the outdoor life."

While Sean couldn't see his brother through the darkness, he imagined the expression of longing on his face. "Mom and Dad are thinking of selling Moss Creek. They're hardly ever here anymore. Maybe they'll change their minds if we both move back."

"I hope so. Moss Creek is our home."

"I still enjoy spending time here," Sean said. "I'll be heartbroken if they get rid of it."

The floor beneath them vibrated. "What's happening?" Cooper said with fear in his voice.

"It's the tornado, bro! Cover your head."

Lizbet stood at the door with her suitcase at her feet and a backpack filled with cherished mementos from her brief marriage slung over her shoulder.

"Where are you going?" Jamie asked, his face a mixture of confusion and concern.

Lizbet hesitated, asking herself if this was really what she wanted. Once she took this step, there was no going back. "Home. To Charleston."

The bottom dropped out of his stomach. "But this is your home now," he said, spreading his arms wide.

"You know what I mean. Tradd Street is where I grew up. It will always be my first home."

"But why do you have to go now? In the middle of a tropical storm?"

Lizbet stared down at the floor, unable to meet his dark eyes. "I need to leave while I have the nerve."

She sensed him moving toward her and saw the toe of his Xtratuf boot when he drew near.

"The nerve for what, Liz? What're you saying?"

She inhaled an unsteady breath as she raised her gaze. "I need some time to myself, Jamie. I'm having a personal crisis."

Emotions marched across his face—bewilderment, anger, and fear. "How long will you be gone?"

"I'm not sure. Indefinitely."

He shook his head, as though baffled. "I don't understand. Are we separating?"

Lizbet bit down on her quivering lower lip. "I don't know."

"You don't *know*? Where is this coming from? We've built a life together."

A beautiful life. Her dream life. "I realize that, Jamie. I'm confused about some stuff right now, and I need to get my head straight."

"What about your job? Are you just gonna walk out on

Annie?" Jamie's voice was tight, and she could tell he was close to tears.

"She'll find someone else." Lizbet fidgeted with the zipper on her yellow raincoat. "Business is way down, anyway. Annie should close the Garden Cafe and let your mom use the space for the wine shop she's always talking about."

"Where will you work when you come back?"

If I come back, Lizbet thought. "I'll find something more challenging. I have a degree from the finest culinary school in the country. I'm overqualified to manage a sandwich shop."

Jamie took her hands in his to stop the fidgeting. "So, this is about your career?"

Lizbet shrugged. "It's about a lot of things."

Outside, a tree branch cracked and dropped to the ground with a loud thud. "I should go before the storm worsens," Lizbet said, reaching for the doorknob. When she turned the knob, the wind blew the door out of her hand, banging it against the wall. She grabbed her suitcase and darted down the sidewalk to her car before Jamie could stop her.

Tears blurred her vision as she drove away from the small house she and Jamie had so lovingly renovated. She smiled through her tears at the memory of them refinishing the floors and painting the kitchen cabinets. They'd put down new tile in the bathrooms and hung fresh wallpaper in the master bedroom. They'd turned the second bedroom into a home office, but she'd had such big plans for the third bedroom.

Lizbet let out a loud sigh as she merged onto the highway, heading for Charleston. Jamie's happiness was all that mattered to her. If she couldn't give him what he wanted, she would step aside so someone else could.

Jamie ran out of the house after Lizbeth, but she sped off down the street before he could stop her. He remained at the end of the sidewalk until her taillights disappeared out of sight and a crack of lightning sent him running back inside.

He wandered around the empty rooms, oblivious to the rainwater dripping from his clothes. Signs of Lizbet were everywhere. The pink lipstick smudge on the coffee cup in the kitchen sink. Her silky bathrobe hanging from the bathroom door. Her phone charger on her nightstand. Why leave behind essential items like her robe and charger? Was she in such a hurry to get away? Or was she not planning to be away for long? He remembered what she'd said when he asked how long she'd be gone. *Indefinitely.*

None of this made any sense. Lizbet had been subdued lately. He'd tried talking to her about what was bothering her. But his wife was a private person. From experience, he knew it was best to give her space when she got in a funk. He felt marginally relieved. Lizbeth needed some girl time with her sister in their Charleston childhood home. Brooke was a level-headed young woman. Jamie trusted her to offer Lizbet the support she needed.

When he could no longer stand the silence, Jamie grabbed his raincoat and hurried out to his pickup truck. He navigated the neighboring streets that were lined with renovated ranchers, much like his own. He turned left onto Main Street and drove slowly through town. He was unprepared for the flooding he encountered as he approached the T-intersection at Main and Creekside Drive. His heart sank at the sight of four feet of water in Sam Sweeney's on his left. His grandparents had started the seafood market over sixty years ago. Fortunately, they owned the land. They'd rebuilt after a fire destroyed it several years ago. They would rebuild again if necessary.

Straight ahead, his headlights illuminated the assortment of boats floating in the parking lot at the Inlet View Marina. If things were this bad in town, Jamie knew the flooding would be even worse for the houses further down the inlet. Some residents would undoubtedly lose their homes. He hoped his mom and Eli were safe. He pulled out his phone to call them, but the cell service was out.

This system turned out to be way more than a tropical storm. Locals would be cleaning up from Hurricane Ian for years to come. At least Jamie would have something to occupy his time while Lizbet was gone. Pain gripped his chest. What if she never came back?

one
lizbet

Lizbet hid behind the kitchen doorjamb, eavesdropping on her sister's conversation with her partner.

"I can't take it anymore," Sawyer said. "You have to talk to your sister. All she does is mope around here, day in and day out. Her negative aura will be detrimental to the baby once I'm pregnant."

"You're being melodramatic. Liz is going through a rough time. We need to be sympathetic."

"I *have* been sympathetic, Brooke. She's been living here for seven months, and she hasn't been on a single job interview. Why can't she live with your dad?"

"You know why. His condo is only one bedroom. Besides, this is my family's home. Liz has as much right to live here as I do."

"Then maybe we should find our own place."

Lizbeth sneaked out the front door, the sting of Sawyer's words continuing to bite at her as she strode angrily down Tradd Street. The truth hurt. She did mope around all the time. She did have a negative aura about her. And she did need to find a job. Sawyer and Brooke were ready to start a family. They shouldn't have to move. Lizbet needed to get her own place. Unfortunately, she was flat broke and couldn't afford the rent.

She could no longer hide out in her house. She would have to look for a job. But how would she explain the seven-month void on her resume to potential employers?

Lizbet tripped over an uneven sidewalk paver, catching herself before crashing into a crepe myrtle tree. She leaned against the tree while she composed herself. She had one option. It wasn't ideal, but desperate times called for desperate measures.

She typed out a text to Annie. *Do you have time for coffee this morning?*

She waited under the tree until Annie's response came a few minutes later. *If you can come by the shop? I'm swamped with work. We have two large parties tonight.*

She took a deep breath. *I'm on my way.*

Lizbet's concerns about working for Tasty Provisions were legitimate. Serving fried oysters on ritz crackers to snooty people at cocktail parties held little appeal to her. The bigger issue was the obvious conflict of interest. Annie was Jamie's half sister. She would be ticked off at Lizbet for leaving Jamie. On the other hand, Annie and Lizbet had been friends before Jamie and Lizbet started dating. And Annie could offer her the temporary work she needed while she finished sorting out her life.

Lizbet took a left at East Bay Street and walked four blocks to Tasty Provisions, the gourmet shop Annie owned with her mother. The renovated warehouse building was also headquarters for their catering company with the same name.

The door was locked, the gourmet shop not yet open. Peering through the window, Lizbet spotted Georgia dusting a rack of wine bottles and waved to get her attention.

Georgia flung open the door and engulfed Lizbet in a bear hug. "I heard you were back in town. I'm disappointed you haven't been to visit me."

Georgia used to live next door to Lizbet's family on Tradd

Street. Not only was she Lizbet's late mother's best friend, Georgia had been Lizbet's confidante during her troubled teenage years. Many times over the past months, Lizbet had been tempted to reach out to Georgia. But how could she explain her problems to Georgia when she didn't understand them herself?

Lizbet pushed away. "I'm sorry. I've been figuring out some things." Truth be told, Lizbet had figured nothing out. Correction, she'd figured one thing out. The most important thing. The thing that complicated everything else. But at least she was here, taking the first step back into the real world.

She stood back to admire the shop. Tasty Provisions sold everything from gourmet pepper jelly to prepared dinners to unique hostess gifts. "The shop looks fantastic, Georgia."

Georgia's face lit up. "Thanks, sweetheart. Heidi has finally turned all the purchasing over to me."

"Good for you. You're certainly doing an amazing job. I'm here to see Annie. I guess she's in the back."

"Either in the kitchen or upstairs in the office."

Lizbet pressed her cheek to Georgia's. "I've really missed you."

Georgia gave her a squeeze. "And I've missed you. Don't be a stranger."

"I won't. I promise."

Lizbet burst through the swinging door into the kitchen where the staff was bustling about, preparing for the evening's events. In the two years since Lizbet was last here, Heidi had expanded her kitchen into the vacant storage room behind the real estate office next door, which gave them more than ample room for all their catering needs.

Lizbet darted up the narrow stairs to the office, where she found Annie seated at her desk with eyes glued to a computer screen and pencils poking through the honey-colored bun atop her head.

"Here." Annie's eyes remained on the computer screen as she

handed Lizbet a coffee. "I'll be with you in a sec. I need to get this email out."

Lizbet accepted the coffee. "Take your time."

The office was cramped with two desks, one facing the window where Annie was working and one on the opposite wall. Stacks of files were piled high on every surface, including the only other available chair. With nowhere to sit, Lizbet leaned against the windowsill while she sipped the lukewarm coffee.

Annie appeared frazzled when she finally turned away from the computer to face Lizbet. "What's up? I was surprised to hear from you after all this time," she said in a frigid tone.

She expected Annie to be angry, but the vibe Annie was giving off was downright hostile. "I need a job, Annie."

Annie lifted a perfectly manicured brow. "You've been in Charleston since early October, and you haven't found a job yet?"

"I've been offered several. But they were the wrong fit." Lizbet couldn't believe how smoothly the lies rolled off her tongue. "But now my savings is gone, and I'm desperate. I'll bartend or be a server, whatever you need."

Annie crossed her arms. "In a foodie town like Charleston, I have a hard time believing you couldn't find the *right* fit."

Lizbet stared down at her coffee. She hated lying to her friend. "I was too ambitious. I don't have the right experience for the jobs I applied for."

Annie studied her for a minute, as though deciding whether she was telling the truth. "I have an opening for a temporary position. Heidi and I thought of you when we created the position. But we have reservations about hiring you."

"Because of Jamie."

"He's part of it. I don't approve of the way you left him for no apparent reason."

Lizbet fingered the lid of her coffee cup. "I needed to get away to clear my head. I had no intention of staying away so long. The days turned into weeks and then into months."

"To clear your head of what, Lizbet?"

"I've been under a lot of stress. I had some health issues I needed to deal with," Lizbet admitted.

Annie's anger morphed into concern. "Health issues? I hope it wasn't anything serious."

"I'm not gonna die or anything like that." Lizbet sipped her coffee. "Being stuck in a dead-end job didn't help. No offense, but you and I both know the Garden Cafe wasn't doing well."

"Which brings us to the other reason I'm hesitant to offer you a job. Your sudden departure from Prospect was timely. The storm damage was the final nail in the Garden Cafe's coffin. But if it weren't for Hurricane Ian, I would've been left without a manager. You didn't just walk out on Jamie. You walked out on me too. I'm not sure I can rely on you, Lizbet. How do I know you won't bail on me again?"

Lizbet's gaze shifted to the window. Two blocks over, she could see the steeple of St. Philip's Church where she and Jamie were married two years ago. "I can't guarantee anything right now, Annie. I'm asking for a favor. I'm flat broke, and I need a job. I don't understand why you need a lifetime commitment when you have servers and bartenders who come and go all the time."

"This position I mentioned would look better on your resume than serving or bartending. It's a project that requires the skills of a trained chef. But even though it's temporary, I can't afford for you to walk out in the middle of it."

Lizbet gulped. Was she ready to commit, even to a temporary gig? "I understand."

"Sit down, and I'll tell you about the job." Annie gathered up the files from the other chair and added them to the mountain on the second desk. "You can see from this mess we need help."

Lizbet's heart sank as she lowered herself to the chair. "I'm not interested in an administrative position, Annie."

"That's not what this is." Annie swept an arm at the files cluttering the room. "Some of these are weddings and event files. But most are menus and recipes we've collected from magazines and various other places. Our catering menu has grown entirely too large. Some items need tweaking and others need to be removed. In addition, we're looking to expand our offering of prepared meals in the gourmet shop."

Excitement stirred inside of Lizbet. The position sounded ideal. "So, I would be your research chef."

"Exactly. You will be testing a lot of recipes. You'll have full creative control, and you can cook until your heart's content. The project estimate is three months."

"And afterward, if I do a good job . . ."

"If you've sorted out your life, and you're planning to stay in Charleston." They talked for a minute about salary and benefits.

Lizbet, relieved to once again be employed, sat up straighter in her chair. "Thank you so much, Annie. I promise I'll do a good job for you."

Annie offers her a sincere smile. "I'm sure you will, Lizbet. But now, I need a favor from you."

Dread overcame Lizbet. She knew the favor would have something to do with Jamie. But how could she deny Annie when she'd just given her a job? "Name it."

"Please talk to Jamie. It's not fair to leave him hanging. The uncertainty is weighing on him. Either give your marriage another chance or file for divorce."

"Giving my marriage another chance means moving back to Prospect, and you just made me promise I wouldn't bail on you."

"If necessary, you can work remotely."

Feeling the onset of a headache, Lizbeth massaged her temples. "I don't know, Annie. I'm still so confused."

"At least explain to Jamie about your health issues. He's a sympathetic guy. He'll understand. You owe him that much."

Lizbet's shoulders sagged. "I guess you're right."

Annie got up and pulled Lizbet to her feet and into her arms. "I'm glad to have you back in my life. I've really missed you. If you'll let me, I'd like to help you work through your problems."

"That really means a lot, Annie," Lizbeth said, even though she wasn't yet ready to discuss her problems with anyone, most of all Jamie's half sister.

Annie held her at arm's length. "When can you start work?"

The idea of going home to an empty house with nothing to occupy her time held no appeal. "Is now too soon?"

"Now is perfect. You can use Heidi's desk."

Lizbeth glanced at the desk. "Are you sure?"

"Positive. She's hardly ever here. She's either out meeting with clients or working from her office at home."

They spent a few minutes dividing the recipe files into separate piles—one for events and the other for weddings. When they finished, Lizbet refilled her coffee from the kitchen and began the arduous task of studying recipes. By the end of the day, she'd identified the recipes she wanted to experiment with.

Georgia had closed the gourmet shop and gone home when Lizbet finally came down from the office. The early May evening was steamy, a promise of the sweltering days to come in the months ahead. She walked south on East Bay Street three blocks before cutting over to her father's waterfront building.

Phillip greeted her with the same long face he'd worn since her mother died several years ago. "Sweetheart! This is a pleasant surprise. Come in," he said and stepped out of the way for her to enter the tiny condo. "I was just microwaving a Stouffer's lasagna. Would you like some?"

"Thanks. But I didn't come here to steal your dinner. I have a favor to ask you." Lizbet sat down at the kitchen counter while he dumped Caesar salad from a bag onto a plate. "Do you ever go out to dinner with friends, Dad?"

"Occasionally. I have a few lady friends I entertain from time to time." The microwave dinged, and her father removed his lasagna, transferring it to his plate. "I know what you're thinking.

But I'm not romancing them. They truly are just friends. Your mother was my one and only."

"You never know what the future has in store. You're still young. And handsome. Some lovely widow would be lucky to get her claws into you."

"Humph. I'm too set in my ways. I'd make her miserable. Don't worry about me, sweetheart. I'm doing just fine on my own."

Lizbet studied him more closely as he tore open the dressing bag with his teeth. He didn't look well. His skin was pale and his eyes sunken. "Are you feeling okay, Dad?"

"As fit as a fiddle." He came around to her side of the counter and sat down next to her with his plate. "You mentioned a favor?"

Summoning the nerve, she blurted, "I need to borrow some money. I'm moving out of the house, and I need money for a deposit and first month's rent on an apartment."

Disappointment crossed his face as he sunk his fork into his lasagna. "So, you're not going back to Jamie?"

"Not anytime soon. There are places that offer short-term leases. I'm in a bit of a bind. I haven't worked in months, and I spent all my savings on living expenses." She crossed her fingers under the counter as she told this little white lie.

"You need to work, honey. Staying cooped up in the house all day isn't good for you mentally," he said, and tapped his temple.

"I got a job, actually. I started today. I'm working for Annie at Tasty Provisions. As soon as I get my first paycheck, I can pay you back.

He shoveled lasagna in his mouth. "But I thought you were happy living with Brooke and Sawyer."

Her throat thickened as tears neared the surface. "They're hoping to start a family, and I'm just in the way."

Phillip's brow pinched in concern. "Did you and Brooke have an argument?"

"Something like that," Lizbet said, remembering the conversation she overheard this morning. *All she does is mope around here, day in and day out. Her negative aura will be detrimental to the baby.* Sawyer was the one so eager to get rid of her.

Her father set down his fork. "I'm worried about you, sweetheart. You ran away from your problems with Jamie, and now you want to do the same with Brooke. You need to work through your issues, Lizbet. You girls own the house *together.*"

Lizbet shook her head as though confused. "But you gave Brooke the house after Mom died, just as Gran and Gramps gave it to you and Mom when you were first married."

"No, Lizbet. I didn't *give* them the house. The deed is still in my name. I told them they could live there rent-free with the stipulation that you are always welcome to stay there. If they are making things difficult for you, they should be the ones to find somewhere else to live."

In Lizbet's mind, the deed was a technicality. The house was the perfect home to raise a family, which Brooke would soon have and Lizbet never would. She slid off the stool to her feet. "Everything's fine. We just had a sisterly disagreement. We'll figure it out." She kissed her father's cheek. "Prepare yourself. My new job requires a lot of recipe testing, and I'm counting on you to be my guinea pig."

He got up to walk her to the door. "I'll never say no to your cooking."

Her father's words weighed heavily on her during the walk home. *You ran away from your problems with Jamie, and now you want to do the same with Brooke.* She'd promised Annie she would talk to Jamie, a conversation that was way overdue. All her life, she'd avoided conflict. But she was a grown woman now. She could no longer run from her problems.

jamie

S am Sweeney's was a beehive of activity as the staff prepared for their first wine tasting on Friday evening. Fortunately, the building experienced minimal flood damage from Hurricane Ian, and Jamie and Sam were able to reopen the market in time for the Christmas rush. But the cafe side of the building was a different story. Once Annie decided not to reopen the cafe, Sam and Jamie began collaborating with a commercial interior designer on plans for the wine shop. These past few weeks, their builder had been working overtime to finish before summer. The completed project was stunning, a sleek space that complemented the upscale gourmet market with sophisticated quartzite tasting bars and custom wine racks painted a handsome navy blue lining the walls.

Jamie observed the team of black-and-white clad servers hustling about, preparing for the tasting. He whispered to his mom, "No wonder Sean and I can't find employees. You've hired them all to serve wine over here."

Sam chuckled. "All my empty-nester friends were looking for part-time work to occupy their free time. Wine tasting is right up their alley."

Jamie took a closer look at the servers. "Now that you mentioned it, these women are kinda old for waiting tables and throwing out dock lines."

"Hey!" Sam sent an elbow crashing to his ribs. "Watch who you're calling old."

"Wait until you meet my new day manager, Winnie. She's twenty-six but looks sixteen. She's a real badass. You're gonna love her. She reminds me of a younger version of you."

Sam cut her eyes at him. "I can't tell if that's a compliment or not."

Jamie laughed. "Badass is my highest level of praise." Through the wall of windows, he noticed a large motor yacht pulling up at the end of the dock across the street. "I should get back to the marina. Is there anything else I can help you with before I go?"

"I think we're in good shape for the wine tasting. But there is something I've been meaning to talk to you about." Sam held the door open for him, and they stepped outside together. "I'm worried about you, son. You've lost so much weight, and you're working so hard. Too hard, in my opinion."

He chucked her under the chin. "I'm a chip off the old block. I inherited my work ethic from you."

She grabbed his hand. "Seriously, Jamie. Have you taken any time off for yourself lately?"

He set his warm brown eyes on her. "I'm fine, Mom. Stop worrying. Hard work never killed anyone."

"That's not true. Stress causes high blood pressure and heart conditions. Have you heard anything from Lizbet?"

Jamie's face tightened. "Not a word."

"If you ask me, you're both being bullheaded. Why don't you try reaching out to her?"

"Because she's the one who left me. I have to wait for Liz to make the next move."

Sam pulled Jamie out of the way of a group of tourists waiting to cross Main Street. "Marriage is a partnership. It's not just about what she wants."

"I honestly don't know what to do, Mom. My emotions are so conflicted. On the one hand, I feel like I'm treading water. If divorce is what she wants, I'd like to know now so I can move on with my life. On the other hand, I'm terrified of losing her." Jamie massaged the back of his neck. "I figured I'd give her until the end of the summer. If I haven't heard from her by then, I will consult a divorce attorney."

"You know I'm not one to judge people, but I still can't believe she walked out on you like that. She sure fooled me. She's not at all the person I thought she was."

Jamie noticed his one dock attendant struggling to tie up the yacht at the marina. "I've really gotta go. My guy needs help. I love you, Mom." He kissed Sam's cheek before darting across Creekside Drive and through the marina parking lot. By the time he'd reached the end of the dock, Jed had secured the boat. Based on the width of his dock, the boat was over ninety feet long. Vessels of this size rarely visited their humble marina, and he wondered if the boat's owner was someone important.

"Welcome to Inlet View Marina," he called up to the prominent looking gentleman behind the wheel on the flybridge. Jamie assumed the man was the boat's owner. "Are you stopping for fuel? Or will you be staying with us overnight?"

"Both," the captain said as he shut down the rumbling diesel engines.

"Do you have a reservation?" Jamie asked.

"Doesn't look like I need one," the captain said with a sweeping gesture at the half empty marina.

Heat rose up Jamie's neck. "No, sir. Just making sure we don't double book. When you're finished fueling, we'll move you to the end of the next dock over."

The captain gave him a thumbs-up. "Once I'm situated, I'll settle up with you in the marina store."

A pair of tanned and toned legs in white shorts came down the ladder from the flybridge, and an attractive blonde crossed the cockpit with hand extended. "Hi! I'm Kirstin Bowman. Sorry we didn't radio ahead. My father and I are on an exploration expedition. We never know where we're going to land from one day to the next."

Jamie shook her hand. "Jamie Sweeney. Welcome to Prospect." He glanced at the stern. The boat's name, *Bad Attitude,* and *Nantucket* were painted across the transom in gold block lettering. "You're a long way from home. We don't get many New Englanders around here. What sort of exploration expedition are you on?"

"We're searching for waterfront property to develop."

Jamie's guard went up. "Develop into what?"

"An upscale shopping and dining complex. Waterfront, of course. Looks like you've got a gracious plenty of land." She inclined her head at the wooded property south of the marina. "How many acres are there?"

Jamie massaged his chin. "Hmm. I'm not sure in terms of acres. The lot extends about a half mile down the road with the inlet to the east and Creekside Drive to the west."

She slid her sunglasses down her nose and stared at him with piercing blue eyes. "Why hasn't anyone developed it before now?"

"I can't answer that. A few buildings used to occupy the vacant land nearest us—a hot dog hut, ice cream parlor, and gift shop. But the hurricane flooded them out last fall. So far, there's no evidence they plan to rebuild."

Kirstin moved to the edge of the dock, shielding her eyes as her gaze traveled the waterfront. "It's the most impressive spread we've seen. Does the same person own all of it?"

"The same family. When the original owner, Jeanne Franklin, died a few years back, the land passed to her three children—two sons and a daughter. I'm not sure if they own it collectively, or if they divided it up into parcels for each of them."

"Do any of the siblings live in town?"

"Not that I'm aware of. I went to high school with Carl, the oldest son. I could get in touch with him through social media if you decide to inquire about the property."

"I may take you up on your offer." Kirstin started up the dock, and Jamie stepped in line beside her. "The marina looks new. Are you the owner?"

"I am. The original marina, built around the turn of the last century, was also devastated in the storm. I bought it from the previous owner, who couldn't get out of town fast enough after the hurricane." Jamie chuckled. "We salvaged the marina store and restaurant, but we had to start over with the docks."

At the end of the dock, they climbed the ramp to the small porch off the marina store. "You did a marvelous job. It has a cozy Lowcountry feel."

"Thank you. This building was way overdue a facelift. For the most part, I'm pleased with the way it turned out, but I still have some changes I'd like to make."

Kirstin rested against the railing, looking out over the marina. "My father will want to know more about the property. Can you join us onboard for dinner later?"

"I promised my mom I'd help her with a wine tasting from six until eight. My family owns the gourmet seafood market across the road."

"Cool!" Turning away from the railing, she squinted as her blue eyes traveled to Sam Sweeney's. "Very nice. How about if I stop in for a sip around seven thirty, and we can walk back to the boat together afterward?"

Her determined tone let Jamie know she wouldn't be deterred. "Sounds like a plan."

She took off her sunglasses and slipped them into her purse. "Since your family is in the seafood business, I don't have to ask if you eat lobster." She furrowed her brow, as though struck by a thought. "Unless, maybe, you have an allergy. Which would be a bummer in your line of work."

Jamie shook his head. "No allergies. And I love lobster. Unfortunately, we don't get enough of it in the Lowcountry."

"Our chef knows just how to prepare it. I think you'll be pleased." She touched his chin with a pink lacquered fingernail. "Well then, Jamie Sweeney. I look forward to seeing you tonight."

He watched her slender figure disappear inside the marina store. The idea of having dinner with Kirstin stirred a desire he hadn't felt in a very long time. He shouldn't feel this way about another woman when he was still married to Lizbet. Then again, he was a normal man with a healthy sexual appetite, and his wife had been gone for seven months. He told his mom he would give Lizbet until the end of the summer to get her act together. Maybe he was more ready than he realized to move on with his life.

Heads turned when Kristin arrived at the wine tasting in a white knit sundress that clung to her shapely body. Jamie, despite being married, was still a man, and she was one smoking hot young woman.

He introduced Kirstin to his mom, and the two women became fast friends. Sam's blue eyes brightened when Jamie explained Kirstin's mission. "That's wonderful! That type of development would boost tourism and be a major draw for the masses moving here from Charleston." Her smile faded. "We're talking about the property south of the marina, right?"

Jamie knew what his mom was thinking. The property north of the marina was not for sale.

Kirstin nodded. "We may eventually want to expand northward, but we love the curving shoreline to the south." A dreamy expression crossed her face. "I can see it now, the meandering boardwalk lined with quaint shops and restaurants with lights twinkling at dusk."

"Just make certain none of your tenants are seafood merchants," Sam teased, but there was a hint of warning in her tone as well.

Kirstin laughed. "Yes, ma'am. I'll keep that in mind."

"We're gonna head out, Mom. Kirsten's father is waiting for us to eat dinner."

"Go!" Sam motioned them to the door. "I've got everything under control here. Enjoy your dinner. And Kirstin, let me know if I can help with your project."

"Will do," Kirstin said, wiggling her fingers at Sam in parting.

"Your mom looks so young. And she's *so* pretty," Kirstin said as they stroll down the dock to the boat.

"She's fifty-seven. But she takes good care of herself. She works harder than anyone I know."

"I can tell Sweeney's is her passion. Do you co-own the market with her?"

"Co-manage. For now, she's the primary proprietor. But it will be mine when she retires. *If* she ever retires."

Kirstin's father, Arthur, was waiting for them at the table on the aft deck. A steward opened a bottle of champagne and served them platters of oysters on the half shell. Arthur was not only knowledgeable about the seafood industry, he was also an avid outdoorsman. With so many shared interests, the men found plenty to discuss during the subsequent salad and main lobster courses. If talking about hunting and fishing bored Kirstin, she didn't let it show.

When they finished dessert, Arthur excused himself for bed, and Kirstin invited Jamie to stay for an after-dinner drink.

Kirstin touched her finger to her lips. "Shh! Don't tell Dad. We can sample his port collection." She poured a splash of clear garnet-colored wine into two snifters, handing one to Jamie.

Jamie sipped the port. The liquid burned his throat, and seconds later, a comforting warmth washed over him.

"We're heading out in the morning," Kirstin explained. "We have a few more places we want to check out near Hilton Head and Beaufort. But I have a hunch I'll soon be back to do more research, at which time I may ask you to contact the property's owner."

"I'm happy to help in any way. I have a vested interest in your development. An upscale shopping complex would bring in a lot of business for the marina. Let me give you my number in case you have questions."

As he recited the number, she keyed it into her phone, but she didn't offer her number in return.

The port went to Jamie's head, and when Kirstin pressed her cheek against his, he resisted the urge to kiss her on the lips. He would never cheat on Lizbet, even though they'd been separated for seven months.

Bidding her goodbye, he left his truck in the marina parking lot and walked two miles to his house. The exercise and night air sobered him up from the effects of the alcohol and the giddiness of Kirstin's presence.

Jamie had had enough. He couldn't wait until summer's end. He'd given his wife more than ample time to work through her problems, and he'd heard not a single word from her since early October. For all he knew, she was shacking up with someone else. He wasn't even sure she was still in Charleston. He remembered his mom's words from earlier. *She's not the person I thought she was.* Jamie wanted to give Lizbet the benefit of the doubt, but she certainly wasn't acting like the woman he'd married. The time had come for him to have a long overdue heart-to-heart chat with her. The problem was finding the time to drive to Charleston to see her.

three
sean

S ean wandered around the restaurant, admiring the newly installed benches, tables, and chairs. When his cousin bought the marina after the hurricane, Sean had jumped at a chance to take over the restaurant's lease. Located above the marina store, the sweeping views of the inlet and downtown area had prompted him to change the name from Pelican Roost to The Lighthouse. In keeping with the nautical theme, he'd installed beadboard wainscoting and painted the walls navy and the ceiling pale blue. He'd completed most of the renovations himself, including restoration of the random width oak floors and teak bar.

Sean entered the refurbished kitchen to find his head chef studying something on her iPad. He'd been lucky to find someone with such talent, and her young age didn't concern him. Carla's resume spoke for itself, even if she had jumped around a lot in the few short years she'd worked as a chef. She possessed the fresh creativity he'd been looking for, and she understood food better than anyone he'd ever met, including his Aunt Sam.

Carla absently toyed with her dark ponytail as she scrolled the screen of her iPad. She was stunningly beautiful, with dimpled cheeks and almond-shaped emerald eyes. But her manner was strictly professional. Whenever Sean inquired about her personal life, her responses were guarded. She reminded him of his mother, in both looks and professional demeanor. He never thought he'd be attracted to someone like Jackie, but there was something intriguing about Carla Grant. Perhaps it was her mysterious aura. She'd told Sean little about her upbringing. She was originally from Columbia, but she was not close to her family. If she had a significant other, she was keeping that a secret. Regardless, Sean realized the potential problems that could arise from being involved with his head chef.

Looking up from her iPad, she flashed him a smile. "I was just sending you the completed menus. As we've discussed, I recommend changing them with the seasons. We can always add items, but I think this is a good place to start. Of course, we'll offer multiple specials every day."

For more than a month, Sean and Carla had been taste-testing dishes. The result was a casual menu offering a modern spin on Southern food.

"Sounds good," Sean said. "Now all we need is staff to run the restaurant. I'm getting worried, Carla. Our soft openings begin in less than two weeks."

"You have me and Randy," Carla said, referencing the bartender who had been with the restaurant for nearly twenty years.

"And I'm grateful for you both. But we need at least six servers, two dishwashers, a couple of hostesses, and a team of line cooks."

Carla snapped her iPad cover shut. "It's the first week of May. College kids will start flocking to the area, looking for summer jobs. I realize you'd prefer full-time employees, but at least they will get you through the summer."

Sean tapped his chin. "Good idea. You might be onto something. Any thoughts on how I might go about finding these college kids?"

Before she could answer, Carla's phone pinged with an incoming text. Snatching it up, she let out a soft moan as she read.

Sean furrowed his brow. "Is something wrong?"

"My babysitter just quit on me," she said, slamming her phone down on the stainless-steel counter.

He chuckled, assuming she was joking. "Since when do you need a babysitter?"

"Since I had a baby four years ago. Is that a problem for you?" she asked in an icy tone.

Sean's hands shot up. "Hold on a minute. There's no reason to get hostile. Of course, I don't care if you have a child. I'm just surprised. We've been working closely for a month. Why haven't you mentioned it before now?"

She let out a slow breath. "I'm hypersensitive about it because of my age."

Sean could understand that. Carla was twenty-six, which meant she had the child when she was twenty-two. He knew from her resume that she'd attended the University of South Carolina. But he couldn't remember if she'd graduated. Did she drop out of college to have the kid? "Is it a boy or girl?"

"A son. Josh." Picking the phone back up, she thumbed off a text and stuffed her phone in her back pocket. "If we're finished for the day, I should get home."

"Of course." He gestured toward the door. "I'll see you in the morning."

After she left, Sean spent a few minutes at his desk in the small adjacent office, going over the menu one last time before sending it off to the printer. After locking up for the day, he hurried down the outdoor wooden stairs to the marina store.

As boys, Sean and his twin brother had loved coming to the marina store with their father. The store had carried everything from fishing tackle and bait, to boat maintenance supplies, to apparel bearing the marina's logo. There'd been a freezer chest in the back filled with ice cream treats. Sean and Cooper had always gotten the same thing—Klondike Cookies and Cream sandwiches.

Jamie was nowhere in sight, and Sean was surprised to see a young blonde behind the counter. "Who are you?"

"I'm the new day manager. Who are *you*?"

"I'm Jamie's first cousin," Sean said. "You can't seriously be old enough to manage the store. Are you even out of high school yet?"

She leveled her gaze on him. "I'm four years out of *college*, thank you very much."

Sean gave her the once-over. "Well, you don't look a day older than sixteen. Jamie must've been desperate if he hired you."

She planted her hands on her hips. "Why would you say that? I'm perfectly capable of managing this store. I'm the only child of an avid outdoorsman from John's Island. I bet I know more about boats and fishing than you."

"I doubt that," Sean said, rolling his eyes. "You never know who's gonna walk through that door," he said, tossing a thumb over his shoulder at the door. "Some tough characters come into this store. Pretty little thing like you will be an easy target for all kinds of verbal abuse."

Her brow hit her blonde hairline. "Pretty little thing like me? Why you—" She was about to lay into him when Jamie emerged from the back office.

"Hey, cuz! I see you've met Winnie," Jamie said, joining Winnie behind the counter.

The corner of Sean's lip twitched. "Winnie? What kind of name is that?"

Jamie's eyes popped. "Sean! Why would you say that? What's wrong with you?"

Her blue eyes flashed with anger. "Let me handle this, Jamie. I can fight my own battles." She glared at Sean. "For your information, my parents named me after my grandmother—Gwendolyn."

Sean considered the name. "Gwendolyn is better than Winnie. Why didn't your parents call you Gwen? Were you obsessed with Winnie the Pooh as a child?"

Winnie looked up at Jamie in disbelief. "Is this jerk really your cousin?"

"He is my cousin, and he's not usually so rude. I don't know what's gotten into him today." Coming from behind the counter, Jamie took Sean by the arm and marched him toward the door, calling over his shoulder to Winnie, "Hold the fort down for me. I'll only be a minute."

On the boardwalk, Jamie turned to Sean. "What was that about? I've never seen you act like that."

Sean shook his head. "You're robbing the cradle, man. You're asking for trouble."

"You're one to talk. Your head chef is only a year older than Winnie."

Sean angled his body toward the railing, looking out over the inlet. "At least Carla looks her age. You know the bums who come into your store sometimes. They will eat her alive."

"I'm not worried about Winnie. She can take care of herself." Jamie squeezed his shoulder. "Is something else wrong? You're not yourself today."

Sean exhaled a gush of air. "I'm freaking out because my restaurant is opening in two weeks, and I don't have any employees."

"I know what you mean. This labor market is lean. I was fortunate to find Winnie."

"I'm thinking of hiring some college kids to get me through the summer. Do you, by any chance, know any?"

"That's not a bad idea. I'm still looking for dock hands and shop assistants myself. Some of my friends have siblings in college. I'll send out some texts and see what I can come up with. What about Cooper? You could hire him to wait tables."

The mention of his twin brother caused Sean's pulse to race. "Cooper already has a job. Although I'm surprised he hasn't been fired. All he does is paint scenery and birds."

Jamie nodded knowingly. "He showed me some of his work. I'm impressed with his talent. Has he mentioned anything about returning to Richmond?"

"Not yet. I have no clue what's going through his mind. I've tried talking to him, but he doesn't have much to say about anything, especially whatever's bothering him." Sean sighed. "I've never seen him like this. He's in a dark place, and I can't lure him out of it."

"I know what you mean. I stopped by the farm to see him the other day. He looks like death."

Sean gave his cousin a playful shove. "You're one to talk. Your clothes are hanging off of you."

Jamie laughed. "Who has time to eat? I've been busy restoring the marina and helping Mom get the wine shop ready."

Sean looked down at the pristine docks below. Approximately half the slips were occupied with charter fishing boats and sailboats. "Well, your hard work paid off. You did an amazing job."

"Thanks. But we're only at fifty percent capacity. I'd feel better if I could fill the empty slips."

"Give it some time. You're lucky to have that many, considering the number of boats destroyed in the hurricane."

"That's a good point. Most of those owners are in the market for new boats."

Sean turned away from the railing. "Have you heard anything from Lizbet?"

"Nope. But I have heard nothing from a divorce attorney either."

"That's a good thing, I guess." Although Sean wasn't so sure.

He didn't approve of the way his cousin's wife had been jerking him around.

Sean pushed off the railing. "I should get going."

Jamie walked him to the parking lot. "I'll let you know if I come up with any summer workers."

"Same. Maybe we'll get lucky if we combine our resources," Sean said and started off toward his truck.

Jamie yelled, "And be nice to Winnie the next time you see her!"

Sean raised his arm over his head and waved.

He was getting in his truck when he received a group text from his mother to Cooper and him. *Your father and I have something important to talk to you boys about. We're coming to dinner on Sunday night. We'll bring a casserole.*

Here it comes, Sean thought. *They're putting Moss Creek on the market.*

He thumbed off a response. *Don't worry about bringing food. Cooper and I will cook for you.*

Sean hadn't seen his parents since Christmas. They'd only spent one night when they'd planned to stay three. If they were upset with Cooper for taking over the master bedroom, they didn't let it show. They led busy lives in Charleston, his father with his medical practice and his mother at her design firm.

Sean drove five miles south to Moss Creek. A sense of peace settled over him as he navigated the winding gravel driveway. The property was in his blood. He was as much a part of the land as the moss-draped live oaks. They'd been fortunate to only lose a few of the majestic trees when the tornado came through during the hurricane.

The plantation style home had been renovated many times since it was built in the mid-1900s. The main living space, including the master bedroom, was on the second floor. Three additional bedrooms occupied the third floor and a game room with a pool table and large-screen television took up the downstairs. Off the living room on the second floor, a covered veranda with daybed swing and comfortable seating extended the width of the house.

Cooper was perched in the corner of the veranda with his easel when Sean arrived home. Passing through the house, he emerged onto the veranda. The brothers were carrot tops as young boys, but over the years, their wavy hair had darkened into a deep reddish-brown. Until recently, they looked so much alike even their parents struggled to tell them apart. But the unkempt shoulder-length hair and full beard covering Cooper's face made them easily distinguishable.

"What're you working on?" Sean peered over Cooper's shoulder at the white bird with the S-curved neck on his canvas. The marsh was a natural habitat for egrets. This one frequented their dock, and Cooper had painted him dozens of times. The pair of binoculars Cooper used to study the bird rested on the railing beside him. "Don't you ever get tired of painting the same subject?"

"Obviously not."

Sean plopped down in the chair nearest Cooper. "Did you get Mom's text?"

Cooper's deep blue eyes remained glued to his canvas. "Not yet. My phone's inside. What'd she say?"

"They're coming for dinner tomorrow night. They have something to talk to us about. I'm sure they're selling the house." Sean watched for his brother's reaction, but Cooper didn't flinch. "We'll have to find somewhere to live. I'll have to rent. I'm stretched thin with the restaurant and can't afford to buy anything right now. What about you? Are you going back to Richmond anytime soon?"

"There's no reason for me to go back to Richmond. I got fired from my job."

"I'm sorry, bro. When did that happen?"

Cooper hunched a bony shoulder. "About a month ago."

Sean's eyes grew wide. "A month ago? Dude! Why didn't you tell me?"

Cooper answered with another shrug. "It's not a big deal."

Sean wasn't surprised to hear Cooper had lost his graphic design job. He was surprised his seniors had allowed him to stay on as long as they did. The big deal was that Cooper kept something so important from Sean for so long. With each passing day, Cooper drifted further away from him. Sean continued to toss out life jackets to him, but Cooper refused to take them.

four
sean

Sean maneuvered the boat while Cooper dumped a dozen soft-shell crabs into a bucket and tossed the trap back into the water. He reversed out of the marsh grass and put the boat in forward. During the short ride home, Sean scrutinized his brother, who sat in the front with his eyes closed and face lifted to the afternoon sun. Cooper seemed content, as he always did when they were out on the water.

Aside from the occasional boat ride, Cooper hadn't been out of the house since . . . Come to think of it, Sean couldn't remember Cooper leaving the house at all since returning to Prospect in early October. He had no reason to leave Moss Creek except to buy groceries. And Sean did all the shopping for him. Staying holed up in the house alone all the time couldn't be good for Cooper's emotional wellbeing. If only Sean could figure out what was going on inside his twin's head.

Back at Moss Creek, Cooper cleaned the soft shells at the sink in the summer kitchen under the carport while Sean went inside the house to start dinner. He was removing a pan of cornbread from the oven when he saw, through the window, his parents talking to Cooper in the backyard. His mother was as stylish as ever in a navy linen blazer and white jeans with her dark hair layered around her striking face, and his father appeared fit and healthy despite his balding head. After a few minutes, Cooper and his father moseyed down to the dock and their mom turned back toward the house.

Jackie entered the kitchen in a cloud of flowery perfume. Opening the refrigerator, she removed a bottle of white wine and guzzled straight from the bottle. "That young man I just spoke to in the yard isn't my son. He's a stranger. What on earth is going on with your brother?"

Sean threw up his hands. "Let me know if you figure it out, because I don't have a clue. I've tried to get through to him, but he keeps shutting me out. This won't help anything." He took the wine from her and returned it to the refrigerator.

Jackie moved to the french doors in the adjacent dining room and stared out at her son. "He looks awful. I don't think he's shaved since Christmas, and when's the last time he got his hair cut?"

Sean went to stand beside her. "When's the last time he *washed* his hair? He informed me yesterday that he lost his job a month ago."

Her hazel eyes grew wide. "What does he do all day?"

"He paints. I'll show you." Sean took his mom's hand and led her down the stairs, through the game room, and into the garage. "I stopped counting at a hundred," he said about the paintings occupying one bay of the two-bay garage.

"My word." His mom touched her fingers to her lips as she moved in closer to inspect the canvases.

Sean followed her into the garage. "My favorite ones are the birds. The egrets, heron, and osprey. But this one is by far the best." He rooted around until he found a painting of a bald eagle, his wings spread wide as he dove for a fish.

Jackie's eyes filled with tears. "It's magnificent. I've been to some of the most prestigious museums in the world, but I've never been so moved by art. Where on earth did he spot a bald eagle?"

"Right out in front of the house. He snapped an image with his telephoto lens. But most of the birds he paints live from his perch in the corner of the veranda. Who knew we had such glorious wildlife at Moss Creek?"

"Who knew Cooper had such talent? I can almost forgive his long hair and beard." She spent a minute flipping through the paintings. "My clients would pay big bucks for these. He should have a show."

"That would require him to leave the house," Sean said under his breath.

Jackie found a painting of a serene sunrise over the marsh she particularly liked and took it with her when they went back upstairs.

She set the table on the veranda while Sean tossed a salad. When Cooper and their dad brought up a platter of crispy fried soft-shell crabs, they sat down to eat.

After Bill offered the blessing, Jackie said, "Cooper, your brother showed me what you've been up to. You're quite talented. I know a couple of gallery owners in Charleston who would love to showcase your work."

Cooper dumped a spoonful of tartar sauce on his plate. "No thanks. Painting is just a hobby."

"Will you at least allow me to show some of your work to my clients? I know several collectors who will be interested."

"If you want. But I don't think my work is that good."

Jackie laughed. "Typical artist. You'll change your mind when you see how much I can get for them."

Sean stuffed a crab leg into his mouth. "I can't stand the suspense any longer. What's this important thing you want to talk to us about?"

Jackie gave Bill the nod. "You tell them."

Their dad set down his fork and wiped his mouth. "Your mom

and I have decided it's time for us to let go of Moss Creek. Our lives in Charleston are growing busier by the day. I've just been promoted to head of cardiology at MUSC."

"Dad, that's great! Congratulations!" Sean said, offering his dad a high five.

Bill smiled. "Thank you, son. And your mother has taken on three large projects."

Sean smiled warmly at his mother. "Congrats to you as well." He was proud of his mother's success. She was currently the most sought-after interior designer in Charleston.

"I'm happy for both of you," Cooper said in a rare, upbeat tone.

"Thank you, son." Jackie sipped her sweet tea. "Retirement for both of us is a long way off. But when that time comes, providing we're in good health, we'd like to travel. We'd rather not be tied down to a property that requires so much maintenance."

Bill continued, "We've been doing some estate planning, and our attorney has advised us to use our gift tax exemption. According to him, we have two options. We can sell the property and gift you boys the proceeds. Or we can transfer the deed to you, also a gift, and let you deal with the maintenance. The upkeep on this place is a full-time job. You can take care of some of it yourself. But be aware, the work you'll have to farm out will get expensive."

Cooper and Sean exchanged a look, each knowing what the other was thinking. Were they ready for such an enormous commitment?

Jackie stabbed at her salad with her fork. "Obviously, you won't both live here once you have a wife and children. When the time comes, one of you will buy the other out. Assuming you both continue to live in Prospect. If you were to both move away, you could split your time here during the summer months and on holidays. Moss Creek is a special place. On the other hand, while your father and I would love for the property to remain in the family, you're young for such an enormous responsibility."

"We don't want to sell," Cooper stated in a matter-of-fact tone. He'd always spoken for his younger-by-five-minutes brother.

"This is not something we have to decide tonight," Jackie said. "You need to talk it through at length. Making these types of important decisions takes time."

Bill looked from Cooper to Sean. "One more thing. You would need to sign an agreement stating that if a dispute over the property were to arise, Moss Creek will be sold, and the proceeds divided between you."

The twins nodded in unison. While they finished eating, they debated the pros and cons of selling versus keeping Moss Creek. They concluded their discussion by agreeing to mull it over during the summer and make their final decision in the fall.

After doing the dishes, the foursome went outside to walk around the premises. Jackie and Bill pointed out things around the home's exterior they needed to watch for, like overflowing gutters and peeling paint on the shutters.

When they reached the dock, Jackie sat down between her sons on the wooden bench. "Sean's new restaurant will keep him tied to Prospect for the foreseeable future. What're your plans, Cooper? Will you be returning to Richmond?"

Cooper shook his head. "I don't think so. That job wasn't the right fit for me. I'm starting my own web design company."

Sean's ears perked up. This was the first he'd heard of this business venture.

Jackie rested her arm on the bench behind Cooper. "Good for you. Web design is something you can do from anywhere as long as you have a computer. If you decide Prospect is too small, you can move to a bigger city, like Raleigh or Atlanta."

Cooper grunted. "That won't happen. I tried big city living, and it's not for me."

Sean blinked hard in disbelief. Who was this guy? His twin

brother had always wanted to expand his horizons beyond their small hometown. Now, with Cooper so uncertain about his career and future, was not the right time to be making major decisions. Their parents meant well, but Sean had a sick feeling co-owner-ship in Moss Creek would lead to major heartache between the brothers down the road.

five
lizbet

The house was empty when Lizbet arrived home from work on Monday evening. She poured herself a glass of sweet tea and plopped down in a chair at the table. Everything about the outdated kitchen reminded Lizbet of her mama. The sunny yellow walls, ancient appliances, and wall clock made from driftwood and seashells. Lula had loved to cook and spent most of her time in here. The kitchen was in major need of a facelift, but even if they could afford to renovate, Lizbet couldn't stand the thought of stripping the last traces of Lula from the house.

Brochures littered the table. She picked up one and then another and another. The subject content of the brochures was do-it-yourself home insemination. Anger surged through her. It was so easy for lesbian couples to make babies these days. They could insert sperm inside their vaginas and boom—they were pregnant.

The back door banged open, and a tornado of flying hair and flailing arms whirled in. Lizbet cleared her throat to make her presence known, and the lovers jumped apart in surprise. Brooke and Sawyer smoothed their hair, straightened their clothes, and wiped away smudged lipstick to make themselves presentable.

The two young women were opposite in personality and looks. Brooke was the prettier of the two with a blonde pixie cut and feminine facial features, while Sawyer's refined good looks—her rich mahogany hair and brown eyes—hinted at her prominent upbringing. Sawyer was serious in nature and Brooke was fun loving. Sawyer, the pediatric resident, was a left-brain thinker while Brooke, the artist, was more creative. Even now, Sawyer's face was dark with anger while Brooke appeared happy to see Lizbet.

"Hey, Liz! What're you up to?" Brooke narrowed her eyes as she studied Lizbet. "Is something wrong? You have a funny look on your face."

"Nothing's wrong. I was just glancing through your reading materials." She gathered up a handful of pamphlets and fanned them out. "Your *do-it-yourself* baby-making projects. It hardly seems fair you two have so many options when I have none."

Brooke's face fell. "Oh, honey. I'm so sorry." She pulled a chair up close to Lizbet and sat down. "So this is why you left Jamie. I worried it might be something like this. Why didn't you tell me?"

Lizbet placed the brochures in a neat stack on the table. "I didn't want to trouble you with my problems."

Sawyer's brown eyes popped. "You didn't want to *trouble* us? You've been moping around here for months? What do you call that?"

Brooke gave her partner a pleading look. "Please don't make this worse."

"I don't know how it could get worse." Sawyer jabbed a finger at Lizbet. "We've been walking on eggshells around her for months. I'm warning you, Brooke. I can't take all this hostility in my house."

Lizbet glared at her. "This isn't *your* house."

"This—" Sawyer started to say something but stopped herself. "Whatever. You deal with this, Brooke. I'm going to bed."

Lizbet watched her go. "Why has she suddenly turned into such a bitch?"

"Sawyer and I have been on edge lately. We've been arguing for months about who will carry our baby. I have my heart set on experiencing pregnancy, but as a doctor, she has better medical care and benefits. She seems turned off by the whole process of pregnancy and delivery."

"Then she shouldn't carry the baby. You have perfectly fine healthcare, Brooke."

"It's nowhere as good as hers. But you don't want to hear about this." Brooke got up from the table. "Let's go outside to the porch." She went to the refrigerator for the pitcher of tea, refilling Lizbet's glass and fixing one for herself.

Lizbet followed her sister outside, and they sat down side by side on the bench swing.

Brooke nestled in close to Lizbet. "I wish you'd told me you were having fertility problems. Is it the endometriosis?"

"Unfortunately. The doctor who performed my surgery in high school warned me it might come back. The pain is getting worse. My periods are almost unbearable." Lizbet bit down on her quivering lower lip. "I'm gonna need a hysterectomy soon. I'm not even thirty years old, and the doctor wants to cut out all my reproductive organs."

Brooke tucked a strand of Lizbet's chestnut hair behind her ear. "How much have you told Jamie?"

"I haven't told him anything. I wanted to see what my options were first. Now that I'm certain I can never bear his child, I'm faced with a whole new dilemma. There's nothing wrong with his goods. He really wants a child of his own, and he should be able to have one."

"What're you saying, Lizbet?"

"I'm thinking of divorcing him."

Brooke straightened. "Whoa. You're getting way ahead of yourself. What about surrogacy?"

Lizbet shook her head. "It's too risky. I would be devastated if the surrogate refused to give up my child."

"Then you should adopt. Jamie loves you, and he will love your adopted baby. You two will be amazing parents. This is a bump in the road, Liz, but it's not worth ending your marriage over."

"I disagree. Jamie will find a new wife who doesn't have faulty female organs and can give him a brood of children. And I will . . ." Lizbet's voice trailed off.

"You'll what, Liz?"

"I'll dedicate myself to my career and become super successful. Once I figure out the right career path."

Brooke leaped off the swing to her feet. "You're being ridiculous, Lizbet. You don't get to make this decision alone. This isn't just your life we're talking about. You're married to Jamie. You're a couple. You decide things together."

"You don't get it, Brooke. Jamie is an honorable guy. He'll feel obligated to stay with me out of a sense of duty."

Brooke let out a humph. "I know Jamie Sweeney. If given the choice between staying married to you and having his own biological children, he'll pick you all day long."

"And that's why I'm going to make it easy for him. If *I* divorce *him*, he'll be free to find that new wife."

Brooke grabbed the swing's chain, stopping it from moving. "If you really feel that way, why haven't you hired a divorce attorney?"

Tears leaked from her eyes and dropped onto her jeans, leaving tiny wet spots in the fabric. "It's complicated."

"If you're so sure about your decision, why is it so complicated?"

Lizbet sniffled as she wiped away her tears. "I'm in a bad place, Brooke. I'm flat broke. I spent all my money on fertility specialists. I can't afford an attorney, any more than I can afford my own apartment. I know how much you and Sawyer want to get rid of me. I asked Dad to lend me some money for an apartment, but he refused to give it to me. I'm sorry, but you're stuck with me for now. At least I got a new job. Hopefully, I can move out by the end of the summer."

"Oh, honey." Brooke sat back down on the swing. "What makes you think I want to get rid of you?"

"I overheard you and Sawyer talking in the kitchen the other day. She thinks my *negative aura* will affect her pregnancy. And you heard what she said just now about me moping around and y'all walking on eggshells."

"Don't listen to Sawyer. I told you we've been on edge lately. You belong here, Liz. This is your home. If Sawyer doesn't like it, let her be the one who leaves."

Lizbet knew Brooke didn't mean that. Sawyer was the love of her sister's life. And Lizbet wouldn't be the one responsible for breaking them up. "Things will be different now that I have a job and will be out of the house more often. I promise to be on my best behavior when I'm here."

"I don't want you to be on your best behavior. I just want you to be yourself." Brooke placed an arm around Lizbet, pulling her close. "From now on, I want you to talk to me about your problems instead of keeping everything bottled up inside. I'm your big sister. I want to be here for you."

"That means a lot, Brooke. Thank you," Lizbet said, resting her head on Brooke's shoulders.

The sisters stayed on the porch for hours, having a long overdue heart to heart. Brooke's upbeat personality and positive attitude were contagious, and by the time they finally made their way to bed around midnight, Lizbet's outlook for the future seemed much brighter. She even promised her sister she would talk to Jamie before making any final decisions.

But a few minutes later, Lizbet was in the hall bathroom brushing her teeth when she heard Sawyer's raised voice. She listened with her ear against their bedroom door. "I can't believe you agreed to let her stay until the end of the summer. It's like a sorority house around here with all her drama. We're a couple, Brooke. Having your kid sister living with us is weird."

"She's my family, Sawyer. And she's going through a tough time. You could be more understanding."

"Are you kidding me? I have been understanding. I've held my tongue for the past seven months. She gives me the creeps. Every time I turn around, she's staring at me with those spooky gray eyes of hers."

"You're being melodramatic, Sawyer."

"And you're being irresponsible, Brooke. Your primary obligation is to me and our unborn child."

Tiptoeing back to her room, Lizbet closed the door and climbed into bed. Sawyer was right. Brooke's primary responsibility was to her partner and their child. Until she could save enough money to get her own place, she would stay out of their way, even if that meant spending her free time in her room.

sean

W hen Sean arrived at the restaurant on Tuesday morning, he was stunned and more than a little annoyed to find a little boy sitting on the floor of his kitchen, beating pans with a wooden spoon. The kid looked like an angel with a halo of white-blond curls and eyes the color of summer grass, but his devilish grin hinted at trouble.

Carla spotted Sean and turned her back to the stove. "I'm so sorry, Sean. I'm having trouble finding a sitter for Josh. He's enrolled in a summer program, but it doesn't start until after Memorial Day."

Josh clambered to his feet and grabbed two metal pot lids off the counter, clanging them together like cymbals. When Carla attempted to take the lids from him, he gripped them tighter and a game of tug of war ensued.

"Mine!" Josh demanded.

"Fine." Carla let go of the lids. "Just don't bang them so loud."

Josh, shooting his mother a defiant glare, started banging the lids and marching around the kitchen as though he were in a parade.

Carla yelled to Sean above the deafening racket. "I realize this isn't ideal. I'm currently interviewing nanny applicants. Hopefully, I'll find one soon."

Sean snatched the lids from the kid. "I'm sorry, buddy. But I can't hear myself think."

Josh folded his arms over his chest in a huff. "You're mean."

"Oh, yeah? Well, you're acting like a brat. How old are you?"

Josh raised his hand, showing four fingers.

"Really? Because I know two-year-olds who are better behaved than you."

Josh picked up the wooden spoons and returned to beating the pans like drums.

Sean and Carla migrated into the dining room, leaving the swinging door open to keep an eye on the kid.

"You handled him brilliantly just now," Carla said. "Everything is a battle with him. I'm an awful parent. He wears me down, and I give into him."

Sean didn't argue. The interaction between mother and child he just witnessed left little doubt that Josh was in total control of the relationship. At least Carla recognized the problem. Maybe she just needed some help in solving it. "Where's Josh's father?"

Carla looked away, her eyes on Josh, who was now running circles around the kitchen island. "I got pregnant in college. My boyfriend and my mother wanted me to have an abortion, but I refused. Now neither of them will have anything to do with us."

Sean frowned. Unsure of what to say, he murmured, "That stinks." When he interviewed Carla, he'd been so impressed with her culinary skills, he didn't think to ask about her personal life. Given the choice, he wasn't sure he would have hired a single woman with a young child. Firing her would give her cause to sue him for discrimination. "If you don't mind me asking, why did you decide to become a chef? The long hours aren't exactly conducive to parenting young children."

"From the time I was a little girl, I've wanted to be a chef. Cooking is what I'm good at. The kitchen is my natural habitat. I figured Josh would eventually become self-sufficient, and I want a career that inspires me. But raising him has proven a bigger challenge than I expected. At this rate, I won't live to see him turn sixteen."

Sean's heart went out to her. He couldn't imagine being twenty-six years old and all alone in the world with the responsibility of a little boy. "Yes, you will. You just need some support. My cousin Bitsy babysits all the time. She's a junior in high school. I don't know what her schedule is like, but I'm happy to check with her to see if she has any afternoons free."

Carla breathed a sigh of relief. "That would be great. If she can't, maybe she knows someone who can."

Sean thumbed off a text to Bitsy, inquiring about her availability. His cousin responded immediately. *Sure! I have some free time. Send me her contact info.*

"We're in luck. Bitsy has some time. I'm sending her your number, and she'll reach out to you." Sean shared Carla's contact info and pocketed his phone.

"That's awesome, Sean. Thank you so much."

"As for today, I'm interviewing several college kids for waitstaff positions this afternoon. I don't want them to think we're operating a daycare around here."

Carla waved her hand, dismissing his concern. "Don't worry about Josh. I brought an air mattress with us. He'll have quiet time after lunch. I downloaded a couple of movies on my iPad for him to watch. I'll make certain he doesn't disturb you."

Sean was skeptical, but he had no other choice but to go along with her. "All right, then. Let's get back to work."

Sean spent the morning in the office ordering enough food supplies to get him through June. And that afternoon, he hit the jackpot with the employee candidates. He filled the server and hostess positions with college kids and hired the brother of a dockworker for dishwasher. He arranged for them all to return the next day for training.

When he came to work on Wednesday morning, Sean found Josh driving Matchbox cars through roadways of flour on the kitchen floor. "Seriously, Carla! I'm training my new hires this afternoon. A busy restaurant is no place for a child."

"No worries," Carla said in a cheerful tone. "I'm meeting Bitsy at my apartment at noon. She doesn't have any classes this afternoon and can stay with Josh until I get home around five."

"Good," Sean said and disappeared into his office. When he emerged around one o'clock, he was relieved to see that Josh and Carla had left and the flour mess on the floor had been cleaned up.

Randy, the bartender he'd hired back from the original restaurant, was the first to arrive for the training session. He was thrilled with the renovations and enthusiastic about ordering new glassware to complement his fancy new bar. Sean, trying not to think about his dwindling bank account, gave Randy permission to order whatever he wanted.

The college kids were a clean-cut, energetic crew who appeared eager to work hard and earn big tip money over the summer. They all got along well, and by the time they left late afternoon, the group was ready for the first day of the soft opening on Monday.

Sean was locking up the restaurant around six o'clock when Bitsy barreled up the stairs toward him. He marveled at how much his cousin had grown up. Their families were close, and he felt overly protective of her—not only because she was like a little sister to him but also because she was the innocent type guys took advantage of. She even looked the part with sandy hair and a sweet, freckled face. At the moment, however, that face was twisted in an angry scowl.

"I take it things didn't go well with Josh," Sean said, stuffing his keys into his pocket.

"That child is the devil himself. Look what he did to my

arms." Bitsy held out her arms, undersides up, revealing several sets of red teeth marks.

Sean looked down at her arms and back up at Bitsy. "What did you do to him to make him bite you like that?"

"I told him he couldn't have a second ice cream sandwich. Apparently, he doesn't like to be told *no*. That kid needs a child psychiatrist."

"That kid needs a strong male figure in his life."

Bitsy rolled her eyes. "Why do all men think they're the answer to every problem?"

"Did you show those marks to Carla?" he asked, choosing to ignore her dig.

"Yep. She barely looked at them. She certainly didn't seem surprised. I told her Josh was too much for me to handle. Can you believe she asked if any of my friends might be interested in babysitting him? As though I would subject my friends to that kind of torture?"

Sean raked his fingers through his hair. "What am I gonna do? I can't have a kid hanging out in my restaurant. But I can't open my restaurant without my chef."

"Maybe you should talk to Mom. One of her residents might be interested."

Sean perked up. "That's not a bad idea, Bits. I'll call her." Bitsy's mom, his aunt Faith, operated a shelter/halfway house for women suffering from homelessness, abuse, and addiction. Faith encouraged her residents to find jobs as they were getting back on their feet.

"This isn't your average babysitting job, Sean. Mom needs to know what the resident will be up against. It will take a special person to handle Josh."

"I understand." Sean took Bitsy by the elbow and guided her back down the stairs. "What are you doing this summer? Are you interested in waitressing? I have an opening on the lunch shift."

"Sounds like a fun gig, but I'm not sure I'll have time. I

promised to help Mom with some projects at the home, and I have several families I'm currently babysitting for."

At the bottom of the stairs, Sean turned to her. "You'd earn more in tips here than babysitting."

"Maybe next summer. I could use the spending money when I go off to college. This summer will be too hectic. I'm traveling with a couple of my regular families." Bitsy stood on her tiptoes to kiss his cheek. "I'm sorry things didn't work out with Carla."

He pinched her freckled cheek. "Thanks for trying, kiddo."

Sean walked Bitsy to her car before heading home, where he spent a sleepless night worried about Carla. He could look for a new chef, but he doubted he could find someone of her caliber at the last minute.

Sean was working in his office the next morning around ten o'clock when Carla bustled Josh into the kitchen. Her eyes were swollen and red-rimmed, as though she'd been crying, and Josh was unusually quiet.

Carla dropped her belongings on the floor in the office. "I'm sorry I'm late. We've had a tough morning." She settled Josh in a chair with a coloring book and crayons and gestured for Sean to follow her into the kitchen.

"I heard what happened with Bitsy," Sean said.

Carla massaged her temples. "I feel awful about that. I encouraged her to check with her doctor about a tetanus shot."

"Don't worry about that. Her stepfather is a doctor. Mike will take good care of her."

She collapsed against the prep table. "I'm not sure how much more of this I can take, Sean. I'm at my wit's end. I hate to dump my problems on you, but I have nowhere else to turn." She quieted her voice. "I'm seriously considering putting him in a foster home until I can get my feet on the ground."

"Are you kidding me?" Sean said, his blue eyes huge. "He's your child. You can't do that. Come here." He pulled her in for a hug, holding her tight while she cried. The restaurant was insignificant compared to her problems. She needed help, and he was in a position to offer it.

When her sobbing subsided, he held her at arm's length so he could see her face. "We'll figure this out together. When exactly does Josh's summer program start?"

Carla wiped her nose with the back of her hand. "The Tuesday after Memorial Day."

"That's two weeks away. We can tag-team until then. If need be, I can stay with him at your apartment while you work."

"You don't understand," Carla said into her balled fist. "I no longer have an apartment. Josh had a screaming fit last night after Bitsy left. And it wasn't the first time. My landlord evicted us. We are now homeless. Things have never been this bad before. I can look for another apartment, but I was out of work for a while before I took this job, and I'm strapped for cash."

"I could loan you the money, but that doesn't solve your child-care needs." Sean pulled her back into his arms. "I have a better idea. You can stay with us. We have plenty of room at Moss Creek." As the words left his mouth, he realized what a potentially drastic mistake he was making. His brother, in his current state of mind, wasn't much better off than Josh. But the feel of this woman's trembling body against his moved him. She was all alone in the world, and she needed his help.

lizbet

L izbet immersed herself in her new job. During office hours, she studied recipes and orders from previous events, which provided intel about the most popular menu items. After the catering staff had gone home, she stayed until late at night in the kitchen tweaking old recipes and testing new ones. She wanted to do a good job and to impress Annie and Heidi, but she was also avoiding Sawyer whose words still stung. *She gives me the creeps. Every time I turn around, she's staring at me with those spooky gray eyes of hers.*

Annie had overestimated the time the project would take. If she continued at this pace, Lizbet predicted she would finish by the end of June. Maybe even earlier. She refused to think about what came next. The monumental decision about the future of her marriage hung over her like a dark cloud. She'd promised Annie she would talk to Jamie, but she wasn't yet ready to tell him the truth. Wasn't yet ready to face his disappointment. Wasn't yet ready to sever the ties to the man she loved with all her heart. But how could she look for a permanent job or rent an apartment with her life so unsettled?

Georgia also worked well into the evening, restocking shelves, taking inventory, and placing new orders. Georgia claimed she was a night owl, but Lizbet suspected she was lonely at home. Lizbet could relate. She was lonely, too, cooped up in her room without even a television to keep her company.

Most nights before leaving Tasty Provisions, Georgia and Lizbet sat down together for a cup of Tasty Provision's specially blended lavender tea. They had quickly settled back into the close friendship they'd shared during Lizbet's turbulent teenage years. She was fortunate to have someone as wise as Georgia as her confidante.

On Thursday evening of the second week of May, while experimenting with a new remoulade-style sauce she hoped Annie would adopt as their signature sauce, Lizbet heard mumbled voices coming from the showroom. She cracked open the swinging door and was surprised to see her father in conversation with Georgia.

Walking toward them, Lizbet said, "Dad! This is a surprise. What're you doing here?"

"I stopped by the house to see you, and Brooke told me you were still at work."

Beads of perspiration dotted his forehead, and he appeared frail, like an old man. "Is something wrong?"

"Not at all." He cast a nervous glance at Georgia. "I just needed to speak with you about something."

Lizbet looked down at her watch. "Wow. I can't believe it's already nine o'clock. Give me five minutes to clean up my mess in the kitchen, and I'll walk you home."

Returning to the kitchen, Lizbet covered her special sauce with plastic wrap, placed it in the refrigerator, and darted up the stairs to retrieve her bag from the office. She said good night to Georgia on her way out and exited the gourmet shop with her father. As they walked south on East Bay Street for a couple of blocks in silence, Lizbet sensed her father was summoning the courage to talk to her.

Finally, Lizbet said, "What's up, Dad? What did you want to talk to me about?"

Her father removed a white linen handkerchief from his pocket and blotted the sweat off his forehead. "Is it me, or are Charleston's summers getting hotter?"

Lizbet's concern deepened. The temperature was mild, with a cool breeze blowing off the harbor. "It's nice out tonight, Dad. I'm worried about you. When's the last time you had a checkup?"

"A few months ago. Everything was fine, aside from my slightly elevated cholesterol levels."

"That's a relief," Lizbet said, although she remained unconvinced he was in good health.

When they reached his street, instead of turning left toward his condo, he continued straight. "Where are we going, Dad?"

"I'm walking you home. It's not safe for a pretty young woman to be walking alone at night."

"You know I'm perfectly safe in this area of Charleston." She stopped and turned to him. "Tell me what's really going on."

"I woke during the night with the strangest feeling."

"About me?" Lizbet asked with a hand on her chest.

Her dad stared past Lizbet at a young woman walking a bulldog. "I think so. Although I'm not entirely sure. I just felt the need to see you, to make sure you're okay."

Lizbet furrowed her brow. "Did you have a dream? Did something bad happen to me?"

He shook his head. "It wasn't a dream. More like a premonition. I wish you'd work things out with Jamie. I'd feel better knowing you were taken care of if anything were to happen to me."

The hairs on the back of Lizbet's neck stood to attention. "But you just said you were in good health."

"I am, as far as I know. But I'm not getting any younger." He cupped her cheek. "I don't mean to alarm you. I'm sure everything is fine. The premonition just unsettled me. I'm glad to see you're okay." He dropped his hand. "Now, about the loan you asked for. If you're determined to move into your own place, I'm happy to give you the money."

Lizbet smiled at him. "Thanks, Dad. But I've had a change of heart about that. I got myself into debt. Now I have to get myself out of it."

"That's my girl. You'll learn a more valuable lesson if you take responsibility for your mistakes." Phillip squeezed her arm. "I enjoy having you in Charleston, but I would prefer for you to work things out with Jamie."

Lizbet let out a sigh as she made the decision she'd been dreading. She could no longer postpone the inevitable. "I'm going to talk to him this weekend. I'm not making any promises. Our relationship may be too far gone. But Georgia has helped me realize we need to at least try."

"Georgia is a wise woman. Marriage is a long journey with lots of ups and downs. You two can conquer any hurdle as long as you love each other."

Georgia and Brooke and her father seemed to feel a reconciliation with her husband was inevitable. But for that to happen, Jamie would have to make an enormous sacrifice. And Lizbet wasn't sure she could let him do that.

Lizbet stood on her tiptoes to kiss her father's cheek. "Thanks for worrying about me, Dad. But you don't need to walk me home. I'll text you as soon as I get there, and I want you to do the same."

"All right," Phillip said after a moment's hesitation. "But if I don't hear from you in twenty minutes, I'm calling the police."

"Fair enough," she said, and waved goodbye to him before heading down Tradd Street.

Her father's ominous premonition unnerved her, and she cast frequent glances over her shoulder as she race-walked home. When she reached the front porch, she sent her father a text before entering the house. He responded immediately that he, too, had arrived home safely.

The faint sound of television noise greeted her in the entry hall. She passed through the kitchen to the family room, where she found Brooke curled in a ball on the sofa with her head resting in Sawyer's lap.

Noticing Lizbet in the doorway, Brooke slowly sat up. "There you are." She aimed the remote at the television and paused her show. "Where have you been all week?"

"Working. I enjoy having the kitchen to myself after the catering staff leaves."

"That makes sense. Did Dad find you? He was here looking for you."

Lizbet nodded. "He came to Tasty Provisions. Can I talk to you alone for a minute? I'm worried about Dad's health."

"Can't it wait? We're in the middle of this show." Sawyer gestured at the television where Beth, the star diva of the hit series *Yellowstone,* was frozen on the screen.

Lizbet stared daggers at Sawyer. "Didn't you hear what I just said? I'm concerned about our father's health. You, being a doctor, should understand that better than anyone."

Brooke gave Sawyer's knee a squeeze. "It's okay. I'll only be a minute." She got up from the sofa and followed Lizbet to the kitchen.

"How did Dad seem to you when you saw him earlier?" Lizbet asked.

Brooke hesitated, as though trying to remember. "Fine. Then again, he was only here for a second, and he didn't come inside. Why?"

Aside from the occasional holiday, their father never came to the house. Lizbet wasn't sure why. Either the memories of her mother were too painful, or he disapproved of his daughter's lesbian relationship.

"He's lost weight, and he's awfully pale. I noticed it when I saw him last week, but tonight he looked frail. I don't think he has much of a social life. He works all day, and then goes home to an empty apartment at night."

"If all goes as planned, he'll soon have a grandchild to dote on."

Lizbet's chest tightened. "*Your* grandchild. Not *mine*."

A pained expression crossed Brooke's face. "I'm sorry, Liz. That was insensitive of me. I wasn't thinking."

Guilt overcame Lizbet. Why did she always make everything about herself? She should be thrilled her sister was starting a family. "No, I'm the one who's sorry. I'm being overly sensitive. Dad will be thrilled to have a grandchild. Until then, though, we should make the effort to spend more time with him."

"I totally agree. He's not getting any younger. I wish we could find him a girlfriend."

"Maybe if we put our heads together, we can think of someone." Lizbet gave her sister a gentle shove toward the family room. "Now go back to your show. I'm sorry I bothered you."

"No bother at all. I'm glad you confided in me about Dad. I'll try to call him more often. Good night," Brooke said, giving her ponytail a tug before scurrying away.

Lizbet was halfway up the stairs to her bedroom when she remembered she forgot to get a cup of water. When she returned to the kitchen, she heard Sawyer's voice booming from the family room.

"This is getting old, Brooke. She's always dragging you into her problems."

Lizbet inched closer to the doorway to eavesdrop.

"He's *our* father, Sawyer. Which makes him *our* problem. Lizbet is going through a tough time. She needs my support right now. You could be a little more considerate."

"But this is a special time for us. I'd like to enjoy it without constantly being worried about offending her. Am I supposed to feel guilty because we're having a baby and she can't?"

"You're a doctor. You're supposed to feel compassion. What's up with you? Lately you've been so self-centered."

"I shouldn't have to spell it out for you. I'm tired of your sister living with us."

"This isn't your house, Sawyer. Lizbet has more right to be here than you. If you ask me to choose between you and my family, you won't be happy with my choice. I'm going to bed. You should sleep on the sofa tonight."

At the sound of approaching footsteps, Lizbet slipped into the walk-in pantry and pressed herself against the wall, holding her breath. She waited until the footsteps had left the kitchen before sliding down the wall to her bottom.

She hated being the source of problems between Brooke and her partner. If things didn't go well with Jamie, she would accept her father's offer of a loan and get her own place. But where? Would she look for a small apartment in an old house or rent a studio in one of the new buildings that offered all the modern amenities? What would she do for furniture and household items? These things cost money she didn't have.

The fog of the past months suddenly cleared, and she began to wonder if she'd made a terrible mistake in leaving Jamie. She loved him more than life itself, and she would give anything to be with him in the cozy house they'd made their home. She had been foolish to run out on him, but she'd needed to explore her options and time to accept the hand fate had dealt her. Dared she hope Jamie would accept her apology and welcome her back into his life?

eight
sean

Sean returned from running errands on Saturday morning to find Cooper in an angry rant, Josh screaming his head off, and Carla dragging suitcases down the stairs.

Sean pulled his brother aside. "What happened while I was gone?"

"I'll tell you what happened." Cooper's nostrils flared as he pointed at the veranda. "Look! That kid destroyed my painting."

Sean's eyes followed his finger to the canvas. The marsh landscape Cooper had been working on all week was now splattered with red paint.

"Do something, Sean. Get that little brat outta of this house."

Calling Josh a *brat* made him scream louder and Carla's face beam an angry red. "Don't you dare talk to my son like that," she said in a low but vehement voice.

"Everyone chill out!" Sean took the suitcase from Carla and parked it near the stairs. "Why don't you take Josh outside? If you need something to play with, there are balls and games in the garage." He remembered the paintings Cooper had stored in the garage. "On second thought, I'll get them out later. You'll never find them in that mess. For now, let him run around in the yard."

Carla hesitated, giving Sean a skeptical look.

Sean encouraged her with a nod. "Go ahead. The fresh air will do you both good. I'll be down after I talk to Cooper, and we'll go for a boat ride."

"Fine." Hoisting the boy onto her hip, she carried him down the stairs and out the back door.

Cooper pinned Sean against the wall with a death glare. "I told you it was a bad idea for them to live here."

"I realize the situation isn't ideal, but I had to do something. I can't afford to lose my chef three days before our soft openings begin."

"My web design business is picking up. How am I supposed to work with that little demon running around? He doesn't understand the concept of *inside voices.*"

Sean considered the dilemma. "Why don't you set up a workstation in your room?"

Cooper threw up his hands in frustration. "So I have to isolate myself in my room while the kid gets full reign of the house?"

Sean narrowed his eyes as he scrutinized his twin's face. Were those crumbs in Cooper's beard? "What's happened to you, Coop? You used to be the kindhearted one. If Annie hadn't miscarried, you would've been a teenage daddy yourself. Can you imagine raising your kid without your family's support?"

Cooper's chin dropped to his chest. "No. You're right. Just tell the kid to stay away from my art," he said, and stomped off to his bedroom.

Sean slathered sunscreen on his face, grabbed life jackets from the storage room, and went outside. He found Carla in the backyard, grinning from ear to ear as though the incident with Cooper never happened, as she watched her son roll around in the grass.

"He'll be filthy dirty and covered in bugs, but I can't get mad at him. He's having so much fun. We've never lived anywhere with a yard before."

"But you take him to the playground and the beach, right?"

Carla's smile vanished. "I . . . um . . . I guess I never thought of that."

"Little boys belong outdoors, Carla." Sean gestured at Josh. "This is how they release pent-up energy. There are plenty of playgrounds around town, and the beach is only a short drive. Does he have a social life, other kids he likes to play with?"

"Not really. We've moved around so much. We never stayed anywhere long enough for him to make friends. His summer program will start soon. He'll make some friends there."

Sean frowned. "But he's been in preschool programs before?"

"Of course," Carla said, but her tone didn't convince Sean. Was it possible this kid had no social skills? That would explain his behavioral problems.

Josh scrambled to his feet and ran over to them. "Can we go for a boat ride now?"

"Sure thing. But you have to wear this." Sean fastened on the life jacket and tightened the straps. "Do you know how to swim?"

"Nope." Josh shook his head, his mop of sandy curls dancing about.

"He's only four," Carla said. "Isn't that too young for swimming lessons?"

Sean hunched his shoulders. "I'm not a parent or a swim instructor. But since he lives near the water now, I wouldn't wait. You should check the schedule of swimming classes at our local YMCA. You could meet some other parents, and he could make some friends."

"You may not be a parent, but you sure know a lot about kids."

"I just remember what it was like when I was one. Playdates and swimming lessons were as important as eating my fruits and vegetables. Now." Sean clapped his hands. "Who's ready for a boat ride?"

"I am! I am!" Josh skipped circles around Sean and Carla as they made their way down to the dock.

With Josh nestled between him and Carla on the leaning post, Sean eased his center console boat away from the dock.

"What was it like growing up on the inlet?" Carla asked.

"Magical," Sean said, as a faraway look passed over his face. "We spent our days swimming in the creek and digging in the mud. In high school, Cooper and I operated our own seafood business. We supplied my Aunt Sam, who owns Sam Sweeney's Seafood Market, with seafood we caught ourselves."

Carla's bow lips parted in a sweet smile. "So you were an entrepreneur at a young age."

"Yep. We were always inventing ways to earn a buck. What about you? Where did you grow up?"

"In a restaurant." Sean gave her a quizzical look, and she laughed. But her face quickly grew serious. "My father left a few months after I was born. My mom waitressed at a Greek restaurant owned by a local family in Columbia. My grandmother took care of me until she died when I was eight. After that, I spent all my free time at Angelo's. I did my homework at a table in a dark corner in the back. Most nights, I slept on a cot in the office until my mom was ready to go home. Usually around midnight, although sometimes they closed earlier."

"So that explains your attachment to the restaurant industry."

"I told you, cooking is what I'm good at. But it's also all I've ever known. My mom busted her butt to send me to college. And I repaid her by getting pregnant. She views my decision to keep the baby as a betrayal."

"That's tough, Carla. I'm sorry." He'd had his fair share of problems in college. When he'd gotten messed up with drugs, his mother had been his rock. Jackie had been hard on him, but she'd also given him the guidance he'd needed. Sean wasn't sure he would've survived that difficult time if not for her.

When they reach the main inlet creek, Sean nudged Josh with his elbow. "Do you wanna go fast?"

"Yes!" Josh squealed.

"Hold on tight to him," Sean said to Carla as he eased the throttle forward and the boat rose out of the water.

It was a gorgeous day with bright blue skies, temperatures in the low eighties, and the ocean slick like glass. When they reached the jetties at the mouth of the inlet, Sean slowed his speed, and they rocked and rolled over the ocean swells. He removed a pair of binoculars from the console and showed Josh how to use them to look at the fishermen anchored in boats near the shore.

"Cool! That man caught a big one," Josh said, pointing the binoculars at a young couple in a Jon boat.

Sean took the binoculars from him and adjusted them for his face. "That's a huge flounder. Would you like to go fishing with me sometime?"

"Yes! Can we do it today?"

"Sorry, bud. I didn't bring any fishing gear with us." When disappointment crossed Josh's face, Sean added, "I promise we'll go fishing soon. We might even talk Cooper into coming with us."

Creases appeared between Josh's eyebrows. "Cooper's mean."

"Normally he's not. He was upset. He had a right to be angry about his painting. He's been working on it for a long time. You must promise not to go near his stuff. Not his canvases or his computer. And don't go near his bedroom."

Josh bit down on his lower lip. "I promise." Snuggling against his mother, the boy dozed off to sleep the minute Sean picked up speed on the way home.

"Monday's the big day," Sean reminded Carla. "I initially thought maybe we could take turns watching Josh, but I don't see how that will work. Especially not the first week when we'll need all hands on deck twenty-four seven. Have you had any luck finding a sitter?"

Carla's expression turned grim. "I've struck out so far. The long hours are the problem. I may have to use multiple sitters, at least until his summer program starts." She kissed the top of

Josh's head. "I'm sorry, Sean. I should never have put you in this situation."

Sean didn't respond. While he agreed she should've been up front with him, there was no point harping on it. "Bitsy's mom operates a women's shelter here in town. I hope you don't mind, but I spoke to Aunt Faith about your situation. Her residents come from all walks of life, some worse off than others. When they reach a certain point in their program, Faith helps some of them find jobs to ease back into normal life. She currently has someone looking for work. Faith thinks she might be a good fit for Josh.

Carla looked sideways at him. "What's wrong with her? Why is she in a shelter?"

"She's homeless. Her husband had a terrible gambling problem. When he passed away, he left her destitute. Her four sons all offered to help, but she's determined to pull her life together on her own. Faith thinks she might make a good nanny for Josh."

Carla looked away. "I don't know, Sean. She sounds kinda sketchy."

Irritation crawled up his back. "As the mother of four sons, she's had plenty of experience. She might be just the person you're looking for. Since you're out of other options, you should at least meet her."

"Maybe you're right. If you share your aunt's contact information, I'll call her first thing in the morning."

"Great."

They rode the rest of the way home in comfortable silence, each lost in thought with the wind whipping through their hair and the sun warm on their faces. Carla was the type Sean could fall for. She was more mature than most of the girls his age. Professionally, she possessed a strong drive, and she had set big goals for herself. But the kid was more than he bargained for. Sean wasn't sure he could raise another man's child, especially one with behavioral issues.

nine
jamie

Jamie ignored his phone when it vibrated in his pocket during the Lord's Prayer at church on Sunday. But when it vibrated two more times, he sneaked a peek at the texts from Winnie.

Angry customer causing problems.

They made a mess of the store. I think they're gone now.

Police are on the way.

Jamie whispered to his mom, "We have a crisis at the marina, and I need to leave."

Narrowing her blue eyes, Sam whispered back, "I hope it's nothing serious."

"I'm sure it's fine. I'll call you later."

Slipping out of the pew, Jamie hurried down the aisle and out the front of the church. He called Winnie on the way to his truck, panic setting in when she didn't pick up. He sped through town, barely slowing down for Stop signs. Two police patrol cars with blue lights flashing were on the scene at the marina, and when he got out of his truck, Jamie spotted three uniformed officers roaming the docks.

Inside the store, fishing tackle and grocery items and T-shirts bearing the marina's logo littered the floors. Jamie's stepfather, Eli

Marshall, was chief of police. Over the years, Jamie had met most of the officers and detectives on the force. He recognized the young police officer speaking with Winnie as Adam Yates.

Winnie described the two troublemakers as scrawny dudes with stringy hair, scruffy beards, and tattered clothes. "When they came in to pay for their gas, the skinnier of the two started hitting on me. I told them to beat it, but they went nuts and began pulling things off the shelves." She slid her nine-millimeter pistol across the counter toward Yates. "I fired a shot at the ceiling, and they took off."

All eyes traveled to the hole in the ceiling above her head.

Officer Yates examined the handgun. "Do you have a permit to carry this weapon?"

"Yes, sir," Winnie said, even though Yates wasn't much older than her. She retrieved her bag from under the counter and showed him the permit.

He scrutinized the permit, then handed it back to her. "Can you describe the boat they were in?"

Winnie stuffed the card back into her wallet and returned it to her purse. "It was an old flat bottom Jon boat, about sixteen feet with an ancient Mercury motor."

"Did the dockworkers see them?" Jamie asked.

Winnie rolled her eyes. "Your dockworkers didn't show up this morning."

Ugh, Jamie thought. Keeping employees was proving to be as difficult as hiring them. "You should've called me."

"I didn't want to bother you on your day off," Winnie said.

Officer Yates finger-typed notes on his iPad. "Did you catch a name?"

Winnie twirled a strand of blonde hair around her finger. "I'm not positive, but I think I heard one of them call the other Roscoe."

"I have security cameras. I can pull the footage and send it to you," Jamie volunteered.

"That would be great. Here's my contact info." Officer Yates handed Jamie and Winnie business cards. "If you can think of anything else, please let me know."

Jamie walked Yates to the door. "Should we be worried about them coming back?"

Yates chuckled, his hazel eyes on Winnie. "She's a looker. Sounds like she scared the daylights out of them with her gun. Still, I wouldn't leave her alone for a couple of days."

Jamie's heart sank. He had no other employees to team up with Winnie except himself.

After Yates left, Winnie came out from behind the counter to survey the damage. "It'll take us forever to clean up this mess."

"It doesn't help that we have entirely too much merchandise in here. We need to reduce our stock."

Winnie looked around. "There's definitely a lot of stuff. But what would you get rid of? People staying on their boats count on us to sell groceries. Same with the fisherman and the tackle. And the marina logo stuff sells like crazy. Instead of scaling back, maybe you should expand the store."

"That would take up too much of the parking lot. The people who rent boat slips count on us to have ample parking."

"That's true." Winnie scooped up an armload of potato chip bags. "I hope you're not upset with me for calling the police. When you didn't answer your phone, I wasn't sure what else to do."

"You did the right thing. I was in church, otherwise I would've picked up right away. Don't hesitate to call for help if you ever feel threatened. Or if you're short-staffed. You shouldn't be here alone. You're stuck with me until I can hire additional employees."

Her face tightened. "You don't have to babysit me, Jamie. I can take care of myself."

"Obviously. You proved that today. Regardless, we should have two people working in the store at all times. Or at least have dockworkers who can fill in for you when you're on a break or have an emergency."

Winnie considered this. "I guess that makes sense."

Jamie gathered up a handful of flounder rigs and threaded them back onto the metal display hook. "With luck, the police can identify the troublemakers from the security footage."

"I hope so," Winnie said, her eyes glistening with unshed tears.

Jamie turned to her. "Hey! Are you okay?"

Winnie fanned her face. "I'm fine."

"You're clearly not fine. You've been through an ordeal. Why don't you take the rest of the day off?"

Winnie shook her head. "No way. I can't leave you to clean up this mess alone."

"I'll be fine until Lester gets here at three. Winnie, I am not asking. I'm telling you to go home and clear your head." He retrieved her purse from under the counter and walked her to the door. "I'll see you in the morning. Hopefully by then, the police will have these punks in custody."

Once she was gone, Jamie began the arduous process of cleaning up. A few minutes later, he was organizing T-shirts by size in the appropriate wooden cubbyholes when Kirstin walked in wearing a flowery sundress and a broad smile.

Jamie abandoned the T-shirts and went to greet her. He was happier than a married man should be to see her.

Kirstin threw her arms open wide. "I'm back! And I come bearing good news. Your charming town far outshines the others. We are moving full steam ahead with our project."

"Congratulations! I'm excited for both of us. Your development will put our little town on the map." Jamie looked out the window. "Does your father need help tying up his boat?"

"He's on his way back to Nantucket on the boat. He's turned this project over to me. This is my chance to prove myself, and I have no intention of letting him down." Her gaze shifted to his left, and her mouth gaped open. "What happened? Did a tornado come through here?"

"A couple of jerks tore the place up earlier."

Kirstin's face registered alarm. "Does this sort of thing happen often? Maybe Prospect isn't the right choice for our project after all."

"Actually, we have a low crime rate relative to other coastal towns. You can research it if you don't believe me. My stepfather is the chief of police. Eli runs a tight ship."

The smile returned to her face. "Oh. That's good to know."

"Are you ready to make an offer on the property? I connected with my friend, the property owner, on social media while you were gone. I'm happy to reach out to him on your behalf."

"I'd like to explore the lot on foot first. Is that possible?"

"There are a few trails, if you know where to look for them. I'm happy to guide you, but I can't leave the store until my second-shift manager comes in at three." He eyed her sundress and high-heeled sandals. "You should change clothes, anyway. Those shoes aren't appropriate for hiking."

"For sure. I've rented an Airbnb a couple miles up the road. I'll get settled and meet you back here at three." She blew him a kiss over her shoulder as she headed for the door.

Kirstin had no sooner left than a couple of lanky teenage boys bounded in. "Hello, sir." The taller of the two boys extended a hand to Jamie. "I'm Drew Edwards, and this is my younger brother, Eric. We saw your sign on the door. Are you still hiring?"

"You bet I am. I'm looking for dockworkers and store attendants." Jamie retrieved two employment applications from the stack by the checkout terminal. He handed an application and ink pen to each boy. "Have you ever worked at a marina?"

"No." Drew grinned. "But we like boats."

"And we love to fish," Eric added. "Are there a lot of hot chicks around here?"

Jamie laughed. "We have our share. You boys remind me of my younger self. How old are you?"

"I'm seventeen," Drew answered. "I'll be a senior in high school next fall."

"And I'm sixteen," said Eric. "I'll be a junior. We're only fifteen months apart."

"Awesome. Are y'all from around here?"

Eric shook his head. "No, sir. We live in Raleigh. Our mother is a romance writer. She's rented a house at the beach for the summer."

"A romance writer? That's cool." As they filled out the applications, Jamie described the responsibilities associated with the job.

When the boys finished, Jamie scanned their qualifications. They'd had little job experience, but he was desperate for employees, and they seemed like nice kids.

"Any chance you can start now?" Jamie gestured at the disorderly store. "We had an unpleasant visit from a couple of thugs earlier, and I could use some help cleaning up."

The brothers snapped to attention. "Yes, sir," one said, and the other added, "We're on it."

When the boys set to work, Jamie pulled a stool up to the checkout counter and accessed the security footage on the store's laptop. His anger boiled as he watched the hoodlums mistreat Winnie, but he was proud of her for standing up to them.

When Lester arrived, Jamie explained what had happened and showed him the footage. "Have you ever seen either of these jerks?"

Lester squinted as he leaned in close to the computer. "Can't say that I have." He pounded his right fist into his left palm. "But I'll teach them a thing or two if they come back."

Jamie chuckled. "You do that. *After* you call the police." With tatted up arms and a solid build, Lester could handle whatever trouble arose.

Drew peered over Jamie's shoulder at the computer. "Who's the babe?"

Jamie craned his neck to see Drew. "Your boss, Winnie. She's the daytime manager. And this is Lester, your second-shift manager." He squeezed Lester's muscular bicep. "If you know what's good for you, I wouldn't get on his bad side."

The brothers looked at each other with wide eyes. "No, sir."

After inspecting the clean-up job, Jamie walked the brothers outside to the parking lot. "I'll see you guys at eight o'clock tomorrow morning. Mostly, you'll be working the docks. I'll provide a marina logo shirt. Wear clean shorts and comfortable shoes."

He was waving goodbye to the boys when Kirstin drove up in a white Mercedes with the convertible top down and her blonde hair blowing about her face. He waited while she parked the car. "Nice ride. Did you rent it?"

"Nope," she said, swinging her car door open. "It's mine. I had one of my father's people drive it down, along with some of my clothes."

"What *people* does your father have?"

Kirstin's long legs appeared in short shorts as she climbed out of the car. "The kind that do everything for him except wipe his behind when he uses the toilet." She secured her hair with an elastic band. "Are you ready? I'm eager to explore this property."

Jamie extended a hand toward the wooded lot. "After you," he said, and tried not to stare at her shapely fanny as he trailed behind her.

At the edge of the parking lot, Jamie located the entrance to the trail. "We'll walk through the woods and circle back along the waterfront. Tell me more about your project. How many tenants will you have?" he asked as he followed her down the dirt path.

"As few as twenty, as many as thirty," she said over her shoulder. "We have a list of over a hundred interested parties, both retail merchants and restaurant owners."

"What type of restaurants?"

"Anything from family-style seafood to upscale Italian. The old ice cream parlor and hot dog stand that were destroyed during the hurricane are on the top of the list."

The additional restaurants would create competition for Sean, but they would also attract more tourists to the area, which would benefit him in the long run. "What about the retail?"

Kirstin hunched a shoulder. "A variety of boutiques and gift shops. I can give you first dibs on location if you're interested."

As Jamie traipsed along behind her, an idea formed in his mind. He could definitely use additional retail space. "I assume the storefronts will be different sizes."

"That's the plan. If you commit early, we'll customize yours to meet your needs."

The narrow path curved to the left, and the waterfront came into view. Kirstin stopped in her tracks. "Wow. This is breathtaking. It's almost too beautiful to build on."

"Instead of clearing the lot, you might leave some of the live oaks. The locals would appreciate it, and it would make for a more charming setting."

Kirstin tapped her chin. "That's not a bad idea. I'll give it some thought. Since the development is located on Creekside Drive, we're thinking of calling it Creekside Village."

Jamie considered the name. "I like it. *Village* implies community, a place where people go to hang out."

"I'm glad you approve. Do you know who owns the undeveloped property north of the marina? It would be ideal for waterfront condos. Maybe even a resort."

"Forget about that property. The owner, who wishes to remain anonymous, will never sell."

"Everyone has a price, Jamie," Kirstin said, and continued onward.

Not this person, Jamie thought.

When they reached the parking lot, Kirstin spun around to

face him. "I look forward to working with you on this project." Hooking an arm around his neck, she stood on her tiptoes and pressed her lips to his.

To his horror, Jamie's body responded to her kiss, and he quickly pushed her away. "I hope I didn't give you the wrong impression, Kirstin, but I'm married."

"Oh god. I'm sorry! I didn't know." Kirstin's eyes fell to his left hand. "You're not wearing a wedding ring."

Jamie stuffed his hand in his pocket. "My wife and I are separated."

She scrunched up her face in confusion. "But you're barely old enough to be married. How long have you been separated?" Her fingers flew to her lips. "Forget I asked that. It's none of my business."

"I don't mind. Lizbet moved out seven months ago. She's currently living in Charleston." Jamie bit down on his lip. Why was he sharing details about his marriage with a woman he hardly knows?

"Your wife left seven months ago?" Kirstin asked, her mouth agape. "That sounds like a divorce, not a separation."

The word *divorce* cut like a knife. Jamie had never considered the possibility. Was that where his marriage was headed?

ten
lizbet

Lizbet took extra care with her appearance to prepare for her trip to Prospect on Sunday. She ran the mascara wand over her eyelashes and smeared on a thin coat of lip gloss. She selected a pale blue sleeveless top to wear with white jeans and blew-dry her hair straight, the way Jamie liked it. During the thirty-minute drive, she contemplated what she would say to her husband when she saw him. She'd tell him about her medical condition and explain why she'd stayed away for so long. The rest would be up to him. She wanted another chance with him more than anything. But she would be asking him to give up the one thing he wanted most in the world.

Lizbet gripped the steering wheel, willing herself to be strong if he asked for a divorce. Regardless of the outcome, they both needed to move on with their lives, either together or alone.

A comforting warmth flooded Lizbet when she entered her old neighborhood. She hadn't realized how much she'd missed her friends and their home. Even though Jamie's truck was missing from the driveway, she parked on the curb in front of the house to admire the improvements he'd made in her absence—the new roof they'd desperately needed and the row of Ligustrum bushes they'd talked about planting to provide privacy from the next-door neighbor. The window boxes spilling over with colorful summer annuals were a woman's touch. Was there someone new in her husband's life?

Lizbet slammed her foot on the gas pedal and sped off toward the center of town.

When she stopped at the red light at Main Street and Creekside Drive, she was surprised to see her mother-in-law's blonde head as she moved around inside the seafood market. They used to be closed on Sundays. Had their hours changed, too, in her absence?

Lizbet took a left onto Creekside Drive and pulled into Sam Sweeney's parking lot. Getting out of the car, she peeked through the glass door at Sam, who was rearranging items on the shelves. When she tapped on the door, Sam looked up, her smile vanishing at the sight of Lizbet.

Sam unlocked the door and opened it a crack. "If you're looking for Jamie, he's not here."

Lizbet was taken aback. She'd never known Sam to be rude to anyone. "You're angry. And I don't blame you."

Sam leveled her gaze on Lizbet. "I'm *disappointed* by the way you've handled the situation. You ran off in the middle of a storm with no explanation. We don't treat people like that where I come from, especially those we love."

"I was confused, Sam. I needed to clear my head."

Sam let out a humph. "After seven months, I hope it's clear as a bell."

Lizbet swallowed past the lump in her throat. "I had a legitimate reason for leaving, Sam. I'm here to talk to Jamie about it now. Do you know where I can find him?"

Sam shot a sideways glance across the road. "He's probably over at the marina."

Lizbet narrowed her eyes. "Is he out on the boat?" she asked, thinking about the center console fishing boat Sam had given Jamie when he graduated from college.

"He's working. He took over ownership of the marina after the hurricane. A lot has changed in your absence." Closing the door, Sam twisted the lock into place and walked away.

Lizbet left her car at Sweeney's and crossed the street on foot.

"Is Jamie Sweeney here?" she asked the giant tatted-up man behind the counter at the marina store.

An appreciative smirk appeared on his lips as he looked Lizbet up and down. "Nah. He's out walking the property next door with some woman. Can I help you with something?"

Lizbeth's skin prickled at the mention of another woman. "No thanks. I need to talk to Jamie," she said, feeling his eyes on her backside as she turned to leave.

As she was exiting the store, she spotted her husband with an attractive blonde on the far side of the parking lot. She continued toward him, calling his name and waving, but he didn't hear her. When the woman kissed him on the mouth, Jamie responded by leaning into her. Lizbet stopped in her tracks, an arm around her midsection as a searing pain tore through her body. Ducking her head, she willed her feet to transport her body back across the road to the car.

Lizbet made it to the outskirts of town before pulling over to the side of the road and vomiting into the gravel. This was all her fault. She'd driven her husband into the arms of another woman. She should've confided in him about her problems, shouldn't have taken so long to reach out. As a result, Jamie had moved on. Not only could this woman make his yard pretty, more than likely, she could give him the family he so desperately wanted.

Lizbet, feeling both emotionally and physically depleted, drove slowly home to Charleston.

She longed for the comfort of her room, to crawl into bed, pull the covers over her head, and block out the world around her. But when she turned onto their block, she saw a crowd of

Brooke's and Sawyer's friends gathered on the front porch of their yellow frame house. They were drinking beer and laughing and dancing to the beat of the pop music blaring from a portable speaker.

In no mood for a party, Lizbet continued driving past the house. The time had come for her to get her own place. She was due a big paycheck at the end of the week. Until then, she would borrow money for a deposit from her father.

She parked beside her father's Buick on the ground floor of his building and rode the elevator to the third floor. She rang the buzzer several times. When her father didn't answer, she let herself in with the key he'd given her for emergencies. A strong stench she couldn't identify assaulted her nose. Was he cooking collard greens again?

She called out, "Dad! Are you home? It's me, Lizbet."

She checked the bedroom and bathroom first before circling back to the kitchen where she found her father lying face down on the floor. Dread overcame her as she dropped to her knees. She shook him gently. "Dad! Are you all right?" When she grabbed his wrist to check his pulse, the feel of his cold skin made her jerk her hand away. As pain gripped her chest, she sat back on her haunches and bellowed out, "No! Dad! Don't die on me now."

With trembling hands, she rummaged through her purse for her phone and clicked on Brooke's number. She called three times before Sawyer picked up. Lizbet could hardly hear her sister's partner over the loud music in the background. "What do you want, Lizbet?"

"Let me speak to Brooke."

"She's busy right now. We're having friends over. I'll tell her you called."

Anger raged through Lizbet. "Let me speak to my sister! Now, damn it!"

"Here we go again," Sawyer said. "Having a tantrum might

work with Brooke, but not with me. Call back when you've calmed down."

Lizbet inhaled a deep breath and willed her voice not to break. "This is an emergency, Sawyer. I just found our father dead on his kitchen floor."

Sawyer's breath hitched. "Hang on a minute." The music faded as Sawyer moved inside the house from the porch. "What happened?"

"I have no idea. He doesn't have a pulse, and his skin is cold. I think he's dead. But what if he isn't? I'm freaking out. What do I do?"

"Hang up and call a rescue squad. Brooke and I will be there soon."

"Hurry!" Lizbet ended the call and tapped 9-1-1 into her phone's keypad. She explained the situation to the operator who promised to send help right away.

Lizbet threw herself across her father's lifeless body. "Please, oh please, oh please. Don't be dead, Daddy. I need you now more than ever."

Ten minutes later, she was still bawling into her father's crisp white shirt when the first responders arrived—a team of two male EMTs and a female police officer whose name tag identified her as Officer Doyle.

Doyle helped Lizbet to her feet and walked her into the living room. "I know you're upset, hon. But you've gotta let us do our job."

Doyle returned to the kitchen, leaving Lizbet alone in the living room. She flung open the french doors and stepped out onto the balcony, gulping in breaths of salty air. This can't be happening.

Ten more excruciatingly long minutes later, Brooke and Sawyer arrived as the EMTs were wheeling her father's body bag out of the kitchen.

"No!" Brooke shrieked, attempting to unzip the bag's zipper. "Let me see him! I need to see him."

Lizbet grabbed her sister's arm. "Trust me. You don't want that image in your mind, Brooke. You can see him later at the funeral home."

"Let her see him if that's what she wants," Sawyer said, shoving Lizbet out of the way.

Lizbet snapped. "Don't you dare push me," she said, slapping Sawyer hard across the cheek.

"I've had about enough of you, you little bitch!" Sawyer went after Lizbet, clawing at her face and pulling her hair.

Doyle broke Sawyer and Lizbet apart, holding them at arm's length. "Pull yourselves together. This situation is difficult enough without fighting."

Lizbet stepped back, away from Sawyer.

"You can take him now," Brooke said to the EMTs with a sad smile. "I'll wait and see him at the funeral home."

Lizbet and Brooke followed the gurney into the hall and watched them load it onto the elevator. Brooke hooked an arm around Lizbet's waist, pulling her close.

"I can't believe this is happening," Lizbet cried.

Brooke stroked her hair. "I know, Lizzie. But Daddy hasn't been the same since Mama died. At least they're together now."

Lizbet sniffled as she nodded.

The sisters walked arm in arm back inside the condo.

Sawyer grabbed Brooke's purse from the chair where she'd dropped it on her way in. "Come on. We need to get you home."

"I'm not going anywhere with you." Brooke got up close to Sawyer's face. "Get out." She extended an arm with finger pointed at the door. "I need some time alone with my sister."

Sawyer's face darkened with anger. "But . . ."

"I want you out. Now." Brooke took Sawyer by the arm and marched her into the hall, closing and locking the door behind her.

The sisters stood in the living room, staring at each other. "What do we do now?" Brooke asked.

"We give him a proper burial, next to Mama in the family plot at Magnolia Cemetery." Lizbet collapsed onto the sofa. "I came over to ask a favor. If not for me, who knows how long it would've been before someone found him?"

Brooke dropped to the sofa beside her. "But you did find him. That's all that matters."

Lizbet shook her head in disbelief. "Maybe he had a heart attack. He hasn't looked well the last few times I've seen him."

Brooke bit down on her balled fist. "I'm sure Mama's already reading him the riot act about something."

Lizbet smiled. "I can hear her now. She's angry because he didn't clean up his apartment before he died."

Lizbet and Brooke remained on the sofa together, crying and talking about old times. They finally dozed off after midnight, their arms and legs entangled like when they were children.

When Lizbet woke at daybreak, she was alone on the sofa and Brooke was coming in from the balcony, her eyes swollen and nose red from crying.

Lizbet eased into a sitting position. "Where have you been?"

"Watching the sun rise." Brooke sat down on the edge of the coffee table. "I just got off the phone with Sawyer. We can go home now if you're ready."

Lizbet rubbed the sleep from her eyes. "After what happened between us yesterday, I think it's better for me to stay here."

"No way! You're coming home with me. I asked Sawyer to stay with a friend for a few days until after the funeral."

Lizbet buried her face in her hands. "I'm so sorry. I keep coming between you two."

Brooke expelled a gush of air. "This isn't your fault, Liz. Sawyer wants to get married, but I'm not ready yet. I love her. At least I think I do. But something is not right with Sawyer. The way she treats you is a red flag. And it's not just you. She was mean to Dad as well. I want this life we've built together. A loving home with marriage and children. But my gut feeling tells me she's not the right one. I want what you and Jamie have."

Lizbet looked up at her sister, her vision blurry with tears. "Jamie and I are over, Brooke. I drove down to Prospect yesterday, hoping to have that overdue heart-to-heart talk with him, and I saw him kissing another woman."

"Oh, honey, I'm so sorry. Come here." Brooke stood to pull Lizbet to her feet and then wrapped her arms around her.

Profound sadness washed over Lizbet, wave after wave like the ocean beating the surf. She'd lost her father and her husband all in one day. How would she ever survive without them?

Brooke cupped Lizbet's face in her hands. "Let's go home. We'll call Georgia. She'll know what to do. She'll guide us through planning Dad's funeral."

Lizbet nodded, not trusting her voice to speak. Georgia always made everything seem better.

eleven
sean

Macy McCall was a female drill sergeant. Despite being only five feet tall, she was built like a tank with mannish features and a deep, booming voice. But she handled Josh with a gentle manner that set Sean at ease.

Macy and Carla played tag with Josh while Sean and Faith talked nearby. Of the three Sweeney sisters, from Sean's perspective—Jackie being the most sophisticated and Sam being the one with all the spunk—Faith was the most feminine. And she had a heart of gold. She handled each of the residents at her women's shelter with tender loving care.

Sean watched Macy chase Josh around the yard. "You were right about her. She appears capable of controlling Josh, but I'm worried about the long hours. Starting tomorrow, Carla and I will be at the restaurant from midmorning until late at night."

"Let's see how it goes. She should be able to handle it. If not, we'll have to find someone to relieve her from time to time." A pensive expression crossed Faith's sweet face. "There is another problem, though. Macy doesn't have a car. She's been at the shelter for months, and she's ready to move on. Ideally, she'd like to find a permanent live-in nanny position. Do you think that's a possibility?"

"Maybe. Carla would have to approve. Josh could sleep in the room with Carla, which would leave the third upstairs bedroom for Macy. Cooper is the problem. He's already unhappy about having Josh and Carla living here. He won't be thrilled about the idea of a live-in nanny."

Faith narrowed her hazel eyes in concern. "Speaking of Cooper, I saw him on my way in. He barely spoke to me. Your mom mentioned he was going through a difficult time, but she didn't elaborate. Is there anything I can do to help?"

"Unfortunately, I don't think there's anything any of us can do. He refuses to talk to anyone about what's bothering him. Including me. And we've never kept secrets from one another."

Faith's gaze traveled to the veranda where Cooper was standing at his easel and staring out over the marsh. "I hate to say this about my own nephew. Goodness knows, I love the boy. But he looks like a homeless bum."

Sean chuckled. "I agree. He's really let himself go. He hasn't left Moss Creek since he got home in October. Not even to go to the grocery store. He eats whatever I leave in the refrigerator. If there's no food in the house, he doesn't eat. He's a zombie. All he does is build websites and paint."

"Maybe he should talk to Big Mo." Big Moses, ex-Heisman trophy candidate for the University of Georgia, was the family's resident shrink. Over the years, nearly every member of the Sweeney family had received counseling from the psychiatrist.

"Believe me, I've suggested it." He smiled as Macy swung the giggling little boy around in circles. "She seems great. I'll handle Cooper. A live-in nanny could solve all our problems. I need my chef's undivided attention at the restaurant, especially during these first crucial weeks. Having Macy living here with Josh will offer Carla peace of mind."

"I don't think you'll regret it."

When they presented the idea to Carla, she jumped at the opportunity, and they made arrangements for Macy to move in first thing the following morning. Sean and Carla agreed to ride to work together so that she could leave her car with Macy for outings and errand running.

After Faith and Macy had left Moss Creek, Sean went in search of Cooper to have the dreaded conversation with his brother. He found Cooper bent over his laptop in his room, his greasy auburn hair shrouding his face, and tapped on the door.

"If you have a minute," Sean said, "I need to talk to you about something." Cooper motioned him in, and he stepped inside the room. "Carla has hired a live-in nanny for Josh. She's one of Aunt Faith's residents, and she seems like a really nice lady. I realize the situation isn't ideal, but it won't be for long. A couple of months, max."

Cooper stared at him, aghast. "You're kidding me?"

"No, bro. This situation is real. The restaurant's opening tomorrow, and Carla needs childcare."

Cooper slammed his computer shut, snatching it up as he jumped to his feet. He grabbed his wallet and car keys off the chest of drawers as he strode angrily out of the room.

Sean hurried after him. "Wait a minute, Coop. Where are you going?"

Cooper kept walking down the stairs and out into the driveway. When he reached his SUV, he turned to face Sean. "I'm moving out. I can't live like this. It's worse than Romper Room with that kid screaming and shouting all the time."

"Won't you please give it a chance?" Sean said in a pleading tone. "Things will be better with Macy here. She's tough. She can control him."

"No one can control that kid. He's the Tasmanian devil." Cooper narrowed his eyes at Sean. "What's up with you, Sean? Why are you going to so much trouble for this woman? Are you in love with her?"

Sean hadn't sorted out his feelings for Carla. He was attracted to her, and he felt sorry for her. But he worried he was attracted to her *because* he felt sorry for her. Regardless, now was not the right time to explore their relationship. He would have to wait until she was more settled, until after the restaurant had launched.

"No! It's nothing like that. Carla is down on her luck, and she doesn't have anyone else to turn to. I'm trying to do right by her, Cooper. Why is that so hard for you to understand?"

"She's carrying baggage, and you're in over your head. I don't want to see you get hurt." Cooper clicked his key, unlocking his car doors. "Either buy me out or we need to sell the house."

"Dude! I'm opening a restaurant tomorrow. I don't have the money to buy you out." Sean wedged his body between his brother and the SUV. "Don't leave like this, Coop. We can work this out. If we talk about it calmly, I'm sure we can come up with a solution."

"Move!" Cooper said, shoving Sean out of the way and reaching for the door handle.

Sean righted himself. "Fine. Go. You won't get far on a flat tire."

Cooper looked down at the flat front tire. "Dang it!"

A smirk appeared on Sean's lips. "That's what happens when you don't drive your car for seven months."

Cooper slumped against the SUV. "I'll call an Uber," he said, tugging his phone out of his pocket.

"And go where?" Sean asked, leaning against the car beside him.

Cooper hunched a shoulder. "To Jamie's, I guess."

Sean caught sight of their neglected guesthouse, tucked away in a cocoon of palmetto trees. "We could clean out the guesthouse for you."

Cooper grunted. "I'm way ahead of you. I thought of that

possibility the day Carla and Josh came to live here. But have you looked in the guesthouse lately? It's full of Mom's crap."

"It can't be that bad." Crossing the driveway to the guesthouse, Sean located the hidden key in the light fixture and unlocked the front door. The living room was crowded with furniture and lamps and accessories—items Jackie had ordered for clients who later decided they didn't want them.

"See what I mean?" Cooper said behind him.

"We can move all this to the garage."

"But my paintings are in the garage," Cooper protested.

"Then we'll move the paintings to one of the bedrooms upstairs."

Cooper considered the idea. "That could work. I'd forgotten there were two bedrooms in here," he said and darted up the stairs with Sean on his heels.

Sean circled the larger of the two bedrooms. "I noticed a small desk downstairs. We can get rid of the bed, and you can make this room your office and art studio."

Cooper opened the door and stepped out onto the balcony. "It's not as large or as open as the veranda, but it's quiet. I guess this could work temporarily until you get rid of Carla and the kid."

Sean glanced at his watch. "It's only three o'clock. If we get to work now, we can have you moved in by dinnertime."

Cooper offered a slight smile. "Okay. Let's do it."

Carla and Josh pitched in to help the brothers clear out the furniture from the guesthouse and transport Cooper's artwork to his new studio. After Cooper moved his belongings from the main house, Sean took over the master bedroom and an exuberant Josh, captivated by the collage of fishing posters covering the walls, claimed Sean's bedroom as his own.

Cooper declined Sean's offer to join them for hamburgers on the grill. "Thanks, but I want to get settled."

Sean was relieved to see his brother upbeat for a change. "I don't blame you. I'll bring you a plate later."

Carla and Josh helped Sean with the Sunday evening chores. After dinner, Sean and Carla finished a bottle of white wine on the patio while Josh played in the yard with the next-door neighbor's mini doodle puppy, Bruno. Sean felt happy, and for the first time in his life, he entertained the notion of one day getting married.

"This is nice," Carla said, kicking her feet up on the ottoman. "I can't remember when I last felt so relaxed." Lowering her tone to a whisper, she added, "I admit, I feel more comfortable with Cooper living in the guesthouse. I know he's your brother, but something about him unnerves me."

Irritation slithered up Sean's spine. "He's not only my brother, Carla, he's my twin. And he's going through a tough time. If you ask me, he's been a good sport about having strangers living in his personal space while he's trying to work through his problems. I'll remind you that Josh destroyed the painting he'd been working on for weeks."

Carla's smile disappeared, and an awkward silence as thick as the Lowcountry humidity hung in the air between them.

After a few minutes, she said, "I'm grateful for all you've done for me, Sean. You're a really nice guy. Are you always so accommodating to every woman who finds herself in a bind?

Sean chuckled. "Let's just say I'm paying it forward. I know what it's like when things don't go your way." He drained the last of his wine. "Although my problem was self-inflicted. I got into drugs in college. I flunked out of Georgia my freshman year."

"That's rough," Carla said with a grimace. "Who helped you get back on your feet?"

"Jamie helped some, but it was mostly my mom. She never gave up on me." Sean realized his mistake as the words left his mouth. "I'm sorry. That was thoughtless of me."

Carla offered Sean a sad smile. "No worries. Moms are

supposed to support their kids through thick and thin. I betrayed my mom by getting pregnant when she'd sacrificed so much for my future." Her gaze returned to Josh and the puppy. "He's been begging me for a dog. This isn't helping any."

"Every boy needs a dog. We grew up with labs. Hunting dogs. All females, some of them yellow but most of them black. We often had more than one at a time."

Sean rested his head against the back of the chair as he thought about all the dogs his family had owned over the years. Sadie had been his favorite, a beautiful red lab they had when Sean and Cooper were about Josh's age. She'd brought Cooper and him such joy. If only Sadie were still around to comfort Cooper now with her quiet presence.

J amie was helping his mom stock the fish display case on Monday morning when Sam asked about his meeting with Lizbet. "Did you two patch things up?"

He jerked his head up, banging it on the top of the display case. "Ouch!" He rubbed his head until the sting went away. "What're you talking about? You know I haven't spoken to Lizbet since October."

"She was here yesterday," Sam said, artfully arranging flounder fillets on a tray. "I sent her to the marina to find you. She left her car in our parking lot. I went into the back for a few minutes. But when I came out, her car was gone."

Jamie puckered his brow. "How long is a few minutes?"

Sam thought about it before answering. "About five minutes, I guess. Since she didn't stay long at the marina, I assumed your talk didn't go well."

"What time was this?"

"Hmm, let's see." Sam drummed her fingers on the counter as she stared up at the wall clock. "I'd say around three thirty."

"That's around the time I was giving Kirstin a guided tour of the wooded property. I must have missed Lizbet. Funny that Lester didn't mention anything about me having a visitor."

Sam slid the flounder tray in the case. "I confess, I wasn't very nice to her."

Jamie's dark eyes were like black coals. "Why would you have been after the way she's treated me? I'm not sure I would've been nice to her either. I have a long list of things I'd like to say to her."

Sam reached for his hand. "You two can't go on in limbo forever. At some point, you and Lizbet need to decide whether to try again or go your separate ways."

The feel of Kirstin's lips on his mouth rushed back to him. "I'm so angry at her. I don't know if I have it in me to give her another chance. She's been gone so long, I doubt she even wants one."

"And she may not. She may have come here to ask for a divorce." Sam pulled him in for a hug. "Living with this uncertainty isn't healthy. Neither is harboring anger. Everyone can see how much this separation is wearing on you. Go to Charleston. See what Lizbet has to say for herself. You have to start somewhere."

"You're probably right. I'll think about it." Jamie pulled away from his mom. "I could use some coffee."

"I have a fresh pot in the back."

Sam disappeared through the swinging door and returned a minute later with two steaming cups of black coffee. As they wandered around the market, making certain everything was in order prior to opening, Jamie told Sam about Kirstin's plans for Creekside Village. "She offered me first choice of locations."

His mom stopped walking and turned to him. "For what? You just rebuilt the marina store."

"I know, but we're already bursting at the seams. I'm calling the second location Sweeney's Outfitters. We would offer high-quality outdoor gear for fishing and other water-related sports. The marina store would become a full-service small grocery store with a deli counter in the back providing made-to-order takeout sandwiches for fishermen."

His mom appeared impressed. "I can tell you've given this careful thought. And I think your ideas are brilliant. But can you afford this new venture with all you've got going on?"

"I would definitely be stretching myself thin. But construction on the village will take a while. Hopefully, by the time the complex is finished, I'll be in a better financial position."

"That's true. Could be a couple of years away."

Jamie and Sam moved over to the window and looked out across the street at the marina. "If you're interested, I'm sure Kirstin would give you a primo location for Sweeney's Market."

Sam spread her arms wide at the intersection of Creekside and Main. "Why would I move when I already have the best location in town? Kirstin's village will attract hordes of new visitors to the area. And they will all drive right past my market as they're coming and going."

"Good point. You're better off staying put. Besides, you own this land." Jamie admired his mother's pretty face, her upturned nose and blue eyes. She was better looking and more energetic every day, as though the clock was turning backward for her. "Kirstin asked if I know who owns the property north of the marina. She has in mind to build waterfront condos on it."

Sam's body stilled. "What did you tell her?"

"That the owner will never sell. Kirstin says everyone has their price. The Bowmans have deep pockets, Mom. You stand to make a fortune. You should consider it."

"I have my own plans for that land. But it's too soon to talk about them," Sam said in an abrupt tone that ended the discussion.

Jamie's phone vibrated with an incoming call from Annie. "Hey, Annie! What's up?"

"Bad news, unfortunately. I thought you might want to know Lizbet's father died suddenly."

Jamie dropped to the windowsill. "I'm sorry to hear that. What happened to him?"

"They think it was a heart attack. Lizbet found him sometime late yesterday afternoon. He'd been dead for a couple of days."

Jamie felt his mother's concerned eyes on him. "God. That's awful. How's Lizbet holding up?"

"She's in shock. Georgia is taking a couple of days off to spend with Liz and Brooke. The funeral is graveside only, which will be held at eleven o'clock on Wednesday morning at Magnolia Cemetery."

Jamie made a mental note of the time and location. "Thanks for letting me know, Annie. I'll see you on Wednesday." He ended the call and broke the news to his mom.

"That's a shame. Phillip was a nice man. Do you think this is why Lizbet left Prospect in such a hurry yesterday?"

"Can't be. She's the one who found him."

"Oh, no! Poor Liz!" Sam sat down next to him on the windowsill. "Now I feel really awful for being so rude to her."

"Don't beat yourself up, Mom. Lizbet knows you love her. I'm not sure what I'm supposed to do since we're not exactly on speaking terms. She's still my wife. Sending flowers or a text is too impersonal."

"You could drive to Charleston to see her," Sam suggested.

"But she'll be busy with funeral preparations and visitors. That could be awkward, considering we're not on the best of terms."

"Then just wait and go to the funeral," Sam said. "I'd like to attend as well. We'll go together."

"Okay. That's what we'll do. It'll be a good way to gauge her feelings for me." Jamie rose slowly and headed toward the door. "I've gotta get to work. My new dockhands are starting this morning, and I need to train them."

With a heavy heart, Jamie traipsed across the road to the marina. While he had little in common with his father-in-law, he found Phillip good natured and easy to be around. Lizbet had grown closer to her father after her mother's death. His absence would create a void in her life. Jamie yearned to reach out to Lizbet. It pained him to know his wife was hurting, and he couldn't comfort her. Their separation had gone on entirely too long.

In the marina store, Jamie found Drew and Eric making goo-goo eyes at Winnie as she showed them how to process a credit card charge on the checkout terminal.

"Come on, boys. A large sport fishing boat is pulling in. This is a good time for y'all to learn," he said and corralled the brothers out of the store.

Eric and Drew had to work hard to keep up with Jamie as he hurried down the dock. "Dude!" Eric said. "Winnie is hot. How old is she?"

Jamie stopped walking and turned to face them. "First of all, I am not your *dude*. I am the man who will sign your paycheck every two weeks. Secondly, Winnie is your superior, and she deserves your respect. If you cross her, I'll fire you on the spot. Are we clear?"

Eric held his gaze, his lips in a thin line and head held high. "Yes, sir! I'm sorry, sir."

Jamie softened, reminding himself they were just kids. "Don't let it happen again."

Drew's eyes got big at the sight of the sport fish behind him. "Wow! Look at that boat. I wanna own one like that one day."

Jamie chuckled. "You'd better choose the right profession, then." He turned his back on them, waving for them to follow him. "Come on. Let's go help them tie up."

The morning flew by without incident. Eric and Drew were eager and hardworking. They took orders well, and by lunchtime, Jamie was ready to let them handle the dock alone on a trial basis. He was heading back to the marina store when he spotted Kirstin getting out of her Mercedes in the parking lot.

She rushed over to him. "I submitted my offer to the

Franklins. I'm a nervous wreck, waiting to hear. You have to talk me off the ledge. Have lunch with me at The Lighthouse. My treat."

Jamie palmed his forehead. "I forgot today is the first day of Sean's soft opening. I'm sure he would appreciate the business."

"Actually, I just went online for a reservation, and they're all booked up. But I called. I got Randy on the phone and sweet-talked him into saving two seats at the bar for us."

Jamie laughed. "I'm impressed with your networking skills."

"I'm the new girl in town. Networking is part of the job. Besides, everyone is so friendly and welcoming in the Lowcountry. Not at all like New England." Kirstin looped her arm through his and dragged him up the stairs to the restaurant.

Sean greeted them at the door of The Lighthouse. "Thanks for coming," he said, giving Jamie a bro hug.

Jamie took in the crowded restaurant. "Look at you, cuz. You're an overnight success."

Sean beamed. "And we didn't even advertise."

Jamie gestured at Kirstin. "Sean, this is—"

"Kirstin. We've met."

Kirstin explained, "I tried to get him to move to Creekside Village, but he refused. I don't blame him. He's got the best view in town from up here."

"No doubt about it," Jamie said, turning in a small circle as he took in the view.

"Sorry, man." Sean slapped Jamie on the shoulder. "I wish you'd called ahead. You're looking at a forty-five-minute wait. Every table is currently occupied."

"No worries," Kirstin said. "Randy is saving us two seats at the bar."

"Perfect." Sean grabbed two menus and walked them to the bar. "Try the soft-shell crab salad special. It's amazing."

Randy's face lit up when he saw them. "Jamie, man! Long time, no see. How are you? And why are you so skinny?"

Jamie laughed. "I've been working hard, my friend."

Randy took their drink orders—sweet tea for Jamie and a glass of sauvignon blanc for Kirstin.

Kirstin's eyes were on Randy's rear as he moved to the other end of the bar. "You and Randy seem chummy," she said. "How do you two know each other?"

"I bartended with him at the restaurant one summer during college, when it was the Pelican's Roost."

"I see. You've done a little of everything, haven't you?"

Jamie smiled. "And I'm just getting started. I've been thinking about it, and I'd like to add my name to your list of potential merchants for Creekside Village," he said and laid out his preliminary plans for Sweeney's Outfitters.

"I love that idea. It's just the type of quality merchandise I'm looking for." Kirstin's phone screen lit up with an incoming text, and she snatched it up from the bar. "This is Carl Franklin. He's accepting our offer. He's calling me to confirm at three o'clock." With a squeal, she dropped the phone on the bar, threw her hands over her head, and did a little victory dance in her chair. "Yay, me! I can't believe this is happening!"

Jamie offered her a high five. "You made it happen! Congratulations. This is a big day for our town."

Their drinks arrived, and as she sipped the chilled wine, her mood grew somber. "I'm sorry about yesterday, Jamie. I would never have kissed you if I'd known you were married. We're going to be seeing a lot of each other, and I hope we can be friends."

"I'm counting on it." Jamie touched his tea glass to hers.

He'd gotten a glimpse of what this formidable woman was capable of, and he was looking forward to watching her in action in the future. She knew what she wanted, and she wasn't afraid to go after it. Unlike Lizbet, who, after seven months, had yet to sort out her problems. Whatever those problems were. He was wrong to compare his wife to another woman. Then again, he hadn't seen Lizbet in so long, he wasn't sure he'd recognize her anymore.

thirteen
lizbet

B rooke did an admirable job of hiding her pain. She exhibited her usual exuberant personality and greeted the many friends who stopped by to offer condolences with a smile. But Lizbet could tell her sister was hurting inside. She heard muffled sobs coming from Brooke's room late at night. She was mourning for their father. But she was also fighting with Sawyer. Whenever Lizbet broached the subject of Sawyer, her sister refused to talk about her partner.

"Let's get through the funeral first," Brooke said. "Our personal problems can wait."

The evening before the funeral, instead of a formal visitation at the funeral home, Lizbet and Brooke invited their friends over to the house. Brooke's girlfriends arrived en masse. But nobody came to see Lizbet. Annie texted an apology about having to miss the visitation because of a big event she and Heidi were catering. Lizbet and Jamie were close to several married couples in Prospect, but Lizbet had lost touch with the wives in the months she'd been away. All her high school friends had moved elsewhere, and she'd made no effort to make any new friends.

Despite the crowd, Lizbet had never felt so alone as she stood off to the side, eavesdropping on the conversations taking place around her. It secretly pleased Lizbet to hear Brooke's friends' brutal assessments of Sawyer.

"You can do better, Brooke. Sawyer has control issues."

"Sawyer is such a bore. You're way more fun."

"Your personalities clash. Sawyer is too uptight. Count your blessings you never married her."

Lizbet's heart went out to her sister. Brooke's breakup was too new, her wounds too fresh, for their harsh words to be of comfort.

Tired of listening to the Sawyer bashing, Lizbet sneaked away to the kitchen. She was nursing a glass of milk when Georgia joined her.

"This is quite the turnout," Georgia said, pouring herself a cup of decaf coffee and joining Lizbet at the table.

Lizbet rolled her eyes. "For Brooke."

"Your life is in Prospect, sweetheart. Do any of your friends down there even know about your daddy?"

She drained the rest of her milk and set the glass on the table with a thud. "This isn't a wake for Daddy. It's a funeral for Brooke's relationship with Sawyer."

Georgia smiled at the roar of laughter sounding from the living room. "It certainly seems that way." Her smile faded. "Have you heard anything from Jamie? I know Annie texted him about your father."

"Nope. He told Annie he's coming to the funeral." Lizbet ran a thumb around the lip of her empty milk glass. "Honestly, I hope he doesn't. I don't want to see him."

Georgia shook her head in confusion. "I don't understand, Lizbet. What happened? Last week, you were ready to work things out with him."

Lizbet exhaled loudly. "I drove down to Prospect on Sunday like I'd planned. When I went to Sweeney's looking for Jamie, I ran into Sam, who couldn't have been ruder to me." Lizbet's eyes fall to the table. "I should've expected it. I'm not surprised she hates me."

"Nobody hates you, sweetheart. I'm sure she's worried about her son. What did she say to you?"

"She told me Jamie was across the street at the marina." She looked up at Georgia. "He bought the marina. Did you know that?"

"Annie might have mentioned something," Georgia said, sipping her coffee.

"Naturally, I'm the last to know. Anyway, I went looking for Jamie, but I couldn't find him, so I came home." Lizbet didn't tell Georgia about Jamie's other woman. His betrayal hurt too much to say the words.

"In other words, you didn't try hard enough." Georgia reached for Lizbet's hand. "I'm gonna shoot straight with you, honey. Just as your mama would if she were here. You have a lot on your plate right now. But once the funeral is over, you need to make your marriage a priority."

"Once the funeral is over, I will make my *future* a priority," Lizbet said, whether or not that included Jamie.

———

Wednesday dawned with hazy skies and thick air, the heat reaching Lowcountry sweltering on the thermostat. A thin coat of perspiration covered Lizbet's face, and her black dress clung to her body as she sat beneath the tent at the cemetery, listening to Minister Sullivan eulogize her father's virtues. The Horne family had belonged to the same Episcopal church for generations. Not only had Sullivan christened Lizbet as a baby, he had also performed the ceremony when she and Jamie married.

Lizbet's mind wandered as her eyes roamed the crowd that consisted mostly of her parents' friends. Her heart skipped a beat when she saw her husband, his handsome sun-kissed face the picture of youth among the oldest and most influential in Charleston society. He'd lost weight since she'd last seen him. The gray suit she'd helped him pick out for their rehearsal dinner hung loosely from his lanky frame. Was she responsible for the weight loss? She'd made so many mistakes in recent months.

Standing next to him was his mother, looking appropriately mournful in a black dress. But when Lizbet saw him again at the house after the lunch reception, Jamie was alone. Only a few funeral attendees remained in the dining room with them.

"Where's Sam?" Lizbet said, because she didn't know what else to say.

"She went home. We drove separate cars. You and I need to talk." Without waiting for her to respond, Jamie led her outside to the garden where the bronze statue of her mother, which her father had commissioned, was verdigrising.

Lizbet had worked countless hours in the garden since last October and her efforts were paying off. There was not a weed in sight, and the rose bushes and other perennials were bursting with blooms.

"Can this wait, Jamie? I just buried my father."

His eyes darkened with anger. "Are you kidding me? I've been patiently *waiting* for seven of the longest months of my life. I've given you the space you asked for to figure out whatever crisis you're dealing with when I don't even know what that crisis is."

Lizbet chewed on her lower lip. There was so much to say, she wasn't sure where to begin. "I came to see you on Sunday."

Jamie's shoulders sagged. "Mom told me. She feels bad for being rude to you."

"She feels sorry for me because my father died."

"Why did you leave the marina without talking to me?"

The image of him kissing the mysterious blonde returned. "I couldn't find you." She inhaled a deep breath, drawing herself to her full height. "I'm sorry, Jamie. I realize this conversation is way overdue, but I'm emotionally spent from the funeral. I'll call you in a few days. We'll figure out a time to talk."

"Let's figure out that time now. How about if I come back to Charleston on Saturday? We'll have lunch and spend the afternoon together."

Lizbet shook her head. "That won't work. I'm working on Saturday."

"Sunday, then. I'll be there at noon." Jamie took her by the arms. "I'm sorry about your father. Phillip was one of the good guys. I'll never forget him crying when I asked for your hand in marriage."

Lizbet's jaw slackened. "He did? You never told me that."

"He seemed embarrassed about it, and it was such a personal moment, I wanted it to be our little secret. He loved you very much, Liz."

Tears filled her eyes as she nodded.

Jamie kissed her cheek. "I've missed you. I look forward to seeing you on Sunday."

A wave of sadness overwhelmed Lizbet as she watched her husband disappear around the side of the house. She grabbed a pair of pruning shears from the garden shed and attacked the roses, removing spent blooms from her mother's prize bushes. Her sense of loss was profound. Both her parents were dead. Her marriage was in jeopardy, and her husband was likely having an affair. She was partially, if not entirely, responsible for breaking up her sister's relationship. And she could never give birth, never hold her biological child in her arms, never see Jamie's smile and beautiful dark eyes on the face of their baby.

Lizbet was still pruning the roses when she noticed Sawyer storm into the house. A minute later, she heard loud voices coming from inside, and Brooke and Sawyer appeared in the window. Sawyer was screaming at Brooke, jabbing her finger at her sister's face. Brooke was backing away from her, shielding her face with her hands as though afraid Sawyer would hit her.

Something inside Lizbet snapped. She returned to the shed, exchanged her pruning shears for a garden hoe, and marched through the house, ignoring the whispers of the catering staff cleaning up the kitchen. The sound of arguing intensified as she stomped up the stairs.

Sawyer yelled, "Why are you doing this to me? To us? I moved here from California to be with you. We were going to get married and start a family. Why are you throwing it all away?"

"I never said I'd marry you," Brooke said in a meek voice.

Was Brooke afraid of Sawyer? Was that why she stayed with her for so long? Because she was afraid to leave her?

"This is about your sister, isn't it? Lizbet has finally gotten to you. Whatever she's telling you isn't true. She's a certified lunatic who should be locked up in a mental hospital."

Lizbet barged into Brooke's room without knocking. With the garden hoe raised over her head, she strode angrily toward Sawyer. "Get away from my sister or you'll see what crazy really looks like!"

"Lizbet! Put down that hoe this instant!"

Georgia's shrill voice stopped Lizbet in her tracks, but she kept the hoe suspended in the air above her head. "Get her out of here before I hurt her."

"Gladly." Georgia took Sawyer by the arm and ushered her out of the room.

Lizbet dropped the hoe, and it fell to the carpeted floor with a thunk. She bent over and placed her hands on her knees as she struggled to catch her breath. "Oh my god. I am crazy. I just went postal on her. If not for Georgia, I might have killed her."

Brooke took Lizbet's trembling body in her arms and held her tight. "Don't be ridiculous. You don't have it in you to commit murder. Sawyer brings out the worst in both of us. I say good riddance to her."

An exasperated and out-of-breath Georgia returned five minutes later. "I finally got her to leave. I had to threaten to call the police, though. She's emotionally unhinged, but I think she's realizing your relationship is over. She's coming at nine o'clock in the morning for her things. I'll meet her here. I assume you'll both be at work. If not, make yourselves scarce. In the meantime, if she comes back, I want you to call the police immediately."

Brooke threw her arms around Georgia. "What would we do without you?"

Georgia stroked Brooke's back. "I'm glad I was here. I'm just sorry you're having to deal with this on top of your father's death." She kissed Brooke's head before pushing her away. "I'm going to check on things downstairs. You two need to get some rest."

The Horne sisters curled up together on Brooke's bed, and within minutes, both were sleeping soundly.

Dusk had settled over the room when a sharp abdomen pain woke Lizbet. Her mind raced as she calculated the dates. Her period wasn't due until next week.

She rolled over to find her sister staring at the ceiling with tears streaming down the sides of her face. "I'm so sorry, Brooke. I feel responsible for your breakup."

Brooke sat bolt upright. "Are you kidding me? None of this is your fault, Liz. I stayed with Sawyer for the wrong reasons. Because I knew the breakup would be unpleasant."

"Has she ever hit you before?"

"No." Brooke collapsed against the pillows. "But there were times I worried she might. I'm the one who owes you an apology. I should have kicked her out when she started picking on you."

"No apology necessary," Lizbet said, her hand on her cramping belly. "You felt trapped. I get that. I hope we've seen the last of her."

"If we're lucky, she'll go back to California." Brooke turned her head to look at Lizbet. "I don't know about you, but I'm starving."

"Me too. I ate nothing at the reception." Relief overcame her. Maybe her stomach was cramping from hunger.

Brooke sat up in bed. "I'm sure the catering staff left us some food. I bet there's some wine left over too. I could use a glass. Or a bottle."

Swinging their legs over opposite sides of the bed, the sisters plodded in bare feet down the stairs to the kitchen. Opening a bottle of rosé, they loaded up two plates with leftovers and went outside to the swing on the front porch.

Brooke touched her glass to Lizbet's. "Well, sis, the funeral is over. Time to put our personal lives in order."

Lizbet sipped the dry pink wine, hoping the alcohol would ease the abdominal pain. "The future can wait until tomorrow. Tonight, let's talk about the past. Do you remember the matching doll houses Dad built for us when we were little girls?"

fourteen
sean

During the first week of soft openings, Sean and Carla worked fourteen-hour days, arriving at The Lighthouse before nine in the morning and returning home after eleven at night. Sean attributed his overnight success to his head chef. Not only was she a creative genius when it came to food, Carla had the innate ability to think fast on her feet, putting out fires quickly and efficiently, no matter the size of the blaze. She placated disgruntled customers—not that there were many—and managed her kitchen staff with a firm but sympathetic hand.

But by the end of the first week, Sean noticed the toll Carla's absence from home was taking on her son. Josh had grown increasingly more argumentative at breakfast, the only shared time mother and son had together. He threw raging temper tantrums when Carla left for work, and he refused to go to bed until she came home at night. The nanny never complained about her disobedient charge, but the dark circles beneath Macy's eyes were telling. She was in over her head. They were all in over their heads. And Sean had no clue how to dig them out.

Friday night proved to be their busiest night yet. The restaurant was still hopping at nine o'clock. Every table was occupied.

The patrons kept coming, adding their names to the hour-long waiting list before fighting for seats at the bar. Sean was working the crowd with Eileen, the head hostess, when Carla stormed out of the kitchen.

She slipped off her chef's coat and slung her purse over her shoulder. "Here!" She threw the coat at Sean. "I've gotta go. Josh is missing," she said and fled the restaurant with no further explanation.

Sean handed Eileen the coat. "Hold down the fort as best you can. I'll be right back."

He took off after Carla, and when he caught up with her in the parking lot, she was pacing up and down the rows of parked cars. "What do you mean, Josh is missing?"

"Macy can't find him. She's looked everywhere." Carla rummaged through her purse.

"I can't find my keys. And where the heck is my car?"

"Macy has your car, remember? I'll drive you home. I'm parked over here," Sean said, sweeping an arm at the full parking lot.

Carla clung to Sean as he guided her to his truck. "I'm so scared. Josh doesn't know how to swim. What if he fell off the dock?"

"I told him not to go out on the dock alone," Sean said, although he was pretty sure the kid wasn't listening when he tried to warn him of the dangers of being on the dock without a grown-up.

They were almost at his truck when Sean spotted Jamie emerging from the marina store. He flagged him down. "Dude! I'm glad to see you. We have an emergency at Moss Creek. Carla's son is missing. Can you cover for me at the restaurant until we get back?"

Jamie appeared concerned. "Of course. I'll head up there now."

Sean was thankful Jamie didn't slow them down with questions. "Thanks, cuz. You're the best! I owe you one."

"Good luck! Text me when you find him," Jamie called out to Sean as he slid behind the wheel of his truck.

"Go faster!" Carla demanded as he sped south on Creekside Drive past the multimillion-dollar homes overlooking the inlet.

"I'm driving the limit. This stretch of Creekside is a known speed trap." He glanced over at Carla. "Speaking of the police, do you know if Macy called them?"

Carla stared at the phone gripped tightly in her hand. "She didn't say. She'd just discovered him missing when she alerted me. She fell asleep on the sofa. When she woke up, he was gone. What kind of nanny falls asleep on the job?"

Sean held his tongue against the sarcastic remarks that came to mind. Maybe a scare like this would finally wake her up to Josh's behavioral problems.

"I'll try Cooper." Sean clicked on his brother's number and brought the phone to his ear. After three rings, Cooper answered in a lifeless voice.

"Cooper. Have you seen Josh?"

Cooper paused a beat. "Josh who? Oh, wait. The kid. No, I haven't seen him. I've been working on a big website design project. Why?"

"He's missing. Carla and I are on the way home. Can you help Macy look for him?"

Cooper groaned. "Yeah. Whatever," he said and hung up.

Sean felt Carla watching him. "*Josh who?* What is wrong with your brother? My son has been living in your house for almost a week, and he doesn't even know his name."

Sean white-knuckled the steering wheel. Cooper may have his share of problems, but nothing compared to her son. "He was just distracted. He's in the middle of working on a project." He hated making excuses for his brother. But Carla was the star of his show. The Lighthouse would fail without her.

They arrived at Moss Creek to find Cooper and Macy roaming around the yard with flashlights, calling out for Josh. Landscape lighting provided dim illumination around the exterior of the house, but the area near the water was pitch-black.

A frantic Macy explained what had happened. "I started a movie for him around seven thirty. I drifted off around eight. When I woke thirty minutes later, he was gone. He's not inside the house. I searched from top to bottom." She threw her arms around Carla. "I'm so sorry. I can't believe this has happened."

Carla shoved the woman away. "I can't believe it either. I'm not paying you to sleep, Macy."

Sean rested a reassuring hand on Macy's shoulder. "Arguing about how this happened won't help us find him. Have you checked the dock?"

When Macy and Cooper shook their heads, Sean sprinted down to the dock and turned on the spotlight. The overhead light helped little as he raced up and down the boardwalk, looking down into the inky water for a glimpse of Josh's blond head. He knew his efforts were futile. A kid who couldn't swim would've drowned instantly.

Sean pulled out his phone and placed a call to Jamie's stepfather. Eli answered in a groggy voice. "What's up, Sean?"

"I'm sorry to bother you, Eli. I'm taking liberties by calling you directly, but I have an emergency, and I need your help. My friend's four-year-old son is missing at Moss Creek. His babysitter fell asleep, and he disappeared." Sean checked his watch. "He's been gone now for over an hour. But he can't swim."

Sounding more alert, Eli said, "I'll gather my search and rescue team. We can be there in thirty minutes. In the meantime, keep looking for him."

Sean located more flashlights in the garage, and the foursome methodically searched the Moss Creek property. A half hour later, a long line of first-responder vehicles paraded down the driveway, and an army of search and rescue workers appeared on the scene.

Eli's gray eyes were somber when he introduced himself to

Carla. "I promise. We will find your son," he said, and began barking out orders to his men and women.

One group searched the wooded lot on the south side of the property while another scoured the neighbors' yards to the north. A rescue helicopter hovered over the inlet, using high-beam lights to search the marsh, and another two-man crew launched an inflatable raft to explore the waters in and around the dock.

Cooper watched the action from the veranda while Macy brewed pots of strong coffee no one drank. Sean and Carla waited on the wicker love seat on the terrace for news of her son.

Sean pulled a shivering Carla close for comforting. "I know you're worried, but we're gonna find him."

"You don't know that. He probably fell in the water and drowned." She cupped her hands around her eyes, blocking the commotion from her sight. "I can't bring myself to look at the water. I keep imagining his lifeless body lying at the bottom of the creek. I signed him up for swimming lessons. He's supposed to start a week from Monday. I should've done it sooner."

"You're doing it now. That's what's important. He's an active boy. He'll be a good swimmer. And you'll have peace of mind."

"If he's not . . ." A sob caught in her throat, preventing her from saying the word.

Sean gave her a squeeze. "He's not dead, Carla. He's somewhere safe and sound, and we're going to find him."

"I'll never be able to trust anyone to look out for him, especially not Macy."

If she fired the nanny, Sean would lose his head chef, and his success would be the shortest-lived on record. "Things like this happen, Carla. Especially with little boys. It's part of growing up. When Cooper and I were about ten, we got caught out in a storm in our Jon boat. We were flying through the marsh at low tide, hoping to beat the storm home, when we ran aground. We tore the motor all to hell. We huddled together in the bottom of the boat as lightning streaked all around us. We were scared out of our minds and praying for our lives. Our parents called the police. They didn't find us until the next morning."

The anecdote was partially true, although slightly embellished for greater impact. There'd been no need to call the police. Their dad had come looking for them. And they'd made it home in time for dinner. But the story appeared to set Carla somewhat at ease. Her teeth stopped chattering, and she exhaled a deep breath as she slumped against him.

Sean's hopes dwindled with every minute that passed. He stared into the black night, imagining the various scenarios that might have happened to the young boy. He marveled at how quickly the balance of life could tip. In the blink of an eye, everything had changed forever.

One by one, the rescue workers returned from their searches to report finding nothing. Just a few minutes before midnight, one of the team leaders climbed through the hedge from the next yard over. Tucked beneath his muscular arm was Josh.

Carla sprang up from her chair and sprinted across the yard, taking Josh from the rescue worker and hugging him close to her body. Sean, a broad grin on his face, followed in her tracks.

The rescue worker explained, "We found him inside your next-door neighbor's house, asleep beside the puppy's kennel. Apparently, he sneaked into the house when the neighbor let the puppy out to potty. The neighbor had no idea he was even there."

"I just wanted to play with Bruno, Mommy," Josh cried, his face buried in Carla's neck.

Carla bounced from foot to foot under the weight of the four-year-old. "Mommy's not mad, sweetheart. We're all just glad you're okay."

Not mad? Sean thought. If Josh were his kid, he'd beat his behind black and blue.

Macy emerged from the house with a hand on her chest and relief covering her face. "Thank the good Lord in heaven. I am so sorry, Miss Carla. From the bottom of my heart. I promise never to take my eyes off the child again."

Carla's emerald eyes were cold and hard. "You won't, because you're fired. Go back to that homeless shelter or wherever it is you came from. Your services are no longer needed here."

Sean gave Macy a sympathetic look. "Come on, Carla. We've all had a long night. Josh is safe and sound. That's the most important thing. Firing Macy won't do anyone any good."

Through clinched teeth, Carla said, "Get this woman out of my sight right now."

Macy pulled out her phone. "I'll call an Uber."

"No need. I'll give you a ride." Sean placed a hand on Macy's back, guiding her toward the driveway.

"Shouldn't I pack my things?" Macy asked.

"Not yet. Let me talk to Carla again in the morning once she's calmed down."

"Okay," Macy said, shuffling along beside him.

Sean waited until they were in the truck, headed back toward town to call Faith. "I have Macy with me, and we're headed your way. We had a minor mishap tonight, but everyone is fine. We'll sort everything out in the morning. But I think it's best if she stays with you tonight."

"Of course, Sean. I was just in the kitchen having a cup of tea. I'll be on the lookout for you."

Sean ended the call and dropped his phone into the cupholder. "She's waiting for us."

"I don't want to lose my job, Sean," Macy said, biting on a fingernail. "But Josh is a bigger handful than I bargained for. I've established some ground rules with him, and we are making progress, but he takes a lot out of me, both emotionally and physically. With you and Carla gone all day, there's no one here to relieve me."

Sean never thought about that. How did the poor woman manage five minutes alone to use the restroom?

"We've been swamped at the restaurant this week with way more business than we dreamed of. Unfortunately, you and Josh are suffering because of our success."

Macy blushed. "I hope we can work it out. But I don't think I can stay on unless some things change."

"I understand." Sean parked beneath the portico at the women's shelter and shifted in his seat toward Macy. "I need to think things through. Maybe I can come up with a solution. I'll be in touch tomorrow."

When Faith appeared in the doorway, Sean waved at her, and she blew him a kiss.

Macy craned her neck to see Faith and then looked back at Sean. "What should I tell her? I don't want her to think I'm incompetent."

"Tell her the truth. Faith's the most compassionate person I know. She won't think you're incompetent. She'll think you're human."

fifteen
jamie

Jamie looked up from the restaurant's seating diagram to see Kirstin waiting for a seat at the bar. A thrill of excitement ran through him. These past few days, he'd been thinking entirely too much about the real estate developer and not enough of his wife. However, at the moment, he needed help managing the restaurant, and Carla was the most resourceful person he knew. Even if she had no restaurant experience, she was at least a warm body.

He tapped Kirstin lightly on the shoulder, and she turned to face him, a dazzling smile on her lips. "Jamie! What a pleasant surprise. Are you waiting for a table?"

"I wish. I'm filling in for Sean and Carla. She had an emergency with her kid, and they had to leave suddenly."

Kirstin glanced around the restaurant. "Must have been urgent for them to walk out with so many guests in the house."

"I assume so. They didn't go into detail." It wasn't Jamie's place to spread gossip about Carla's missing son.

Glancing around, Kirstin said, "It's mayhem in here. Do you need some help?"

"I could use an extra set of hands. But I hate to interrupt your dinner plans," he said, more curious than he should be about who she was meeting for drinks and/or dinner.

"I don't have any plans. I was gonna grab a glass of wine and see if I could order dinner from the bar."

"In that case . . . If you don't mind . . ."

"I don't mind at all. I'm not much of a cook, but I'm good with people. Why don't I greet customers while you check on things in the kitchen?"

"That'd be awesome. Just do the best you can."

He introduced Kirstin to Eileen at the hostess stand before making his way through the crowded restaurant to the kitchen, where he discovered absolute chaos. Orders were screwed up. Cooks were fighting. Someone had left a skillet unattended and started a small fire. His experience working in the kitchen at Sweeney's kicked in, and he soon had things under control.

When the last patron had gone, the staff pitched in to clean up. It was almost midnight by the time the last employees left for home.

He gave Kirstin a hug. "I owe you one. I couldn't have survived without you." He gestured at the bar. "If you still want that drink, I remember enough from my bartending days to pour a glass of wine."

Kirstin laughed. "Thanks, but I won't sleep if I drink wine at this hour."

"We could raid the refrigerator," Jamie suggested. "I have a hunch we might find some tempting leftovers."

"I'm not really hungry either. But I could use some fresh air and advice about the local housing market." Her gaze drifted to the window. "Fancy a walk on the docks?"

"Sure! What're we waiting for?" he said, stepping out of the way for her to walk ahead of him.

Locking the door behind them, they descended the stairs and strolled out onto the main dock.

Kirstin inhaled a deep breath as she tipped her face to the

night sky. "Marinas are so peaceful at night, when all the boat owners are tucked away in their cramped staterooms."

Jamie shoved his hands in his pockets as he lumbered along beside her. "Sounds like you're speaking from experience."

"I've spent much of my life in marinas. My mother died when I was young. As his only child, my father insisted I travel with him on his many business trips. You name it, and I've been there. From Australia to Singapore to China and Japan."

"That's amazing. What did you do about school?"

Kirstin tucked a strand of hair behind her ear. "I was home-schooled. My tutor traveled with us. She spoke nine languages. I learned more from Nala than I would've in any classroom."

"I bet. How many languages do you speak?"

"I speak a little of many languages, but I'm only fluent in English." When they reached the end of the dock, they gazed out over the moonlit inlet. "No matter where I am, I never get tired of looking at the water. Since I'll be working in Prospect for the foreseeable future, I'm going to need a home. And I prefer buying instead of renting. A swanky condo overlooking the inlet would be ideal. Obviously, such unicorns don't exist in this area. Which is why I will eventually build a complex on the land north of the marina." She winked at Jamie. "But that doesn't help me any now."

Jamie refused to be baited into a conversation about the land north of the marina. "I keep an eye on the local housing market. One day I hope to buy something on the water too. The best properties are south of the marina. You can spend anywhere from three hundred thousand for a fixer-upper to several million for a large home on a significant spread of land."

"That's pretty much what my Realtor told me. Problem is, I don't need a McMansion. Nor am I interested in renovating a fixer-upper."

Turning, they started back down the dock. "There are a row of townhouses that front the creek a couple miles north of here,"

Jamie says. "My grandmother used to live there. I wouldn't call them swanky, but—"

"No thanks. The one I looked at today was a dump."

"Have you considered looking for something at one of the nearby beaches?"

"I don't want to commute. I need to be hands on at all times."

"Then your choices are limited, Kirstin. Your best bet is to look for a small house in a nice neighborhood. You'll get your fill of water views during the day. At night, you can go home and listen to the crickets chirping in your garden."

"Ugh. That sounds way too domesticated for me." Kirstin stopped walking and peered over the top of a center console fishing boat. "What's that over there?"

"Where?" Jamie's dark eyes followed the end of her finger to a custom-built houseboat on the next dock over. "Oh. That's my inheritance."

She lifted a manicured eyebrow. "Someone left you a floating heap of junk in their will. Sounds more like a curse than a bequest."

"It kinda is," Jamie said with a laugh. "I have no clue what to do with it, so I parked it over there, hoping some fool would come along and buy it."

"That fool might be me." Kirstin, with Jamie on her heels, navigated the maze of docks to the houseboat. "Tell me more about your benefactor."

"Uncle Mack wasn't technically my uncle. He was my grandfather's best friend. He loved this boat, lived on it for the last ten years of his life."

"What's it made of?" Kirstin asked, walking up and down the dock as she inspected the vessel from every angle.

"The hull is fiberglass and the siding solid teak. Technically, it's a house barge since it doesn't have an engine."

"What's it like inside?"

"Pretty tricked out, surprisingly. Mack loved to tinker on his barge."

"Can I see it?" Kirstin bounced on her toes, pressing her hands together under her chin. "Pretty please."

Jamie narrowed his eyes as he studied her face. "I can't tell. Are you being serious?"

"I'm totally serious. This is just what I'm looking for. It has a killer vibe, and you can't beat the location."

"I think you're crazy, but whatever," Jamie said, pulling his keys out of his pocket.

Kirstin's breath hitched when she entered the main cabin. "This heart pine is scrumptious," she said while admiring the reclaimed wood covering the floors and walls of the salon and galley.

"I cleared out all Mack's furniture except this." He ran his hand across the pine wood of the custom-made built-in dinette. "Mack built these himself. Along with the queen-size bed in the loft bedroom."

"Clearly, your Uncle Mack was a master craftsman. I want to see the bedroom," Kirstin said, and climbed up the wooden ladder to the only bedroom. "I just love it, Jamie." She opened the door and walked out onto the small covered deck. "I'll pay you cash for the boat right now. How much do you want?"

Jamie chuckled. "I have no clue how much it's even worth. I've never considered selling it. Why don't you rent it from me? Heck, you can live here for free. Just pay the dockage fees."

"No way. I want to make it my own, and you won't like what I have in mind." She winked at him. "My plan involves a lot of pink."

"Would you get rid of the heart pine?"

"Not a chance. The wood is the best part."

Jamie exhaled a slow breath of air as he considered her offer. "I don't know, Kirstin. I've kept it all these years for sentimental reasons. I need to talk to my mom first. She was closest to

Mack." He stood at the railing, the twinkling lights of the marina giving him a peaceful feeling. "I'll show it to you again in the morning. You might not find it as appealing in the light of day. The confined quarters will get old, fast. The bathroom features are minimal. Your days of soaking in bubble baths would be over. And the storage space is limited. I'm certain a woman with your sophisticated taste has an extensive wardrobe."

Kirstin laughed. "You'd be surprised. I grew up a tomboy. I don't spend hours on end admiring my reflection in the mirror. I admit I like to shop. But I don't horde my clothes. I clean my closets out regularly."

He looked sideways at her. "A tomboy, huh? You *are* full of surprises, Kirstin Bowman." His arm touched hers and a shiver ran across his skin.

"You can't possibly be cold in this heat. The sun set hours ago, and it's still eighty degrees," she said, consulting her Apple Watch for the temperature.

Jamie eased down to the edge of a chaise lounge. "The truth is, I'm attracted to you. I'm trying my best to ignore my feelings, but they keep creeping up on me. We're gonna be seeing each other a lot, and I want us to be friends. I'm not sure what to do about it."

"Maybe it will help if you tell me more about your wife." Kirstin stretched out on the matching chaise lounge next to him. "You said she's been living in Charleston since October. How does she fit into your life?"

"That's a good question. Liz and I are long overdue a talk. I spoke with her briefly at her father's funeral on Wednesday. We made a date to spend the day together on Sunday."

Kirstin's expression grew grim. "Was her father ill for long? Is that why she went back to Charleston? To take care of him?"

"Actually, Phillip died suddenly from a heart attack." Jamie leaned back against the chair. "I'm not sure why she left, honestly.

She was having a life crisis of some sort. She said it was personal, and she needed some time alone."

Kirstin scrunched up her nose. "Personal? Is she having an affair?"

Jamie shook his head. "Liz would never do something like that. Best I can tell, her problem is career related. She's a trained chef with a degree from the CIA. She felt unfulfilled managing a sandwich shop."

Kirstin turned her head to the side to look at him. "Why didn't Sean hire her at The Lighthouse?"

"The position would've been perfect for her, but she'd already left by the time he took over the restaurant."

"I can see where she might have more professional opportunities in Charleston. What's she doing now?"

"She's working for Annie, my half-sister, who runs a catering company she owns with her mother."

Kirstin snorted. "Doesn't sound like much of a job upgrade to me." She rolled her head back and stared up at the metal roof. "Your wife is up to something, Jamie. If I were you, I'd find out what it is. You're a nice guy. Sounds to me like she might be playing you for a fool."

Jamie responded with silence. Kirstin had never met Lizbet. Naturally, she would assume his wife was involved in something nefarious. The circumstances certainly suggested it. Was it possible? Was he too blinded by love for his wife to recognize the obvious?

sixteen
sean

S ean wondered what he had ever seen in Carla as he sat across the breakfast table from her on Saturday morning. He'd been arguing with her for thirty minutes, but she refused to give Macy another chance. While she was a creative genius, she lacked a lick of common sense when it came to anything outside of her culinary domain.

Sean set his coffee mug down on the table with a thud. "What's your plan then, Carla? You've exhausted your search for babysitters, and we're way too busy at the restaurant for Josh to come to work with you."

"I'll figure something out. I just need a few days."

Sean planted his elbow on the table and raked his fingers through his auburn hair. "We don't have a few days. We need to capitalize on the success we've seen this week. We have to be on our A game. Now is not the time to slack off."

Carla stared down at her coffee, her hands wrapped around the mug. "I'm sorry, Sean. But my son comes first."

He glanced over at Josh, who was too busy slurping down Froot Loops to pay attention to what the grown-ups were saying.

"If you're so concerned about your son, why do you let him eat that garbage?"

Sean realized he'd crossed a line, and he prepared for Carla's wrath, but she didn't look up from her coffee. "I'm too exhausted from last night to make him breakfast."

"And you call yourself a chef," Sean grumbled as he pushed back from the table. He snatched up the cereal bowl and dumped the contents down the disposal.

Josh jumped up and rushed over to the counter, staring into the sink as the Froot Loops went down the drain. "Hey! Why'd you do that?" the kid asked, staring up at Sean with his mama's emerald eyes.

"Because I'm cooking you eggs for breakfast." He opened the refrigerator and removed a carton of eggs. "They'll make you strong so you can do all the cool stuff big kids do."

Josh peered over the top of the counter, watching Sean beat two eggs with a fork. "Will you put cheese in them like Macy does?"

"You bet," Sean said, returning to the refrigerator for the grated cheddar cheese.

Josh stuck his lower lip out in a pout. "I don't understand why Macy had to leave. I really like her."

Sean gave Carla a scornful look. "I do too, buddy." He tousled the boy's sandy curls before returning his attention to the stove.

When the eggs were done, Sean scooped them onto a plate and carried it to the table for Josh. "Carla, I need a word with you in private." Without waiting for her response, he turned his back on her and walked out onto the veranda.

Carla waited a few minutes before joining him. "I know what you're gonna say, Sean, but I won't change my mind about Macy."

Sean could no longer hold his tongue. He refused to pay Carla to stay at home with Josh. So what if he made her angry enough to quit? At least he'd be rid of her. "You're being hardheaded, Carla. Accidents happen, and Macy feels awful about it. But you and I are also at fault. We were MIA this week while Macy was taking care of him around the clock. There was no one here to relieve her, not for a thirty-minute dinner break or to even use the bathroom. I can see why she fell asleep on the sofa while he was watching a movie. She was exhausted."

Carla's green eyes turned cold. "If she's not equipped to handle him, maybe she shouldn't have taken the job."

Sean's temper spiraled. "Would you listen to yourself? Not even *you* can handle him, Carla. He's an active little boy with anger management issues. I've gone above and beyond the call of duty for you. I invited you to live in my house. My brother's barely speaking to me because of it. You should've told me from the beginning you were a single parent. Especially given the long hours our industry demands."

Carla jutted out her chin in defiance. "You wouldn't have hired me if I'd told you the truth."

"Probably not." Sean leaned against the wooden railing. "Which might've been the best thing for everyone involved."

"Are you firing me?" Carla asked, her eyes wide.

"I'm considering it," Sean said to alarm her. He couldn't fire her, even if he wanted to. She would slap him with a discrimination lawsuit before the day was out.

"But The Lighthouse is a success because of me."

Sean dug his thumb into his chest. "I've poured my blood, sweat, and tears into this restaurant. I deserve some of the credit for its success. Despite what you might think, you're not the only talented chef in the Lowcountry. I can't run a restaurant without a chef. We can't afford for you to take a few days off to look for a new nanny. You need to make things right with Macy." Sean pushed off the railing. "I'm going to work. If you're not there by noon, I'll assume that means you quit."

"But . . ."

Sean stormed off the veranda, leaving Carla staring after him with her mouth wide open. He gathered his belongings, said goodbye to Josh, and left the house. On the way to his truck, he felt Cooper watching him from the guesthouse balcony, but he didn't stop. He was tired of Cooper and Carla not taking responsibility for their own problems.

When he arrived at the marina, he stopped in at the store to thank Jamie for covering for him last night.

"Happy to help, cuz," Jamie said. "I assume you found the kid?"

Sean smiled. His cousin's cheerful mood softened his sour one. "Not until after midnight. He'd sneaked into the neighbor's house to play with their puppy and fell asleep beside the kennel. The neighbor didn't know he was there until the police knocked on his door."

Winnie came from behind the counter. "Speaking of puppies, my friend's red lab had a large litter, all females. He still has four available if you know anyone who might want one."

Sean kept a straight face, even though the mention of red labs piqued his interest. Cooper and Sean often dreamed of getting a pair of red lab puppies from the same litter. Sisters or brothers, they didn't care which as long as they were the same gender.

Winnie babbled on. "In case you didn't know, a red lab is a yellow lab with a darker coat similar to a fox."

Sean rolled his eyes. "I know what a red lab is, Winnie." He hadn't spoken to Winnie since the day he was so rude to her. What was it about her that got under his skin?

Winnie dropped her smile. "Whatever. I'm just spreading the word, helping my friend out. The puppies have excellent pedigrees."

Sean experienced a pang of guilt. Why was he being a jerk to Winnie for no apparent reason? "Who's the breeder?"

"The guy's name is Oliver Gray."

Sean nodded. "I know Oliver. I grew up with him. His family always had the nicest, most well-trained dogs around."

Winnie absently straightened a display of breath mints. "I'm going to see the puppies again after work, if you'd like to come."

A flicker of excitement stirred inside of him. Sean had always been a sucker for a puppy. "Do you mind if I bring a friend along? He's just a kid, and he's puppy crazy."

"That'd be awesome. The more the merrier," Winnie said, and they made arrangements to meet in the marina parking lot when her shift ended at three o'clock.

Jamie, who had been eavesdropping on their conversation, said, "Puppies are a lot of work, Sean. And you just opened a restaurant. Are you thinking of getting one?"

Sean's blue eyes twinkled with mischief. "Maybe. If I wait for the right time, it may never come," he said, play-punching his cousin's arm.

Sean realized how crazy it was for him to even consider getting a puppy, but he could think of little else as he worked in the kitchen, concocting the day's lunch special—a grilled chicken sandwich with his own secret aioli sauce.

He kept one eye on the clock, watching the second hand tick toward noon. Relief overcame him when Carla showed up a few minutes after twelve. "I assume you worked things out with Macy?"

"You didn't give me any choice." Carla hung up her purse and slipped on her chef's coat. "And it took some convincing. Macy doesn't seem to really want the job. I have a bad feeling about this, Sean. If anything happens to my son, I'm holding you personally responsible."

Sean glanced around to see if anyone had overheard Carla before dragging her into his office. "Don't you dare threaten me, Carla. If something happens to Josh, it's not on me or Macy. It's on you. You're his mother." He sucked in a deep breath, willing himself to calm down. "So here's the plan. You and I will take turns going home to Moss Creek to spend time with Josh and give Macy breaks. I'm taking him on a surprise outing at three. Why don't you take them dinner around five thirty before our evening rush?"

"Whatever. You've made it clear I have to play by your rules if I want to keep my job."

Sean stared at her, aghast. "I'll remind you, this is *your* son we're talking about. I'm trying to do what's right for him."

Something had drastically shifted in his relationship with Carla. They were no longer friends, and Sean sensed a rocky path ahead of them as boss and employee.

Josh was thrilled at the prospect of a surprise outing, and Macy appeared content to have a few minutes to herself. When he and Josh left Moss Creek, she was sipping a glass of sweet tea while sunning on the patio.

On the way back to the marina, the four-year-old peppered him with questions about the excursion, but Sean gave little away. "You'll have to wait and see. But I'm pretty sure you're gonna have fun."

When they picked up Winnie, she played along with Sean. "I'll give you a hint," she teased. "We're not going to the circus."

Josh's face flushed in irritation. "That's not fair. Give me a hint about where we *are* going."

"We're going to someone's farm. And that's all I'm gonna say," Winnie said, drawing an imaginary zipper across her lips.

They arrived at Oliver's family's farm to find the eight puppies frolicking in the grass inside a portable pen beside the barn. Winnie opened the gate to let Josh in. "Be careful now. They're still babies."

"Aww. They're so cute." Josh dropped to his knees, and the puppies surrounded him, nipping at his hands as they crawled on top of him.

Sean watched Winnie as she inspected each of the puppies,

calling them by name and kissing their noses. He was so mesmer-ized by her, he didn't hear Oliver approach.

"Is she your girlfriend?" Oliver asked, his eyes on Winnie.

Sean startled. "Who, Winnie? Heck, no. She's just a kid. That would be like robbing the cradle. I thought maybe she was dating you."

"I wish. I'd rob the cradle any day for a piece of that action. Besides, she's twenty-six, only a couple years younger than we are."

Sean turned to face his old friend. Oliver had gained some weight and lost a lot of hair in the few years since he'd last seen him. "Good to see ya, man," he said, shaking Oliver's hand. "How do you know Winnie?"

"Our parents are old friends. My parents invited her to dinner when she first moved to town. I've been hitting on her for months, but she won't go out with me." Oliver chuckled. "Maybe if I had four legs and a red fur coat, she'd be more interested. She's been to see those puppies every day. She's even named them."

Sean and Oliver moved closer to the pen. "They all look the same to me." He called out to Winnie, "How can you tell them apart?"

Winnie grinned up at him. "I have special puppy-whispering powers." She stood up, a puppy in each arm. "These two are my favorites. This one is Emmie." She handed Sean the puppy. "She's aggressive. She'll be a good hunting dog. And this one is Willa." She handed him the second puppy. "She's the chill puppy in the litter. She's a space cadet but super sweet. She's going to make an excellent pet."

Oliver let out a humph. "With their pedigrees, they'd better all be excellent hunters," he said, and told Sean the price of the puppies. "That's a bargain for dogs of this caliber. Maisy, the mama, is the best dog I've ever owned. I bred her for the sole purpose of keeping one of her offspring. Unfortunately, the puppy market is flooded right now. Everyone got pets during the pandemic. Which is why I still have four available."

Sean nuzzled with the puppies, letting them lick his chin and neck. "I may be interested in two. I'm thinking of getting one for Cooper. We've always talked about getting labs from the same litter."

"That'd be cool. You would get the fifth and sixth picks."

Sean knelt down, setting the puppies loose in the grass. "When will they be ready to go home?"

"On day forty-nine, which falls on Memorial Day," Oliver said.

"What about training?" Sean rolled a puppy onto her back and stroked the soft skin on her belly. "I just opened a restaurant. A puppy doesn't exactly fit into my hectic schedule."

"I heard about the restaurant. Congrats!" Oliver snatched up the second puppy when she tried to escape. "You've had dogs before, Sean. You know the drill. You'll need to crate-train her. Just get a small crate for your office and let her out several times a day. Then send her off for training when she's about five months old. I have an excellent trainer if you're interested. Scooter Kello. He owns West Wind Retrievers in Virginia. It's out of the way, but worth the drive. In my opinion, a dog can't have too much training. Makes for a better hunter and pet."

Winnie flashed Sean a grin. "We'll all pitch in to help. She can be our marina dog."

Sean looked down his nose at her. "Not with her pedigree. You're welcome to help take care of her. But she will not be your marina mutt."

Josh scrambled to his feet, let himself out of the pen, and threw his arms around Sean's neck, nearly knocking him over. "Please, Sean! Can we get a puppy?"

The child's eager face pulled at Sean's heartstrings. He longed to make this kid happy by getting a puppy. But the puppy wouldn't belong to him. And it would devastate Josh when Carla rented an apartment and he had to leave the puppy behind at Moss Creek.

Sean got to his feet. "We'll see, kiddo," he said, placing a hand on Josh's head. "A dog is an enormous responsibility and expense. I need some time to think about it."

But the more Sean thought about it, the more he warmed up to the idea. Nothing could compare to the love he felt for his previous dogs. And Cooper could sure use a big dose of the joy and comfort a pet provided. Things would be hectic for a while until he sent her off to the trainer in a few months. He remembered what he'd said to Jamie earlier. *If I wait for the right time, it may never come.*

The days following their father's funeral were traumatic for the Horne sisters. When Sawyer arrived at nine o'clock on Thursday morning, Georgia greeted her at the door, showed her to Brooke's room, and returned to the kitchen, allowing her privacy while she collected her belongings. But while Georgia was straightening up the house and organizing leftovers in the refrigerator, Sawyer was ripping Brooke's bedroom to shreds with a pair of sharp scissors. She slashed her draperies and pillows and Brooke's favorite dresses. By the time Georgia realized something was amiss, Sawyer had fled the scene.

Georgia reported the incident to the police, who promised to investigate the matter.

Around nine o'clock that night, Lizbet was helping Brooke restore order to her bedroom when they heard a commotion outside. They peeked through the window blinds to see a disheveled-looking Sawyer stumbling about and blabbering incoherently in their postage stamp of a front yard.

Brooke's lip curled in disgust. "She's drunk. I can't understand what she's saying, can you?"

Lizbet raised the blind and leaned against the glass, listening to the stream of obscenities coming out of Sawyer's mouth. "Nothing nice. She wants you to come outside and talk to her."

Uncertainty crossed Brooke's face. "Maybe I should. If for no other reason than to make her stop disturbing the neighbors."

Lizbet had never seen her sister so vulnerable. Brooke had confessed to Lizbet that she no longer loved Sawyer, but that she feared Sawyer was on the brink of an emotional breakdown. A fierce determination to protect her older sister overcame Lizbet. She couldn't let Brooke give in to Sawyer.

"I'll deal with her. You stay here and call the police." Turning away from the window, Lizbet marched out of the room, down the stairs, and out the front door.

She addressed Sawyer from the edge of the front porch. "Lower your voice, Sawyer! Unless you want to add disturbing the peace to the list of complaints I plan to file with the police when they get here. By the way, Georgia reported your vandalism from earlier. We're pressing charges. Did the police talk to you about your rampage yet? If not, they will soon."

Sawyer's flicker of concern was quickly replaced by smugness. "Ha! The police are too busy fighting real crime to worry about me."

"I wouldn't be so sure about that. I suggest you beat it. Otherwise, you'll be spending the night in jail," Lizbet said with more confidence than she felt.

"I'm not leaving until I talk to Brooke." Tilting her head back, Sawyer cupped her hands around her mouth and screamed more lewd comments at Brooke.

"Fine. If you wanna be difficult. Two can play at your game." Stepping down off the porch, Lizbet held her phone up as she videotaped Sawyer's drunken rant.

Sawyer grabbed at the phone. "Give me that."

"No way," Lizbet said, holding the phone over her head.

When Sawyer lunged forward, Lizbet took a giant step backward. Sawyer stumbled and wrapped her arms around a porch column to prevent herself from falling.

Lizbet pushed play on the recording. Out of her phone came the sound of Sawyer's loud and obnoxious voice.

Sawyer's eyes grew wide. "What're you gonna do with the video?"

"What do you think? I'm gonna post it on social media. Then all your friends and coworkers can see what a raving lunatic you are."

Sawyer's hands shot up in surrender. "Okay, chill, Lizbet! No reason to get your little feathers ruffled. If you promise not to post it, I'll leave Brooke alone."

Lizbet turned up her nose. "I'm not promising you anything."

"If you care about your sister, you'll delete that video," Sawyer said, gesturing toward the phone.

Lizbet's brow hit her hairline. "Is that a threat?"

"Damn right, it's a threat." Sawyer backed down the sidewalk until she reached the street and then hurried off on foot into the night.

Lizbet waited until Sawyer was out of sight before going back inside. She checked the locks on all the doors and climbed the stairs to her room.

She was brushing her teeth in the hall bathroom when a terrified Brooke appeared in the doorway. "What'd she say?"

Lizbet spit toothpaste into the sink, dried her mouth with a hand towel, and took Brooke's trembling body into her arms. "She got the message. She won't be bothering you anymore," she said, even though she was certain they hadn't seen the last of Sawyer.

Brooke sobbed into Lizbet's neck. "I'm such an idiot. How could I have been so wrong about her?"

"She did a good snow job on you. On all of us. Even Mom approved of her. I'm just glad you had the good sense not to marry her," Lizbet said, walking Brooke to her room and tucking her into bed.

In her own bed down the hall, Lizbet lay awake well into the night, watching the video footage of Sawyer over and over. She'd captured enough of Sawyer's tirade to incriminate her. Her face was visible and her voice clear when she called Brooke the stream of vulgar names. Lizbet possessed the evidence to destroy Sawyer's reputation, both professionally and personally. Question was, did she have the courage to use it?

Lizbet, after a mostly sleepless night, rose early the next morning for work. She emerged from the house to find *Bitch* spray painted in red on the black porch floor. The fog of sleepiness vanished as fury took control of her body. Sawyer had made Lizbet's decision easy. Sawyer had made it clear she had no intention of leaving Brooke alone. To protect her sister, Lizbet would have to resort to drastic measures. If Sawyer got hurt in the process . . . Well, she would have brought it on herself.

Lizbet drove the short distance to MUSC, parked in visitor parking, and located a map of the campus. She explained the situation to the uptight receptionist in the office of the head of oncology.

In a squeaky voice, the receptionist said, "I'm sorry, but Dr. Robinson is busy today. If you'd like to file a complaint, you can find the form online."

"If I don't see Dr. Robinson today, I will post this video on social media, tagging your office." Phone in hand, Lizbet leaned across the desk and showed the receptionist the video of Sawyer.

The color drained from the receptionist's face. "I . . . Leave your name, and I'll have someone contact you."

Down the hallway a short distance, she spotted on a door a nameplate that designated its occupant as Antonia Robinson. The door opened, and out walked the head of oncology, an attractive woman in her late fifties with a blunt-cut silver bob.

Lizbet clicked the video play button again and strode toward Dr. Robinson. "I need to speak with you about one of your interns. She's harassing my sister. It would be bad press for the hospital if this little footage were to find its way to social media."

Robinson glanced around the reception area before motioning Lizbet to her office. "Let's discuss this in private."

The head of oncology was appalled at her resident's behavior, and she assured Lizbet she would take care of the matter. In turn, she asked Lizbet not to post the video on social media.

"I can only make that promise as long as Sawyer stops harassing my sister."

"Understood," Robinson said, and walked her to the door.

Later that evening, Lizbet and Brooke were sipping margaritas on the front porch when Sawyer's silver BMW pulled to the curb, and Sawyer, dressed in a long, black linen sheath, sauntered up the sidewalk.

"I'm here to say goodbye," Sawyer said in an arrogant tone with chin lifted and head held high. "I've requested a transfer. I never liked living in the South. I start at Mass General in Boston on Monday."

Lizbet heard a sniffle beside her and was shocked to see her sister was crying. So she did still love Sawyer. Even after everything that had happened.

Lizbet got up from the swing and slipped inside the house to give them privacy, but she hovered near the storm door in case Brooke needed her. Sawyer and Brooke exchanged a brief hug and kissed a little too long for Lizbet's liking. Sawyer palmed Brooke's face one last time before making a dash to her car.

Lizbet's heart sank. Had she driven her sister's soulmate away? Was it possible Sawyer and Brooke could've worked out their differences? What would Brooke think if she found out what Lizbet had done? Ratting Sawyer out to her department head would be a secret Lizbet carried to her grave.

Lizbet took an Uber to Leon's on upper King for lunch on Sunday. The weather—low humidity and brilliant blue skies—was amazing, and she would walk home afterward.

Jamie was waiting at a table in the outdoor seating area. He stood to greet her, placing a perfunctory peck on her cheek. He gestured at the platter of raw oysters and frosty mugs of craft beer on the table. "I hope you don't mind. I ordered our favorites for starters."

"Not at all. This is nice." Taking the chair opposite him, she studied his handsome face. The weight loss looked good on him. His smoldering eyes were as sexy as ever.

An awkward silence settled over them as Jamie devoured the oysters, while Lizbet, her stomach too nervous to eat, sipped beer. They'd blocked off the afternoon to spend together. They needed time to ease into the purpose of this meeting.

When the waitress arrived, they ordered another round of beers and their entrees—grilled fish sandwiches with cucumber salad slaw. They kept the conversation lighthearted while they ate. Lizbet told him about Brooke's breakup with Sawyer, and he told her about the shopping village being built on the property south of the marina.

"If you're still interested in opening a restaurant, Creekside Village would be the ideal place."

Lizbet's heart fluttered. Did this mean he wanted her to move back home?

He paused, as though waiting for her to respond. When she remained silent, he continued. "I'm leasing space for a retail store specializing in outdoor gear," he said and described his plans for Sweeney's Outfitters.

"Sounds cool. But isn't that a lot to manage along with the marina and seafood market?"

Jamie shrugged. "Staying busy helps keep my mind off of you. Of us."

Lizbet glanced around at the nearby tables. There were too many people around to discuss their marital problems here.

The waitress brought the check, and Jamie paid. "Where to now? Do you wanna go for a walk?"

"Sure! But what about your truck? It might get towed if you leave it here."

"Annie is using it to move some furniture. She's gonna pick me up later, whenever I'm ready."

Lizbet pushed away from the table. "In that case, let's head back downtown."

They strolled a few blocks south on King Street in silence. Finally, Jamie said, "I've been patient, Lizbet. I've given you ample time to figure out your problem. I need to know where we stand."

"That's a good question. I'm not sure where to begin."

In a patient tone, as one might speak to a child, Jamie said, "Let's start with your new job. Is it all you'd hoped it would be?"

Lizbet scrunched up her face. "What do you mean? My job is only temporary, a special project more than a job. I would never have taken a full-time position without consulting you first."

"How was I supposed to know that? You didn't tell me why you were leaving, and you've been gone so long, I assumed you were having a career crisis."

She shook her head, bewildered. "I admit, managing a sandwich shop wasn't challenging. But I enjoyed working with Sam."

"So this was never about your career?"

Lizbet took a deep breath for courage. "Not at all. I came to Charleston to address my fertility problems."

Jamie shook his head, as though confused. "What fertility problems? We only tried to get pregnant a few times."

"True, but I suspected there was an issue. And I was right," Lizbet admitted.

Jamie's jaw tightened. "I assumed it was something personal, a *you* problem. But fertility is a *we* problem, Lizbet. Something that involves both of us. Something we work through together."

"This is a *me* problem, Jamie." She jabbed her finger at her chest. "I'm the one with faulty reproductive parts."

"But having children is something *we* do together. Whatever the problem is, we'll fix it. *Together*."

Lizbet lowered her gaze to the sidewalk. "I developed endometriosis as a teenager. My first surgery got rid of it for a while. But it's come back with a vengeance. I moved home to Charleston to be closer to MUSC. I've seen every fertility specialist, and they've run every test. Not only is my problem unfixable, I will soon need a hysterectomy. I'm so sorry, Jamie. I know how much you wanted to have your own child."

Lizbet held her breath, praying he would assure her everything would be fine and they would adopt a brood of children. After several painfully long moments of silence, he said, "I'm sorry too, Liz. For both of us."

They arrived at Marion Square and located an empty park bench.

"Getting pregnant isn't our biggest issue, Lizbet. You keeping this vital information from me that affects our marriage, our future, is an enormous concern, a gigantic red flag. We're supposed to be a team, but you betrayed my trust," Jamie said, his tone a mixture of anger and disappointment.

"And you betrayed mine," Lizbet snapped. "I saw you kissing a woman in the marina parking lot last Sunday. Is she your girlfriend?"

Jamie appeared confused at first, and then a knowing look crossed his face. "That was Kirstin Bowman, the property developer I told you about, the one who is building Creekside Village. For your information, she kissed me. Not that it's any of your business. You're the one who walked out on me, remember?"

He jumped up, and she stood to face him. "Where are you going?"

"Home. I'm too angry to talk to you right now." As he strode off, he tugged his phone from his pocket and pressed it to his ear.

Lizbet wondered if he was calling Annie to pick him up. Or if he was making dinner plans with Kirstin. He claimed Kirstin had kissed him, but he didn't deny they were involved.

That went as expected, she thought as she headed south down Meeting Street. Why would Jamie want damaged goods when he had Kirstin Bowman, property developer of Creekside Village, waiting in the wings? So what now? Does she give him a few days to calm down and try talking to him again? Or does she move forward with a divorce?

eighteen
jamie

J amie forced the throttle forward until his boat was at full speed. The wind whipped through his dark hair, and saltwater spray coated his face, but the fresh air helped clear his mind. When he reached the mouth of the inlet, he turned off the motor and let the tide carry him back inland. Friends called out as they cruised by on their way in from a day of fishing in the ocean, and he waved back at them. A pang of jealousy hit him. He had had little time lately for the extracurricular activities he enjoyed. Lizbet had always gone along on his fishing expeditions. While she wasn't a fan of fishing, she loved to stretch out in the front of the boat with one of her novels. Sadness overwhelmed him. He'd been so hopeful for a reconciliation. But now he didn't know what to think about her infertility. About her keeping this *we* problem to herself.

After coasting for over an hour, he started the engine and navigated the inlet creeks to his mom's house. Sam was a good listener, fair and nonjudgmental, and he kept few secrets from her. She would have advice for him, whether or not it was the advice he wanted to hear.

Sam was watering flowers in the containers on her patio when he pulled up to her dock. She set down her hose and walked out to greet him. "This is a surprise. I didn't expect to see you today. How did your lunch go?"

"Not great," he said, as he secured his lines around the cleats.

Sam's smile vanished. "I'm sorry, son. Come on up to the house, and I'll fix us some sweet tea."

Jamie waited on the patio while she went inside for the tea. When she returned, she handed him a glass and sat down in the chair next to him.

"So what's the big mystery? Why has Lizbet been hiding out in Charleston all these months?"

"She went to Charleston to be close to MUSC. She's been seeing fertility specialists. She can't have children. In fact, her endometriosis is so bad she needs a hysterectomy."

"Oh no! That's awful. Poor Lizbet." Sam rested a hand on top of his. "This is a huge blow for you, son. I know how much you want to have children."

"Of course, I'm disappointed. But I trust God has a different plan for me regarding being a father. There are plenty of orphaned children who need homes, and I'm totally open to adopting. But Lizbet betrayed me. She didn't trust me enough to tell me the truth. I'm not sure I can get over that."

"I agree. She should've confided in you. But she's going through a difficult time, and we shouldn't judge her. She's so young. She didn't run off to Charleston to hurt you, Jamie. I'm sure she was scared about her health, and without her mama to support her, she naturally turned to her sister."

"Maybe you're right," Jamie conceded. He hung his head. "What do I do now?"

"Wait a few days before you do anything. Give yourself a chance to process everything. And then talk to her again. If you still love each other, decide whether you have what it takes to make your marriage work. Ask yourselves if you can put the past behind you and focus on the future."

"I still love her. Question is, does she still love me?" Jamie guzzled down his tea and stood to leave. "Thanks for the advice, Mom."

Sam rose out of her chair. "Anytime, sweetheart." She placed an arm around him and squeezed him tight. "I only want what's best for you. And I believe in my heart that Lizbet is it. I feel bad for being so tough on her. I'll work harder to be a better mother-in-law in the future. Next time, maybe she'll come to me with her problems."

"You're an outstanding mother-in-law, Mom. She would never have come to you with this. She knows how much you want a grandchild."

Sam appeared crestfallen. "We talked often about her having a baby, about giving me a grandchild. I didn't mean to put such pressure on the poor girl. If only I'd known."

"But you didn't. No sense beating yourself up about it. I'm sure Lizbet doesn't hold it against you."

Mother and son walked arm in arm to the dock. When they reached the boat, Jamie turned to face her. "By the way, I've been meaning to ask you about Mack's houseboat. Kirstin wants to buy it. Are you okay with me selling it to her?"

"Why on earth would she want to buy a barge?"

Jamie smiled. "She wants to pimp it out and live on it. She grew up traveling the world with her father on his boat. She's spent more time in marinas than at home."

Sam narrowed her eyes as she studied him more closely. "Are those stars I see in your eyes? Do you have feelings for this woman?"

Jamie stared down at his feet. He'd never been able to hide his feelings from his mother. "I may have a little crush on her. I can't help myself. She's super cool."

Sam tilted his chin up to look at her. "Listen to me, son. Don't let the shiny new object in the toy store window distract you from your beloved stuffed animal at home."

Jamie chuckled. "Nice analogy, Mom." He bent down to untie his lines. "Is there harm in having a crush if I don't act on it?"

"Absolutely! You're flirting with disaster. If you get caught up in the heat of a moment, you might not be able to control yourself."

"Then I'll have to avoid such moments." Jamie jumped in his boat and sped off across the still water, replaying his conversation with his mom on the way back to the marina.

He was too preoccupied securing his boat in his slip to notice Kirstin standing on the dock, watching him.

With hands on hips, she said, "Where have you been? I noticed your boat was gone, and I've been trying to call you. Do you not get cell service out on the water?"

"Depends on where I am." Grabbing his phone off the console, he scrolled through the missed calls, relieved to see none were from the marina store but disappointed none were from Lizbet either.

"I went to see my mom," he said, stepping off the boat to face her. The object in the toy store window was exceptionally shiny today in a flowing blue linen dress with her blonde hair dancing about her shoulders.

"How'd it go with your wife?"

Jamie looked away. "I don't want to talk about it."

She removed her sunglasses and studied his face. "That doesn't sound good. When you are ready to talk about it, I'm happy to listen."

"Thanks," he muttered.

"Did you mention to your mom about selling me the houseboat?"

"Yes. And she's fine with it."

Kirstin's face lit up. "That's fantastic." She threw her hands above her head and victory danced a circle around him on the dock.

He waited until she finished celebrating to tell her the price, which she readily agreed to. "I have one stipulation. If you decide to sell the barge, I want first right of refusal."

"Done." She pulled out her checkbook and rummaged through her purse. "I'll write you a check now. Do you have a pen?"

He laughed. "I don't typically carry ink pens with me when I go out on the boat. But there's no rush. We can do the transaction tomorrow."

"Okay." She held out her palm. "Can I at least have the key? I'm dying to see it again."

"Sure!" He removed the key from his key ring and handed it to her. "I'll go with you. There are a few things I need to show you about the boat."

As they walked over to the far dock, he explained about garbage collection and the septic system. Detecting her skepticism, he suggested she live on the boat rent-free for a couple of weeks before buying it. "Try it out. See how you like it. If you change your mind, there's no harm done."

"No way! I'm certain about this. Besides, I've looked at countless apartments and houses for sale. The boat is the only cool place I would consider laying my head."

Jamie laughed. "I'll remind you of that when the first big storm comes through."

A flicker of uncertainty was quickly followed by determination. "You won't scare me off, Jamie Sweeney."

He threw up his hands. "Just want you to be aware of potential dangers."

When they reached the boat, she unlocked the door, and they entered the salon. Jamie ran a hand down the pine wall paneling. "And you promise you won't paint the pine."

She drew an *X* across her chest. "Cross my heart. It's the best feature."

"Are you planning to work from here as well?"

"No way. I'm not a work-from-home kinda girl. I need more

structure in my life. I've rented office space in a charming converted warehouse. The exposed brick walls are fabulous. I considered living there, but the commercial zoning forbids it."

Kirstin wandered around the salon. "All I really need to do is add a few colorful accessories, like rugs, pillows, and lamps." She climbed the stairs to the bedroom. "I envision white linens with mounds of decorative pillows." She gestured at the row of transom windows above the bed. "The natural light in here is lovely."

She opened the door and exited onto the upper deck. "I'm gonna hang fairy lights all around the canopy. Maybe purchase a more comfortable reading chair with a little table and lamp."

"Where will you store your chair, table, and lamp when it storms?"

"In the downstairs cabin. Stop worrying, Jamie. I know what I'm doing. I'm just so happy. Thank you," she said, throwing her arms around his neck.

He molded his body to hers. She felt so good, and it had been so long since he'd held a woman in his arms. Unable to control his desire, he tightened his hold and pressed his lips to hers. She kissed him back, and his hands slid down her shapely figure to her bottom. She was smoking hot and setting him on fire. He was walking her backward toward the bedroom when she pushed him away.

"Slow down, partner. You're married, which makes you totally off limits. This is my fault. I got carried away."

"I'm equally to blame." Jamie collapsed onto the lounge chair. "We need to address this attraction between us. Ignoring it isn't working."

"Tell me about it." Kirstin moved over to the railing. "I'll be the one who gets hurt when you get back together with your wife."

Jamie buried his face in his hands. "I'm so confused. I honestly don't know if Liz and I *can* work things out. Or if I even want to."

"But you owe it to each other to try," she said.

"I guess. Regardless, the last thing I want is to hurt you. I truly enjoy your company. You make me laugh and forget about my problems."

"What you need is a friend to talk to." Kirstin turned to face him. "Tell me what happened when you saw her today."

"She confessed why she left me. I thought she was having a professional crisis. But it wasn't like that at all," he said and filled Kirstin in on what he'd learned about Liz's fertility problems.

"That's awful, Jamie. You must be devastated to learn she can't give you a child."

He nodded, not trusting his voice to speak. He waited a few minutes until the lump in his throat went away. "No one seems to care how I feel. It's all about Lizbet. I guess that's fair, since it's her body. Naturally, I'm sympathetic toward her, but I resent being kept out of the loop."

Kirstin stretched out on the other lounge chair. "I've never been married, so I have no clue what I'd do in her situation. But the way she handled things doesn't seem right to me. I guess the bottom line is, Do you still love her?"

"Very much so." Jamie propped his hands behind his head and closed his eyes, trying to imagine a life without Lizbet in it. During the last seven months, there were times he thought he'd go out of his mind from missing her. But then other times hadn't been so bad. "I'll always love her, whether or not we stay together."

"Do what's right for you, Jamie. Ask yourself what will make you happy. Will you be satisfied not having children or raising another man's child if you choose to adopt? If you want to make a clean break, now would be a good time."

Jamie sat up straight as her words hit home. He appreciated Kirstin's brutal honesty. Even though he refused to admit it, these questions were already in the back of his mind.

nineteen
sean

Sean left work early on Sunday to take Josh fishing. As he pulled up to the house at Moss Creek, he noticed Cooper painting on the dock. He turned off his engine but remained in his truck, watching his brother attack the canvas with his brush. Cooper typically painted with calculated brush strokes, but today he looked more like a composer directing a lively musical composition. Sean had never seen his brother work with such reckless abandon.

He got out of his truck and walked quietly down the dock so as not to disturb the artist. Cooper, despite the heat, was dressed in heavy green Mountain Hardware pants and a long-sleeved black shirt. His face was covered in sweat. Or were those tears? Sean studied Cooper more closely. His face was twisted in anguish as he dipped his brush and slung more paint onto the canvas. Sean's gaze shifted to the masterpiece, a series of black and red slashes.

"Cooper! Bro, what's wrong?"

Cooper startled, and slapped his paint-brush clad hand across his chest. "Geez, Sean! Don't sneak up on me like that."

"If I'd paraded out here leading a marching band, you were so engrossed in your work that you wouldn't have heard me."

Setting down the brush, Cooper turned to face him, shielding the painting with his body while wiping his face with his sleeve.

Sean closed the distance between them. "I'm really worried about you, man. We're twins. Why won't you talk to me? Why won't you tell me what's wrong?"

"Give it a rest," Cooper said, his face red with anger. "You sound like a broken record. For the millionth time, nothing's wrong!"

"Really? Then what's up with that?" Cooper gestured at the painting.

"I was having a moment. Expressing myself. That's what artists do." He removed a hunting knife from his pocket and ripped the canvas to shreds. "There." He slid the knife back into its leather sheath. "All gone." He looked up at Sean. "Why are you here anyway? Why aren't you at the restaurant?"

Sean let out a frustrated sigh. There was no sense in pressing Cooper. He would open up when he was ready. "I'm taking Josh fishing. Wanna come?"

The first flicker of excitement he'd seen from his brother in months flashed in his blue eyes. "Fishing for what?"

"Flounder, I think. Unless you have a better idea."

Cooper looked out across the marsh. "Tide's right for flounder. I'm in. I'll get some gear." He gathered up his art supplies and headed up the dock toward the guesthouse.

Sean went inside the main house to collect Josh. When they returned a few minutes later, Cooper was waiting for them on the dock with three fishing rods, their tackle box, and a cooler filled with ice. He'd changed into board shorts and pulled his hair back, his man bun protruding from a camouflage baseball cap.

They loaded everything into the boat and untied it from the dock. Sean was behind the wheel with Josh perched on the leaning post beside him and Cooper up front.

As they picked up speed, Sean yelled to Cooper, "Where should we go?"

"The ledge," Cooper hollered back and gave him a thumbs-up.

Josh tugged on Sean's T-shirt. "What's the ledge?"

"An underwater ridge where the fish like to hide when the high tide is falling." Sean brought a finger to his lips. "It's our secret fishing hole. You can't tell anyone about it."

Josh's face lit up. "I won't. I promise."

Sean navigated through the marsh creeks to the spot. He explained the trolling process to Josh while Cooper got their lines ready. From the minute they dropped their lines, they began catching fish. For the next two hours, Cooper reverted to his old self. He was smiling and laughing and surprisingly patient in helping Josh reel in fish and take them off the hook.

Two hours later, when the fish stopped biting and the cooler was full, they started back toward home.

"I can clean the fish if you want," Cooper volunteered as they were unloading the boat.

"That would be great," Sean said. "I need to shower and get back to the restaurant."

"Can I help clean them?" Josh asked Cooper, bouncing on his toes.

Cooper gave the brim of the boy's baseball cap a tug. "Sure thing, Champ."

Champ? Sean could hardly believe his ears. Who knew an afternoon of fishing would work such wonders? Over the past few months, he'd asked Cooper to go fishing many times. But Cooper always had an excuse. Sean should've insisted he come along. His brother needed diversions to distract him from his problems. And Sean knew just the thing that would keep him distracted for a good long time.

Back at the marina, Sean spotted Winnie coming up from the dock and did a double take. She looked hot in white cutoff shorts and a blue-striped bikini top. She had an athletic build with tight abs and small but perfectly rounded breast.

Winnie waved at him and called out, "Hey, Sean!"

Her chipper greeting brought a smile to his face. "What's up? Have you been out on the water?"

"I just got back from waterskiing with some friends." She gestured to a ski boat down the dock. He recognized the occupants as members of the grade below him in high school.

"That sounds like fun. The weather is incredible. I just got back from fishing."

When he moved toward the restaurant, she stepped in line beside him. "What did you decide about the puppies? Are you getting one?"

Sean held up two fingers. "One for me and one for my brother. Emmie and Willa if they aren't already spoken for. I've just decided. I haven't told Oliver yet. I need to text him and send the deposit."

"Yay!" Winnie said, punching the air. "I'll help you shop. You'll need crates and leashes and food bowls. Oliver will send you home with some food, but you should have some treats on hand. Oh! You have to buy one of those snuggle puppies with the beating heart that mimics the mama dog. You can get them from Amazon."

Sean stopped walking and turned to her. "You're making my head spin, Winnie."

Her eyebrows shot up above the rim of her sunglasses. "I know! It's a lot to think about. But the transition will go more smoothly if you're prepared. And since you're getting two dogs, you'll have to buy two of everything."

The lines on Sean's forehead deepened. "I'll need to figure out where to hide everything from Cooper. I want it to be a surprise."

"Aww." Winnie patted her chest. "That's so sweet. I haven't met your twin. Does he look like you?"

"Not at the moment. If he'd get his hair cut and shaved his

beard, you wouldn't be able to tell us apart." Sean started up the stairs to the restaurant.

Hurrying after him, Winnie said, "I can help with potty training. I've been watching YouTube videos. I can keep the puppy for you during the day, during your lunch rush. I promise, she won't be a marina dog. No one will handle her except me. Which one are you keeping? Emmie or Willa?"

While her excessive chatter exhausted him, Winnie's enthusiasm was contagious. "I'm not sure. Cooper and I will make that decision together. I appreciate your offer to help. I will definitely take you up on it."

"Awesome! When do you wanna go shopping? You should have everything set when you bring the puppies home."

"I guess sooner rather than later if I'm getting the puppies next Monday. How about tomorrow afternoon? What say we meet in the parking lot when you get off at three?"

"Perfect! I'll see you then." She started back down the stairs.

He called after her. "By the way, don't mention this to Josh if you see him. No way can he keep a secret this big."

"Understood," Winnie said, with a salute before hurrying off.

Sean found Carla in the kitchen, deep in conversation with one of the line cooks. "You two look so serious. Is there a problem?"

Carla's head jerked up, as though surprised to see him. "No. Everything's fine. We were just tweaking one of our specials."

He waited for her to ask him about fishing. When she didn't, he volunteered, "In case you're interested, our fishing outing was a success. Josh had a blast. We even got Cooper to tag along. We all caught a bunch of fish."

Carla leveled her cold eyes on him. "Your brother is a head case. I don't want my son anywhere near him."

Sean's blood boiled, but he managed to hold his temper in check. "Too late. I left them cleaning fish together. They're getting along well, actually. Maybe they're kindred spirits."

Carla's mouth dropped open, but she quickly composed herself. "Whatever. At least Josh will be tired and won't notice if I don't make it home for dinner."

"Suit yourself. But you're missing out. Cooper is frying some of the flounder. He's a pretty good cook. Of course, he's nothing like the great Carla Grant," he said, winking at her before disappearing into his office.

What a piece of work she turned out to be. He admired her ambition. He wanted employees who were committed to their careers. But everything else in her life played a secondary role. Including her son. Sean made a mental note to never let his career control his life to such an extreme.

Lizbet and Brooke had been putting Band-Aids on several home maintenance issues since taking over the house after their mother died. All those Band-Aids fell off at once on a stormy Tuesday night, the last full week of May. They were cooking a bake-at-home Margherita pizza when the oven died its final death, and all their proven tricks to restart it failed.

Brooke slammed the oven door shut. "This is just great! I don't have the money for a new oven. Do you?"

"No. I'm flat broke. But there's nothing we can do about it tonight. We'll worry about it tomorrow." Opening the freezer, Lizbet examined the neat stacks of frozen casseroles delivered by their parents' friends after their father died. "How does chicken and wild rice sound for dinner?"

Brooke planted a hand on her hip. "How're you gonna cook it without an oven?"

"In the microwave, duh."

"That'll take forever and taste disgusting. I'm not really that hungry anyway. I'll just have a snack," Brooke said, rummaging through the pantry. She located a bag of popcorn and left the kitchen for the family room.

Lizbet grabbed two orange sodas from the refrigerator and followed her.

Aiming the remote at the television, Brooke said, "Let's watch *Yellowstone*. We're several episodes behind."

Lizbet had never watched *Yellowstone*. The series about the Montana ranching family was Brooke's and Sawyer's show. But Lizbet thought it best not to bring that up.

They'd no sooner gotten comfortable on the sofa when rain gushed through the ceiling.

"Dang it!" Brooke leaped to her feet, searching around the room for a vessel to collect the water. She dumped an orchid out of a cachepot and placed the porcelain container under the torrent of water. "This won't be enough. Find some buckets and towels from somewhere."

Lizbet dashed to the laundry room and was back in a flash with an armload of buckets and towels. The buckets were small and filled up quickly. For the next forty-five minutes, they took turns making trips to the kitchen sink until the storm finally died down.

Lizbet checked the weather on her phone. "The rain's gone for now, but the forecast shows a high chance of storms every day this week. We can make do without a stove, but we have to get the roof fixed."

Brooke got to her feet. "Like you said earlier, let's worry about this nightmare tomorrow. I'm exhausted. I'm going to bed."

The sisters locked up the house and trudged up the stairs to the second floor where a wall of stifling hot air greeted them.

Brooke's body deflated. "Ugh. You've gotta be kidding me. The air conditioner's gone out."

"It can't be. Nobody has luck this bad." Lizbet raced to the thermostat. "Good grief! It's eighty-four degrees up here." She pushed buttons, hoping to hear the loud hum of the ancient compressor, but nothing happened.

"I'll check the fuse box." Brooke retraced her steps down the stairs, returning minutes later with a long face. "It's not a fuse. We're screwed."

Lizbet slumped against the wall. "We were having trouble with this unit when Mom was sick. At least we got a few more years out of it."

"Maybe we should sleep downstairs," Brooke suggested.

"And have a crick in my neck from sleeping on that lumpy sofa tomorrow? No, thank you. Why don't we sleep in your room? You have a ceiling fan, and we can open the windows."

"I guess that's our best option."

Across the hall in Brooke's room, the girls stripped off their clothes, threw open the windows, and stretched out on top of the bedcovers in their bras and panties. "You realize it may not be feasible for us to keep this house," Brooke said. "You'll soon be moving back in with Jamie, and I'll be stuck with the financial burden of maintaining the house and paying the taxes. Living here made sense when Sawyer and I were planning to start a family. Now that I'm single again, I'm not sure I can handle the responsibilities alone."

Lizbet stared up at the ceiling. "I seriously doubt Jamie and I will stay married. Why would he want to be stuck with a wife who can't bear his children?"

"You're being ridiculous. Because he loves you, of course."

"He doesn't love me anymore. I haven't heard from him since Sunday, when I told him I'm infertile."

Brooke reached for Lizbet's hand. "Give him some time to work through his feelings."

"If he loved me, he wouldn't need time." Lizbet rolled onto her side, facing her sister. "Fast forward forty years. You and I are still living in this house together—the old spinster sisters who all the kids on the street fear and the adults make fun of."

"At least we'll have each other."

"We'll be better off without the heartache caused by our significant others. Hey!" Lizbet shook Brooke's arm. "Why don't we adopt our own child? Or get a sperm donor and impregnate you?"

Brook burst out laughing. "It's not a bad idea. Maybe unconventional, but anything goes these days."

Lizbet paused as she imagined the sound of children's laughter coming from down the hall. "We're meeting with Dad's attorney in the morning. Maybe there's enough money in his estate to make the repairs and renovate the kitchen."

"Maybe. It would be nice if we could stay in the house. Neither of us should make any major changes for a while. We just lost our father and our significant others. We'll focus on fixing up the house."

"Then we'll get a better price if and when we decide to sell it," Lizbet said. "We also have Dad's condo to deal with. We should keep it for now. One of us may want to live there at some point. Maybe we should find a tenant to lease it."

Brook nodded. "That would be the smart thing to do."

The sisters stayed awake for over an hour, talking about the improvements they would make to the house if money weren't an object. But when they met with the estate attorney on Wednesday morning, it devastated them to learn their father had been living paycheck to paycheck.

Brooke blinked her eyes hard. "Are you saying Dad was broke?"

Mr. Evans, whom the sisters had known most of their lives, steepled his fingers on top of his desk. "Not broke exactly. Phillip had a small savings account, enough to cover his funeral expenses. And there was no mortgage on his condo. Once his estate goes through probate, you're free to sell it, if you so choose."

Evans briefly explained the probate process before walking the sisters to the door.

When they reached the parking lot, Lizbet turned to her sister. "What now? We'll have to sell the condo, but you heard Mr. Evans, probate could take up to a year."

"We'll rent it in the interim. At least that'll bring in a little extra money." Brooke fished her car keys out of her purse. "I set aside some money for the baby, which I obviously won't be using anytime soon. We can use my savings for the repairs."

"That would be great. You'll get reimbursed when we sell the condo. Thank you." Lizbet hugged her sister in parting.

Lizbet experienced a pang of guilt as she drove to work. She had a job now. She was earning a paycheck. With no mortgage or rent to pay, she could easily help cover these expenses. But she needed her money for something else. Something even more important than air conditioning.

Georgia was behind the counter at Tasty Provisions, inspecting a new shipment of French table linens. "Morning, Georgia. Any chance you can spare a few minutes for me after work today? I could really use your advice."

"Of course. Is this about Jamie? How did your lunch with him go on Sunday?"

Lizbet glanced nervously at two customers hovering nearby. "I'll tell you when we talk later."

"Okay. Should we go to The Rooftop at The Vendue for a glass of wine?"

"Sure. Why not?" Lizbet said without hesitation. There was nothing waiting for her at home except a broken oven and air conditioner and leaky roof.

Georgia, as though sensing Lizbet's turmoil, offered her a sympathetic smile. "I'll be free after closing at six."

"Perfect." Upstairs in the office, Lizbet spent the rest of the day organizing the stack of recipes into binders. Her temporary job was nearly complete. Soon, she'd be asking for a permanent position. If Annie and Heidi couldn't accommodate her, she'd have to go elsewhere. And she'd keep looking until she found a situation that inspired her. Her career was the only thing in her future she had to look forward to now.

At the onset of more stomach cramps, she removed the bottle

of ibuprofen from her purse, shook three into her palm, and gulped them down without water. She couldn't afford a hysterectomy without medical insurance.

At six o'clock, Lizbet and Georgia walked down the street to The Vendue and took the elevator to the top floor. They located a table on the railing and ordered two glasses of rosé.

"Here's to summer." Georgia clinked Lizbet's glass and sipped the pale pink wine. "How're you holding up, sweetheart? Your father's death was such a shock."

"I'm hanging in there. I'm grateful to have Brooke. Thank you for helping us deal with Sawyer."

"You're most welcome." Georgia folded her hands on the table. "So, what's on your mind, sweet girl? Tell me about Jamie."

Lizbet inhaled a deep breath to steady her nerves. "Our marriage is over, and I need a divorce attorney. I was wondering if you would share the name of the one you used."

"Divorce? Whoa." Georgia sat straight up in her chair. "Back up a minute. You went to lunch hoping for a reconciliation and now you're talking about divorce. What happened?"

Lizbet looked out over the rooftops of downtown Charleston, where the sun was transitioning the sky from orange to pink. "When I told him about my fertility problem, he got angry and blamed me for not confiding in him. He said it was a red flag that I kept it from him, that we were supposed to be a team. He just walked off, left me alone in the park. And I haven't heard from him since."

"It's only been a few days. You dealt him a major blow. Give him time. He'll come around."

Lizbet slumped back in her chair. "No, he won't. In the seven months I've been living in Charleston, he never once came to see me. If he cared about our marriage, he would've tried harder."

"That's unfair, Lizbet. He was giving you the space you asked for. Sounds to me like you're both being stubborn. Do you still love him?"

"Of course," Lizbet said. "The problem is, *he* doesn't still love *me*."

"What makes you say that?"

"Remember, I told you I didn't see Jamie when I drove down to Prospect the day Daddy died? Well, I lied. I saw him kissing another woman. I confronted him about it when we met for lunch on Sunday. He made up some bogus excuse about her kissing him, but he didn't deny they were in a relationship."

"Jamie doesn't seem the type to cheat on you, Lizbet. Even if you are separated."

Lizbet looked up. "This woman, this Kirstin person, is developing the land south of the marina into a shopping village. Sounds like they've been spending a lot of time together. When I asked him about the kiss, he told me it was none of my business." She stared at Georgia with vision blurred by tears. "I'm doing Jamie a favor by divorcing him. I'm setting him free so he can move on with his life with a new wife and children of his own."

In a scornful voice, Georgia said, "I'm disappointed in you, Lizbet. I never took you for a quitter."

Lizbet set her eyes on Georgia. "I'm not quitting, Georgia. I'm moving on with my life. Now, if you won't tell me the name of your divorce attorney, I can ask someone else."

"Her name is Inez Erickson, and she's the best around. But I urge you to talk to Jamie one last time before you take this drastic step."

A tear slid down her cheek and into her glass of wine. "There's nothing left to talk about."

twenty-one
jamie

On Saturday of Memorial Day Weekend, vacationers crowded the small town of Prospect on their way to the beach for the first week of summer. They stopped in for lunch at The Lighthouse, shopped for fresh produce at the farmer's market, and loaded up on seafood at Sweeney's.

Jamie spent the morning in the courtyard behind the market steaming large pots of crabs on gas burners. He was thankful for the mindless work—a job to focus on and keep his thoughts off his marital problems. And sensing his foul mood, the other employees were considerate enough to give him his space.

He'd been an emotional basket case since his lunch with Lizbet nearly a week ago. He needed to follow up with his wife. They'd left too many things unsettled. If only he knew what to say. His anger toward Lizbet had softened. She was a private person and would naturally keep something as personal as her female problems a secret. It was the infertility itself that was the issue. Kirstin's words played over and over in his mind like a broken record. *If you want to make a clean break, now would be a good time.* A part of him wanted a fresh start with someone who could give him his own children. Someone like Kirstin.

Sam stuck her head out the door. "I need more crabs, Jamie. How much longer on this batch?"

"Fifteen minutes. By the way, this is the last batch. You're out of crabs."

"What?" Sam stepped out of the doorway and into the court-yard, letting the screen door bang shut behind her. "How is that even possible? I ordered ten bushels to last the weekend."

"The bushels were puny. Where'd you get them?"

"A young fella from Johns Island." She nudged Jamie's arm. "My normal supplier's bushels are higher quality and more plenti-ful, but he's taking a leave of absence."

Jamie slammed the lid on the pot and tossed the oven mitt onto the stainless cart. "Give it a rest, Mom. I'm doing the best I can."

"Calm down, son. I'm teasing you." Sam turned his body to face her. "You've been on edge all week. It's not good to keep all this anger bottled up inside of you. Have you spoken to Lizbet yet?"

"Nope. I've been too busy," Jamie said in a sulky tone.

"I'm here if you need to talk."

Jamie averted his eyes. It pained him to see how much his problems affected his mom.

Sam cupped his cheek. "If not me, then at least talk to a friend."

Kirstin popped into his mind. While she was a good listener, her perspective was one-sided. She'd never met Lizbet. And he suspected Kirstin would love for Jamie and Lizbet to divorce, so he would be free to date her.

His phone vibrated in his back pocket. Setting down his tongs, he tugged it free and accepted the call from Winnie. "What's up?"

"The troublemakers are back," Winnie said in a low voice. "The store is crowded. I doubt they'll cause a scene with so many people here. Do you think I should call Officer Yates?"

"I'll call him. I'm over at Sweeney's. I'll be there in a second."
Jamie ended the call and scrolled through his contacts for Yates's
number. "I need to go, Mom. Can you finish with this batch of
crabs?"

"Of course." Sam grabbed the oven mitt and lifted the lid off
the pot. "Be careful, son."

With phone pressed to ear, Jamie exited the enclosed court-
yard, went around the corner of the market, and hurried across
the street. When he explained the situation to the police officer,
Yates, who was in the area, promised to come right away.

Jamie inhaled a deep breath to calm himself before entering
the marina store. He didn't want to provoke the troublemakers
unnecessarily. By the time he arrived, the only customers
remaining in the store were an older couple at the checkout
counter. While she processed their credit card charge, Winnie
said to Jamie, "You just missed them. But they're still tied up at
the fuel pumps, if you wanna get a look at them."

Jamie sprinted to the end of the dock, but he only glimpsed
their dilapidated Jon boat as it pulled away.

When he returned to the store, Officer Yates had arrived and
was questioning Winnie. "I heard their names," she told the officer. "The taller of the two is Roscoe. The other one is Buck. They
were shoving each other around and making wisecracks. And
their eyes were bloodshot. I think they were stoned."

"Do you have any clue where they were going?" Yates asked.

"They said they were going offshore fishing."

Jamie shook his head. "God help them if a storm comes up.
They'll capsize in that battered heap."

"That would solve our problem," Winnie said with a mischievous grin. "While they didn't cause any trouble this time, I got
the impression they will be back."

Sean, with alarm etched in his face, burst through the door.
"What's going on? Why are the police here?"

Jamie told his cousin about the troublemakers.

"Are you okay, Winnie?" Sean asked in a concerned tone.

Her blue eyes twinkled when she smiled over at Sean. "I'm fine."

Jamie's head swiveled back and forth as he studied Sean and Winnie. When did these two make nice? They were not only friendly, they were actually flirting with each other.

A customer stepped up to the cash register, dumping several grocery items on the counter. Officer Yates backed away, so Winnie could assist the customer. When she bent over to retrieve a bag from under the counter, Jamie noticed Sean staring at the holstered pistol tucked in the waistband of her shorts at the small of her back.

Sean leaned in close to Jamie. "Dude, she's packing heat."

"She's fine. I gave her permission to carry. She has her concealed carry permit anyway."

Closing his iPad cover, Officer Yates said, "You did the right thing in calling me. I left my blue lights flashing on purpose. Hopefully, they saw them. If they know we're on to them, maybe they'll stay away. Call me if they come back." He tipped his hat to Winnie and left the store.

Sean, his eyes on the bulge at the small of Winnie's back, said, "Do you think you could actually shoot someone with that gun?"

"If necessary. In self-defense," she said in a tone that belied her worried expression.

Sean's smile faded. "Let's hope it doesn't come to that."

"Are we still on for the . . ."—Winnie cast an uncertain glance at Jamie—"surprise on Monday?"

Sean nodded enthusiastically. "Sure thing. Pickup time is four o'clock. Plan on eating dinner with us. I'll grab some burgers to cook on the grill."

Jamie looked from Sean to Winnie. "What surprise? What're you two up to?"

"I . . . uh . . . we—" Sean clammed up when Kirstin sauntered in.

"Did I interrupt something?" Kirstin asked in response to the awkward silence.

Jamie rolled his eyes. "Ignore them. They're keeping secrets. I'm going out in the boat to put out some crab traps. Wanna ride with me?"

"Sure," she said, the wide brim of her sun hat bobbing up and down as she nodded her head.

"Cool. Give me a minute to gather a few things," Jamie said, and went to the back of the store to get a bag of frozen fish heads from the freezer.

Sean called after him, "Say, Jamie, what do you think about having a cookout for our moms' birthdays at Moss Creek next weekend? I'm hoping a party might pull Cooper out of his funk."

Jamie wondered if he could invite Kirstin to the cookout. Or if that would look too much like a date? "That's a great idea. Count me in. We'll get together later in the week to make a plan."

He grabbed several bottles of water and two packages of peanut butter crackers, dropping them into Kirstin's beach bag on their way out of the store. Jamie retrieved his crab traps from the storage shed behind the store, loaded them onto a dock cart, and wheeled the cart onto the dock.

Once they were underway, Jamie yelled over the sound of the motor, "I'm surprised you didn't go home to Nantucket for the holiday weekend."

"Prospect is my home now. Besides, I've been busy getting settled on the houseboat. I absolutely love it. You were right about the limited storage space, however. I may have to rent a storage unit for my off-season clothes."

"Maybe not. You won't need heavy winter clothes in the Lowcountry."

They rode in silence as Jamie navigated the curving marsh creeks. When the water shallowed, he slowed his speed and tilted the motor. He packed the bait box with fish heads and strategically dropped the traps into the water over his most productive spots.

The fresh salt air improved Jamie's mood, and he drove slowly back to the marina. "Can I ask you a personal question?"

She nestled closer to him, her thigh pressing against his. "Of course. What's on your mind?"

"How do you feel about having children?"

"I want at least four. Maybe even five. Being an only child is lonely. I'd never do that to a kid on purpose. But who knows? God may only bless me with one. That's out of my control."

"I know what you mean. I was an only child too."

"What about your half sister?" Kirstin said.

"Annie and I didn't meet until we were teenagers. I've always been envious of the closeness Cooper and Sean share. As children, they spoke to each other in their own special language."

Kirstin laughed. "Twin speak. My father and I were close, like you and Sam. But it's not the same as having a sibling."

"What would you do if you couldn't have children? Would you adopt?" Jamie asked, his eyes on the water in front of him.

"I don't know, honestly. I'd have to do some serious soul searching. What's with all the talk about babies? Have you spoken to your wife again?"

"No. Lizbet has had plenty of time to adjust to her new reality. Now it's my turn."

Kirstin placed a hand on his shoulder. "You don't have to adjust, Jamie. You have other options."

"You mean divorce," he deadpanned.

She lifted a sun-kissed shoulder as if to say why not. "You've already been separated for nearly a year."

"Seven months is not a year, Kirstin."

"The point is, you're used to being on your own. And you don't have children to complicate a divorce."

Jamie tightened his grip on the steering wheel. "Right. Like you said the other night, if I want to make a clean break, now would be a good time. I should just throw my old wife away and get a new one because she can't give me children."

"Ouch," Kirstin said, removing her hand from his shoulder. "I've never met your wife, but I'd be willing to bet there's more to this separation than her fertility problems. Women don't leave their husbands because they can't have babies. They leave because they're seeing someone else. Or because they no longer love them. Or because they no longer want the same things in life. Open your eyes, Jamie. Don't be a fool."

"You don't know Lizbet like I do. She's a very private person. She went to Charleston to seek treatment." As the words left his mouth, Jamie wondered if maybe his wife was hiding something else, something that had nothing to do with infertility.

"I'm tired of talking about my wife." He settled back on the leaning post next to Kirstin. "How are the plans coming for Creekside Village?"

While she talked about clearing land and breaking ground, he admired her toned arms, round breasts, and tanned legs extending from hot pink short shorts. He imagined what it would be like to take her to bed. He was so lost in thought, he ran aground on a sandbar he'd been dodging all his life. Fortunately, he didn't damage the motor. As he tilted the motor and paddled the boat into deeper water, he berated himself for daydreaming about having sex with Kirstin. His attraction to her was complicating his marital problems. For his own sanity, until he could get his head straight about Liz, he needed to stay far away from this woman.

twenty-two
sean

S ean was glad he waited until they were on the way to pick up
the puppies on Monday afternoon to tell Josh about the
surprise. The boy had been spending a lot of time with Cooper
this week—fishing and string crabbing and working on small
projects. Josh would never have been able to keep something this
big to himself.

"Tell me where we're going," Josh demanded from the back
seat of Sean's truck.

Sean locked eyes with him in the rearview mirror. "I told you,
it's a secret," he teased.

"Ugh!" Josh kicked the back of the seat. "I promise not to tell
anyone."

From the passenger seat, Winnie shot Sean a scolding glare.
"Put the poor kid out of misery already."

Sean let out a reluctant sigh. "All right. We're going to Oliver's
farm to pick up puppies."

Josh's mouth fell open and his green eyes doubled in size.
"*Puppies?* You mean more than one?"

"Correct. One for me and one for Cooper. But Cooper doesn't
know about the puppy. We're going to surprise him."

"Yippee." Josh punched the air with his tiny balled fists. His smile vanished. "Can I keep a puppy too?"

Sean chuckled. He knew this was coming, and he'd prepared his response. "Two puppies are enough for now. Puppies are a big responsibility and require a lot of attention. We want you to play with them and help us take care of them, but you must follow our rules."

Josh's grin returned. "I understand."

Winnie shifted in her seat to see Josh. "Puppies love to play, but they also sleep a lot. And when they are sleeping, we must be careful not to wake them."

Josh squished his brows together. "Because they'll be grouchy."

Winnie smiled. "That, and because they need their rest to help them grow."

"I promise not to wake them up," Josh said.

The scene at Oliver's farm was chaos, with children chasing puppies while new pet owners peppered Oliver with questions. Sean and Winnie had visited the puppies several times during the week, and they'd decided for certain that Emmie and Willa were the right dogs for the brothers.

Sean paid Oliver the balance, and they collected their paperwork, food samples, and flannel fabric remnant with the mama dog's scent. They separated their puppies from the rest of the pack, but instead of placing them in the travel carrier Sean brought, Winnie insisted on holding them during the ride home.

"They'll be fine. We're not going far. Besides, Josh will help me." Winnie sat in the back seat next to the kid, and they passed the puppies back and forth during the short drive.

When they arrived at Moss Creek, they spotted Cooper painting on his balcony. Winnie remained in the car with the puppies while Sean and Josh lured him down.

Cupping his hands around his mouth, Josh called out to Cooper in a singsong voice. "Oh, Cooper. We have a surprise for you."

"Not now, buddy. I'm at a critical stage with this bird I'm working on."

Josh gave Sean an exasperated look, and Sean nodded for him to continue.

"But, Cooper, wait until you see what we got for you. You're gonna be super excited."

Cooper looked down at Josh.

"Please," Josh begged, pressing his hands together. "I really want you to see your surprise."

"All right. Give me a minute to clean up, and I'll be right down."

Sean and Josh helped Winnie out of the car, and they took the puppies over to the yard to play. Emmie and Willa were romping around in the grass when Cooper finally emerged from the guesthouse.

"What's all this?" he asked with a bemused expression.

Sean grinned like a little boy. "I bought puppies, red labs, one for each of us from the same litter like we've always talked about."

Cooper's blue eyes widened. "You're joking." He knelt down to get a better look. "Who'd you buy them from?"

"The mama dog belongs to Oliver Gray. He mated her with a phenomenal stud dog in Arkansas. Their pedigrees are impeccable."

Cooper rolled a puppy over on her back. "Are they both females?"

"Yep. Thanks to Winnie, they already have names." Sean smiled at Winnie. "She's the one who told me about the litter. Willa is wearing the pink collar and Emmie the purple."

"I like those names. Come here, Willa." Cooper picks up the puppy and nestled her against his chest. "You're a cutie." He looked up at Sean. "Whose is whose?"

Sean shrugged. "I figure we'll decide that together."

Winnie chimed in, "Emmie is the aggressive one, although she is super sweet too. Willa is the chill puppy in the litter."

"Chill works for me."

"Fine by me." While he wanted Cooper to have the first pick, he'd secretly had his eye on Emmie. "We can switch in a day or so if we change our minds."

Cradling the puppy, Cooper got to his feet. "This is crazy, Sean."

Sean laughed. "Impulsive, maybe. But not crazy. This is our dream, Coop. You're not going to send her back to the litter, are you?"

"Not a chance," Cooper said, inhaling the puppy's sweet breath. "I'm attached already. But I insist on paying for her."

"No way! My treat. But you're not getting a birthday or Christmas gift from me for the next ten years."

"Deal. But at least let me buy the supplies for both of us."

Sean shook his head. "Winnie and I have already bought the basics. We stored everything in the garage." When Cooper appeared wounded, he added, "If it means that much to you, you can Venmo me back for your supplies."

Seemingly appeased, Cooper said, "Cool," and dropped to the ground with his puppy.

Sean sat down next to him. "By the way, Oliver hooked me up with his trainer in Virginia. I've already spoken to Scooter a few times. Willa and Emmie can go for training as early as four months. He'll train them to hunt. He can even make them master hunters if we want."

"That'd be awesome," Cooper said. "We can take turns driving them up for training."

Macy came out of the house to meet the puppies, and the small group stood on the edge of the lawn, watching Emmie and Willa wrestle and chase each other through the flower beds until they conked out.

Josh curled up in a ball beside his new little friends. "I'm tired too, little puppies," he said, closing his eyes.

"Why don't we set up the crates while they're sleeping?"

Winnie suggested.

"I'll watch these three while you do that," Macy said, dragging a lounge chair from the patio to the grass.

The brothers opened the garage and perused their purchases. "We'll fix up the guesthouse first," Sean said, carrying a wire crate across the driveway.

After a quick walk-through of the small quarters, Winnie chose the kitchen as the ideal place for the crate. "You want to confine the puppy to a small space at first. It helps with potty training. You can easily close off the kitchen from the living room with baby gates." She flashed Cooper a grin. "We bought some of those too. If she has accidents, it won't hurt the hardwood floors."

Sean went back to the garage for the baby gates. When he returned, Cooper and Winnie were busy setting up the crate. He experienced a pang of jealousy as he watched them from the doorway. He was used to Winnie's bubbly personality, but there was something more in the way she interacted with Cooper. Was she flirting with him? And what about Cooper? Sean hadn't seen his brother smile like that since . . . since he couldn't remember when.

In high school, Cooper and Sean had often fallen for the same girl. And understandably so. They were both naturally attracted to outdoorsy types. And Winnie was the girl next door with those charming freckles and her warm, fuzzy personality. If Winnie could save Cooper from his demons, Sean would put his own feelings for her aside. Grudgingly, because he was finding her irresistible as of late.

But his brother appeared to have it bad for Winnie. Cooper hung on her every word as she rambled on about potty training. "How do you know so much about dogs?" Cooper asked, visibly impressed.

"I've watched a lot of YouTube videos. I would've gotten a puppy myself, except my apartment complex has a strict no pet policy."

When they finished in the guesthouse, the threesome moved over to the main house. "I've given this some thought, and I believe the game room is the best place for our puppy," Sean explained. "There are too many people living in this house. The crate will be in the way in the kitchen."

"That makes sense," Cooper said.

They moved the furniture out of the way and rolled up the rug in the game room. Cooper and Winnie set up the second crate while Sean positioned an indoor pet pen in a circle around it.

By the time they'd finished, the puppies had woken up and were whining for food. Winnie and Cooper fed them while Sean made hamburger patties for their dinner. They'd just sat down at the rectangular table on the patio to eat when Carla's car screeched to a halt in the driveway.

"I can't believe this," Carla said, her face flushed with anger. "You're having a picnic with *my* son when I haven't had a day off in two weeks."

Sean looked at her over the top of his burger. "You should take a day off. You've been working hard. Grab a burger and join us. We're celebrating the two new additions to our family." He gestured at Emmie and Willa napping in the grass near their feet.

Carla glanced down at the dogs and then shot Sean a death glare. "I need to have a word alone with you," she said, and strode across the lawn toward the dock.

"Ooh. You're in trouble," Josh said with a mouth full of potato chips. "Is Mommy gonna spank you?

"Let's hope not. She's not my mommy." Sean left the table and followed her out to the dock where she was pacing angrily back and forth.

"What's with the temper tantrum, Carla? We were enjoying a perfectly fine evening until you showed up."

"You crossed the line, Sean." She stopped walking and pointed at the yard. "How dare you bring those puppies home without consulting me first."

A surge of anger overcame him. "This is *my* home, Carla. I'll do whatever I damn well want. You are a temporary guest here."

"Exactly. And when we finally get a place of our own, Josh will be heartbroken to have to leave those puppies. Couldn't you have waited?"

"No. The right litter presented itself to me. I didn't go looking for it. Regardless, I won't put my life on hold for you. My brother is going through a tough time, and I thought a puppy would make him feel better."

"Speaking of your brother. I specifically told you I don't want Josh hanging around with Cooper. Yet all Josh talks about anymore is Cooper." Her lip curled up in a snarl as her head bobbed back and forth. "Cooper this and Cooper that. Those two are joined together at the hip."

Sean held her gaze. "You should be grateful. Josh's behavior is drastically improved. Or haven't you noticed? Oh, that's right." He snapped his fingers. "You're never around long enough *to* notice. You expect everyone to take care of your child until they do something you don't approve of. Then you cause a scene. Well, I'm growing tired of your drama, Carla. You're not the only talented chef around. I'm your boss. You work for me. If you ever talk down to me like you just did, I'll fire you on the spot."

Tears welled in her eyes, but Sean didn't stick around to console her. He felt pounds lighter as he returned to the others. The conversation with Carla was long overdue. He'd given her an inch, and she'd taken a mile. She'd been down on her luck, and he'd invited her into his home. And she'd been making his life miserable ever since. He would document this incident and make her sign it. Now that he'd warned her, the next time she caused trouble, he would have grounds to fire her.

Josh was a good kid. Sean had grown fond of him these past few weeks, and he would miss Josh when he left. But the price of having to deal with his mother was too high.

twenty-three
lizbet

Lizbet waited for the right opportunity to talk to Annie about a permanent position with Tasty Provisions. Late afternoon on Tuesday, she finally summoned the courage. She rolled her desk chair close to Annie's. "Can I have a word with you? I'm in the final stages of the project, and I would appreciate your feedback regarding wrapping things up."

"Sure thing," Annie said, swiveling her chair away from the computer.

"Here are the final menus. I hope you approve of them." Lizbet presented her with a sheaf of printed menus, and Annie took a few minutes to study them.

"I'm impressed, Lizbet," Annie said, setting the menus on her desk. "These are outstanding. And you delivered the finished product in half the time. Well done. I can't wait to show them to Heidi."

Lizbet beamed. "I need to find a real job, Annie. Is there any potential for a permanent position with Tasty Provisions?"

Uncertainty crossed Annie's face. "Are you staying in Charleston? I was hoping you and Jamie were working things out."

This surprised Lizbet. She thought Jamie told Annie everything. "Not exactly. You borrowed his truck the day we had lunch. Didn't he tell you what happened?"

"He was in a bad mood, and I got the impression he didn't want to talk about it."

"Things are complicated, Annie." Lizbet hesitated, considering how much to reveal about her marriage. Annie would never hire her full-time if she thought Lizbet might move back to Prospect. And she desperately needed a job. "I have good reason to believe Jamie is having an affair. Our marriage is over."

Annie scoffed in disbelief. "That's ridiculous. No way would Jamie ever cheat on you! He's the most honorable guy I know."

"I agree. He is. But I saw him kissing her with my own eyes. Kirstin Bowman is the real estate developer, building a shopping complex on the land next to the marina."

The color drained from Annie's face. "Right. He's mentioned her. I'm sure there's a logical explanation about what you think you saw. But who am I to interfere with your marital problems? You should talk to Jamie."

"I did. He didn't deny it." Lizbet picked at a loose thread on her gray pants. "If you don't have anything permanent, I could bartend or serve at catering events until I find something else."

Annie crossed her legs and leaned back. "Our events are growing increasingly more elaborate as our clients try to outdo one another. We're hiring a catering chef to coordinate food and beverage, which will free Heidi and me up to handle the logistics. We've talked to a few people already. You obviously have the right credentials. If you're absolutely certain you want to stay in Charleston, we'll get you in soon for a formal interview."

A formal interview? Is she serious? Heat flushed through Lizbet as she moved to the edge of her chair. "I'm the obvious candidate for the job. I just designed the menus this *catering chef* will use to coordinate your food and beverage." She jumped up and began gathering her belongings. "Talk to Heidi and let me know what you decide. In the meantime, I'll look elsewhere. I assume I can count on you for a reference."

"Of course. You did an outstanding job, Lizbet. There will be a handsome bonus included in your last paycheck."

Even the mention of a bonus didn't soften her anger as she strode across the office on her way out. Lizbet was nearing the doorway when a sharp abdomen cramp caused her to double over.

Annie rushed to her side. "Liz? Are you okay?"

Lizbet gripped the doorjamb as she slowly straightened. "I'm fine," she said, even though she was far from fine. On top of everything else, the cramps were getting worse by the day.

She hurried down the stairs and through the catering kitchen. She didn't even stop to speak to Georgia as she passed through the gourmet shop. The catering chef job was rightfully hers. She'd worked extra hard on the project, and she'd earned it. She wasn't sure she could work for Annie anymore. Not if she couldn't separate business from her personal life.

Lizbet started toward home, but remembering the technicians were installing their new air-conditioning compressor, she headed in the opposite direction, wandering aimlessly around historic downtown.

She'd enjoyed the few brief years she'd spent in Prospect. She loved their quaint neighborhood and weekends spent on the water with Jamie. But she'd lived in Charleston most of her life. These cobblestone streets, churches, and ancient cemeteries were part of who she was.

Lizbet paused in front of Husk, the restaurant renowned for artful food indigenous to the Lowcountry. The restaurant was housed in a converted old wood-framed home with double-decker porches. Next door was the historic brick building featuring their indoor bar and exterior garden patio.

Lizbet had always dreamed of working her way up the ranks in an upscale restaurant like Husk. It was why she'd attended culinary school. But after graduation, she married Jamie, moved to

Prospect, and took the first job that came along, managing Annie's Garden Cafe. But there was nothing preventing her from pursuing that dream now.

Drawing herself to her full height, Lizbet marched down the brick path separating the two buildings to the back of the restaurant. She pressed herself against the side of the building near the kitchen's screen door as she eavesdropped on the team of cooks preparing for dinner. The sounds of clanging pots and cheerful chatter warmed her heart, as though she'd found her way home after a long journey.

Lizbet was caught red-handed when a gray sports car whipped around the corner of the restaurant and into a reserved parking spot in front of her. She stepped away from the building, trying to look innocent, as an attractive man got out of the car. He wore checkered pants and a black chef's shirt with a skullcap covering his blond hair.

He approached her with an extended hand. "Hello. I'm Dana Ramsey, one of Husk's sous chefs. Can I help you with something? Or are you on a spy mission for our competition?" he asked with a smirk tugging at his lips.

Lizbet laughed, his humor setting her at ease. "I'm Lizbet Sweeney. I was passing by on my way home and wondered if you had any openings."

"We're always looking for fresh talent. Do you have a resume?"

"Only a digital copy. I just finished updating it. I can email it to you." She accessed the document on her cell phone and handed the phone to him.

Dana thumbed down the document. "Are you still working for Tasty Provisions?"

"I just finished a temporary project. I'm in negotiations for a full-time position."

"I see." Dana continued reading her resume. "You have good experience. Just not the right experience." He handed back her phone. "You'd have to start in an entry-level position. Although our turnover rate is high. If you're diligent, you can work your way up in no time."

"I'll do that," Lizbet said with a determined nod. "I'm skilled and dedicated. Can you tell me about the salary?"

"It's competitive, but probably not what you're used to." He told her the amount and outlined the benefits.

While the base salary was low, the benefits package was attractive. She would have the healthcare coverage she needed for her hysterectomy when the time came.

A loud crash followed by the sound of angry voices came from inside the kitchen. Dana gestured at the screen door. "As you can hear, this is a busy time for us. We'll be opening soon. Can you come back in the morning and talk to our head chef?"

Lizbet remembered her meeting with the divorce attorney at nine. "I have another interview in the morning. But I'm free early afternoon."

"Great. Let's say around one o'clock." He handed her a business card. "Be sure to email me the copy of your resume."

"Will do." Pocketing the business card, she hurried back up the side of the restaurant to Queen Street.

Excitement buzzed inside her as she walked home. Lizbet could hardly believe her luck. When she married Jamie, she'd lost her way on her path to professional success. Beyond any doubt, working in a restaurant was where she belonged.

Her phone vibrated with a text from Annie. *Can you come in tomorrow for an interview with Heidi and me?*

She thumbed her response. *I have other interviews in the morning and early afternoon. I'm free around four.*

Annie texted back right away. *We can make that work.*

"I'll bet you can," Lizbet said, and dropped her phone in her bag.

She was rounding the corner at the end of her street when another sharp pain took her breath. She hugged a crape myrtle tree while she waited for it to pass. Her periods were getting worse with each passing month. And now she was having cramping in between. She was on borrowed time. She would need to work for the restaurant for several months before having the surgery. At this rate, she wasn't sure she'd make it through the summer.

When she arrived home, Lizbet was relieved to discover the HVAC technicians had finished, and the upstairs was blissfully cool. She crawled beneath the covers and fell into a deep sleep. Hours later, she woke in excruciating pain, and when she got up to go to the bathroom for ibuprofen, it alarmed her to see her sheets covered in blood.

twenty-four
sean

Sean and Cooper, wearing yesterday's wrinkled clothes with eyes half shut, sipped coffee on the back lawn while watching the puppies wrestle in the grass. The sun had barely broken the horizon, but Emmie and Willa were eager to play.

Cooper moaned as he massaged his lower back. "Sleeping on the sofa is killing my back. Now that the puppies are used to their new environment, I suggest we separate them into their own kennels tonight."

For the past two nights, the twins had slept on the sofas in the game room so the puppies could be together in the same kennel. They'd taken turns getting up to let them outside when they cried.

"I agree," Sean said. "Having them sleep together seemed like a good way to avoid separation anxiety. But when one whines, she wakes the other up."

Sean studied his brother's profile while Cooper stared out at the marsh. He'd been keeping a careful eye on his brother these past couple of days. Cooper seemed happy one minute, almost like his old self again, but then his sullen mood would return.

"A dog is a lot of responsibility," he said. "It wasn't fair of me to drop this puppy in your lap without asking if you wanted one. If it's too much, we can try to find another home for Willa."

Cooper swiveled his head toward Sean. "Are you kidding me? I love this little dog." He set down his coffee mug and picked up his puppy, nestling her to his chest.

Sean rubbed the puppy's head. "Good. "I'm glad you're happy. We'll have fun watching them grow up together. To be honest, I've become equally attached to Willa. I couldn't give her up, even if you wanted to. I'd end up raising both puppies."

Cooper held the puppy up in front of him. "I just need to get you on a schedule, little girl, so I can get some work done." He set the puppy back down in the grass. "Winnie's a tremendous help. She played with Willa for a couple of hours yesterday while I worked. But I can't keep asking her to dog sit for me. I tried to pay her, but she refused."

Sean's gut hardened. Watching Winnie and Cooper become a couple wouldn't be easy. But he would make the sacrifice if it meant bringing his brother happiness. "Winnie loves these puppies. She's happy to help."

"She suggested we take them for their first boat ride on Saturday. We could anchor at one of the beaches and introduce them to the water."

"That would be fun. But we have that cookout for Mom's birthday on Saturday."

Cooper groaned. "I forgot about that. Who all is coming?"

"Just the family. Mom and Dad, of course. Sam, Eli, and Jamie. Mike and Faith. Bitsy is a maybe."

Cooper nodded toward the main house. "What about your houseguests and Macy? Josh is fine, but I'm trying to keep my distance from Carla."

Sean chuckled. "Don't worry. Carla will be working. And since Josh doesn't know the others, I'll probably have Macy bring him over for cake."

"That works. What're we cooking?"

Cooper's willingness to take part encouraged Sean. A month ago, his brother would have refused to even come. "You and I will handle the main course. I'm thinking about beef tenderloin and soft-shell crabs. The husbands are contributing side dishes. Mike is bringing a salad. Eli is making his famous cornbread. And Dad is in charge of the cake."

"That sounds manageable." Willa sat down at Cooper's feet and stared up at him with pleading eyes. "I think someone is hungry."

Sean checked his phone for the time. "Right on schedule." They carried the puppies inside to the game room. Sean measured out the kibble while Cooper refilled their water bowl.

"I don't see why we can't still go out in the boat on Saturday," Cooper said while they watched the dogs devour the food. "We just won't stay long. Winnie doesn't get off work until three anyway."

"Saturday is our busiest day. I'll need to stay at the restaurant through the lunch rush, but I can probably leave around then."

Cooper pulled up the tidal chart on his phone. "The tide should be right to go to Ghost Island."

"That works. Josh will get a kick out of a haunted island."

Cooper stuffed his phone back into his pocket. "Maybe we should ask Winnie to stay for the cookout since she'll already be here."

"Fine by me, bro. If that's what you want." Sean shrugged off his irritation. He would need to learn how to put his feelings for Winnie aside.

———

Carla's angry voice greeted Sean when he entered the restaurant later that morning. He paused outside the kitchen door, listening. Best he could tell, she was screaming at a line cook who'd dared to disobey her orders.

With his puppy tucked under one arm, Sean barged through the swinging door. "Good morning," he said in a cheerful voice. "What's all the yelling about?"

"Never mind. We figured it out." Carla, her lip curled in disgust, glanced down at Emmie. "That dog does not belong in *my* kitchen. The health department will shut us down."

"It's *our* kitchen. And I've already spoken to the health department," Sean lied. "The puppy is fine as long as she's in the kennel in *my* office."

"May I have a word with you in *our* office?" Without waiting for his response, Carla spun on the heels of her black chef's clogs and strode angrily across the kitchen.

One of the line cooks said in a loud whisper, "Good luck, boss. She's in a rotten mood."

"I can tell," Sean murmured and went to face the firing squad.

Carla waited for him at the door, tapping her foot on the floor and gripping the knob. When he entered the office, she slammed the door behind him. "I deserve a day off."

"And I'm happy to accommodate you." Sean slipped the puppy into the kennel and sat down at his desk. "We should both have regularly scheduled time off to avoid getting burned out. I'm taking Saturday afternoon off. Would you prefer Friday or Sunday?"

She grimaced. "I want Saturday."

His skin prickled. "Do you have plans for Saturday? Because it's my mom's birthday and I'm hosting a family cookout."

She folded her arms over her chest. "I'm taking Josh to the zoo."

"Oh really? What zoo?" The Edisto Island Serpentarium was the only zoo worth visiting in the Lowcountry. And Carla didn't strike him as the reptilian type.

"I mean, the Aquarium in Charleston."

Sean raised an eyebrow. "Have you bought your tickets yet? The Aquarium sells out quickly, especially on summer weekends."

He'd recently considered taking Josh there, but at thirty bucks a head, he'd changed his mind. In his opinion, Carla should save her money for an apartment instead of blowing it on extravagances. There were plenty of affordable options for spending an after-noon with one's four-year-old son. The beach was nearby and free.

Carla ran her finger across a grease stain on her chef's coat. "I was planning to get them at the door."

"So you don't have a concrete plan. You can just as easily go on Friday or Sunday?"

She leveled her gaze on him. "As easily as you can have your cookout on Friday or Sunday."

"Not without inconveniencing my entire family. Pick a day, Carla. Any day but Saturday." Sean knew he was being a jerk, but he needed to establish some boundaries with her. He was the restaurant's owner, and she was his employee. Her uppity attitude of late was getting under his skin.

"Fine. I'll take Friday. But I want the following Saturday."

"Noted." He scrawled a reminder on a sticky pad to create a wall schedule of their days off for the summer. He tossed the pen on the desk. "As of now, I have nothing else important planned for the rest of the summer. We're in the early days here, Carla. Working overtime is expected. If the schedule is too rigorous for you, perhaps you should look for another job elsewhere."

"You don't mean that. I'm responsible for your success."

Sean stood to face her. "Maybe so. But you let that success go to your head, and it's not a good look. For the past week, you've been bullying everyone around. Including me. And it stops now. I own The Lighthouse, Carla. Therefore, I call all the shots." He lifted a file on his desk. "I have a stack of resumes of chefs with more experience than you."

Carla opened her mouth to speak, but only an exaggerated huff came out.

"As for the puppy, she'll only be here a few weeks, until she's old enough to go away to training. So you might as well get used to her." He swept his hand at the door. "You can show yourself out of *my* office."

After she stormed out, Sean dropped back down to his chair. He hated being the bad guy, but he needed to put Carla in her place. He opened the file folder and sifted through the resumes until he found Carla's. He thought back to the day he'd hired her. He'd been so impressed with her knowledge and professionalism, he hadn't bothered to check her references. Pulling out his cell phone, he tapped in the number for the last place she worked in Columbia—an Italian place from the sound of it—and asked to speak to the manager.

"How could I forget Carla Grant?" the manager said. "She has plenty of talent. She was a real gem in the beginning. But then everything went south, like a switch flipped inside her head. She just couldn't seem to get her personal life together. She was consistently late to work and was constantly having childcare problems. I let her stay on longer than I should because I felt sorry for her. But I finally had to let her go."

"That sounds like what I'm dealing with now. Thanks for your feedback," Sean said and ended the call.

He dropped the phone on his desk and buried his face in his hands. He blamed himself for not checking Carla's references. Even if he had grounds to fire her, that was not what he wanted. He felt sorry for her too. She had no family to support her, no significant other to take some of the responsibility for the kid. Then again, Sean had been good to her. He'd given her a place to live and helped her find childcare, and she'd turned on him. What if she had legitimate mental problems? What if Josh's life was in danger? What if all their lives were in danger? Sean assured himself he was being melodramatic. But an uneasy feeling warned him to proceed with caution where Carla was concerned.

twenty-five
jamie

J amie tossed out the anchor, pulled his shirt over his head, and stretched out on the bench seat in the front of the boat. The sun warmed his face and the salt air tickled his skin. He could take a quick break to clear his mind. No one would miss him. And he desperately needed a minute of peace to himself.

Inevitably, thoughts of his wife interfered with his tranquility. He still hadn't heard from Lizbet in the ten days since their lunch meeting at Leon's. He'd expected her to be the one to reach out to him. He'd accused her of betraying his trust, and he felt she owed him an apology. Or perhaps he used that as an excuse not to contact her. Like his mom said, they were both being stubborn.

Jamie propped himself up on his elbows. Why was he waiting for Lizbet? He needed answers, and he knew where to find them. He would go to Charleston to see her. This time, he would surprise her. He would find out if she was seeing someone else. If so, he would file for divorce. If not, he would ask Lizbet if she still loved him and suggest they seek marriage counseling. Together, they would deal with her fertility problems.

Swinging his long legs over the side of the bench, he got to his feet and began hauling in the crab traps. He dumped the live

crabs into coolers and reset the traps with fresh bait before dropping them back into the water.

He pulled in his anchor and started the engine. On the way
back to the marina, he thumbed through his text messages. He
blinked hard in disbelief as he read the note from his wife. *I met
with an attorney this morning. I'm filing for divorce.*

Fury racked Jamie's body as he stared down at his phone. The
urge to hurl it across the water into the marsh grass was powerful.
But he ran two businesses, and he couldn't afford to be without a
phone. He tossed it to the safety of the console.

He slammed the throttle forward and flew at full speed atop
the water the rest of the way. Transferring the coolers to a dock
cart, he pushed the cart across the street to Sweeney's, where he
found his mom in the kitchen stirring a pot of potatoes on the
commercial stove.

"Here are your crabs, Mom." Jamie gestured at the coolers in
the cart outside the screened door. "I've gotta go to Charleston.
Someone else will have to cook them."

Sam set down her spoon and turned to face him, her smile
vanishing when she saw his distraught face. "What's wrong, son?"

Jamie raked his fingers through his dark hair. "Lizbet texted to
tell me she's filing for divorce. Can you believe that?" He flashed
his phone in his mom's face. "She *texted* me. She couldn't even give
me the courtesy of a phone call."

Sam let out a sigh. "You're upset. You shouldn't be driving. I'll
go with you."

"No, Mom. I'll be fine. The drive will give me some time to
think about what I want to say to her. I'll call you later." Kicking
open the screen door, he unloaded the coolers from the cart and
hurried back across the street to the marina.

His mind reeled on the drive to Charleston. He had much he
wanted to say to his wife, but when he saw her standing in the
doorway of their home, he was at a complete loss. She was profes-

sionally attired in gray pants and a starched white blouse, but her face was pale and bruises outlined her eyes.

"You got my text," she said in a deadpan tone.

"We were married two years. You could've given me the courtesy of a phone call." He tilted his head as he looked more closely at her. "Are you okay? You don't look well."

"I'm having a bad period." She straightened her spine. "But I'll be fine."

Even though they'd been apart for seven months, Jamie could tell when his wife was lying. She definitely wasn't fine. "Can we talk? I deserve an explanation about the divorce."

"I guess. Although there's not much to say." She stepped out onto the porch, pulling the storm door closed behind her.

"Shall we sit down?" He gestured at the bench swing, but Lizbet remained standing.

"I don't have much time. I have an appointment in an hour." Lizbet's breath hitched, and she placed a hand on her belly.

Jamie rubbed her back. "Have your cramps ever been this bad? Maybe you should see a doctor."

"I've seen every doctor in Charleston, Jamie." She smacked his hand away. "I just took some Advil. The pain will go away once it kicks in." She grimaced as another cramp ripped through her gut.

Jamie leaned against the railing beside her. "I'm not ready to talk about divorce. I believe our marriage is worth salvaging. Why don't we try counseling? If it doesn't work out, *then* we'll consider filing for divorce. I still love you, Liz. Do you still love me?"

She hesitated, biting down on her lower lip.

"It's not a hard question, Liz. You either love me or you don't."

"It's more complicated than that. I can't give you the children you want, Jamie."

He shrugged. "So we'll adopt. It's not the end of the world."

Lizbet's face flushed red, and she bent over slightly.

A concerned expression crossed his face. "You're obviously in pain. Maybe you should cancel your appointment and get some rest."

"I can't. It's an important job interview."

Jamie's anger returned. "Last time we talked, you said you would never take a full-time position without consulting me first. What's changed?"

She stared down at the porch floor. "I'll never have children, and my marriage is over. My professional life is all I have left."

He shook his head in disbelief. "What's with the defeatist attitude, Liz? You used to be more of a fighter."

Her head jerked up. "I have been fighting. For seven months, my body has been poked and prodded and scanned. And look where it got me." She pushed off the railing. "I'm moving on with my life, Jamie. You should do the same."

He grabbed her by the arm and squeezed hard. "Listen to yourself. *I'll* never have children. *My* marriage is over. *I'm* moving on with *my* life. How come you get to decide our future without consulting me?"

"Ow, Jamie! You're hurting me," she said, trying to wriggle free of his grip.

An attractive blond man with a baby face appeared at the door. "Hey, man! Is there a problem here?"

Jamie let go of Lizbet's arm. "I'm talking to my wife. Not that it's any of your business."

The guy emerged from the house with biceps bulging from his blue uniform shirt and fists clinched by his side. "It's my business if you're hurting her."

Jamie gestured at the man. "Who is this guy, Liz? Your boyfriend?"

"Duh, Jamie. He works for the appliance company. He's installing our new oven."

Jamie felt like a fool. Of course, she was telling the truth. The man was wearing a uniform bearing the logo, Palmetto Appliance. He hated feeling so on edge, so defensive.

Lizbet smiled at the appliance guy. "Everything's fine here, Ben. But thank you for your concern."

Ben returned her smile. "If you're sure." He aimed his thumb over his shoulder. "I'm finished installing your oven. If you don't mind, I need to show you one thing before I go."

"Sure thing," Lizbet said and followed him inside.

Jamie sat down on the swing to wait for her return. After five minutes, he was considering sneaking around back to spy on them when she came out of the house.

She stood in front of the swing, her steely gaze on him. "How dare you accuse me of having a boyfriend when you're the one having an affair."

Jamie jumped up to face her. "Give me a break. Kirstin is just a friend."

"Right. Friends with benefits. As I told you after our lunch at Leon's, I saw you kissing her with my own eyes. Now, if you'll excuse me, I need to get ready for my interview." Lizbet went back inside, closing the door in his face.

Jamie raised his hand to pound on the door and then thought better of it. There was no point in arguing with Lizbet when she was being so irrational.

Suddenly weary, Jamie trudged down the sidewalk to his truck. He drove aimlessly around downtown Charleston, neither knowing nor caring where he was going. He hardly noticed when he crossed over the Cooper River Bridge, and he drove all the way to Georgetown before he realized he was going in the wrong direction. Turning around, he made the long trip back through Charleston to Prospect.

L izbet forced Jamie from her mind as she race-walked toward Queen Street. The air was heavy with humidity, and she yearned for air conditioning, but she was too doped up on ibuprofen to drive. Her body was a noodle. She envisioned herself slumping over in her chair during the interview. She'd been popping pills like candy all morning. Finally, after triple the recommended dosage, the pain was finally under control. She was planning to come home between interviews, but just in case, if she should run out of time, she'd stuffed her shoulder bag with fresh tampons.

Gerald Weber's booming voice intimated Lizbet at first. But she quickly warmed to Husk's head chef. Beneath his gruff exterior was a man whose passionate love affair with food was like none Lizbet had witnessed in her many years in the industry. For more than an hour, he grilled her with technical questions, which she felt she answered to his satisfaction.

When he rose out of his office chair, she assumed the interview was over, but he surprised her when he asked, "Would you like to prepare a dish for me?"

"You mean now?" Lizbet asked, glancing at her watch.

"Of course. I understand if you're pressed for time. It's not a requirement . . ."

Lizbet heard the but in his voice. If she wanted this job, she would cook for him. She had an hour to spare before her interview with Annie and Heidi. "I'd like that," she said, and followed him into the kitchen where dinner preparations were in full swing. "Do you have anything specific in mind?"

"Not at all. Whatever you're in the mood to make. We should have everything you could need. If not, I'll send one of my line cooks out to the store." He chuckled, as though the possibility his kitchen lacked any ingredient was preposterous.

Weber turned her over to Dana, who gave her a brief tour of the kitchen before setting her up at an out-of-the-way cooking station.

In the interest of time, Lizbet needed to keep her presentation simple. She'd managed Annie's Garden Cafe for two years. She was the queen of sandwiches. While Po'Boys weren't unique to the Lowcountry, she was certain the Fried Shrimp and Okra Po'Boy recipe she'd brought home from her honeymoon in New Orleans would wow him.

She located all the ingredients. She typically made her own creole mustard from scratch, but she found a jar of Arnaud's from the famous French Quarter restaurant in the pantry, which would do just fine in a pinch. She felt like a top dog as she worked at the cooking station. The bustle of the kitchen lit her up with excitement.

Lizbet served the sandwich to Chef Weber at a table in the main dining room on the first floor. Seated across from him, she held her breath while he took his first bite. He said nothing, but dove in for another bite, this time letting out a groan of satisfaction. To Lizbet's delight, he devoured every crumb.

He wiped his lips and placed his linen napkin on his plate. "You've outdone yourself, young lady. I don't ask all of my interviewees to cook for me. And I rarely finish what they offer. But that was scrumptious."

Lizbet beamed. "I'm so glad you enjoyed it."

"That's an understatement." He propped his elbows on the table with fingers entwined. "I sense you're way overqualified to be a line cook. Unfortunately, that's all I have to offer you at the moment."

Lizbet sat up straight with head held high. "I appreciate the opportunity, Chef Weber. Because of my lack of experience in a fast-paced upscale restaurant like Husk, I expect to start at the bottom. I have a lot to learn, and I would very much like to be a member of your team." She playfully wagged a finger at him. "But watch out. I intend to work my way up quickly."

The chef chuckled. "I believe you will." His expression turned serious. "I'm interviewing a couple of other candidates. We'll be in touch in a few days."

Lizbet took this as her cue to leave. "I look forward to hearing from you," she said and went to the kitchen for her belongings.

The menstrual cramps had started back up while she was cooking. She'd managed to ignore them until now, but by the time she exited the kitchen through the back door, she could hardly walk for the pain. She fumbled in her bag for her ibuprofen and popped three into her mouth. She checked the time again. Her meeting with Annie and Heidi started in ten minutes. So much for going home first. With one hand gripping her belly, she stumble-walked over to East Bay Street, arriving at Tasty Provisions with only enough time to use the restroom before heading upstairs to the office.

Heidi and Annie went silent when she entered the room, and Lizbet wondered if they'd been talking about her.

Heidi jumped up to greet her. "Lizbet, honey, are you okay? You're so pale, and you're sweating profusely. Is it that hot outside?"

"Yes!" Lizbet fanned her face. "And extremely humid."

"Here, sit down," Heidi said, and dragged a chair over from the corner for her.

"Thank you," Lizbet said, gripping the arms of the chair as she eased down.

"So." Heidi sat back and crossed her legs. "Annie and I agree you're the best person for the catering chef position. However, we want someone long term. The uncertainty in your marriage prevents you from making that commitment."

Anger seized Lizbet's body, worsening the cramps. "Annie made that clear already. If you're not going to hire me, why'd you drag me down here for an interview?"

"Because you did such a spectacular job for us, and we didn't want to end our arrangement on a sour note."

Given the choice, Lizbet would much prefer to work at Husk. The frenetic energy in the kitchen made her feel alive in a way no other job ever had. But there was no guarantee Chef Weber would offer her a job.

Lizbet moved to the edge of her chair. "It's highly unprofessional for you to deny me this job because of my personal life. In fact, a discrimination attorney would find good reason to sue you."

Annie glared at her. "Is that a threat? Because you would never win in court. Our circumstances are unique. You were once my best friend, and you're married to my brother. Our estranged relationship could cause friction in the workplace."

Lizbet gawked at her. "Since when is our relationship estranged? Everything was fine between us until I asked for a permanent position."

"Our relationship has been strained since you walked out on Jamie last October. At least it has on my end." Annie stood and left the office.

"I apologize for her behavior," Heidi said, her eyes on the top of her daughter's head as Annie disappeared down the stairs. "She loves you and Jamie so much. She's struggling to separate her personal feelings from her professional life."

Annie returned with three glasses of sweet tea. "I can speak for myself, Heidi," she said, handing a glass to each of them. "You and Jamie have something special, and I hate to see you throw it away. I believe your love is strong enough to work through anything." She sat down in her chair. "I'd love nothing more than to see you in this role. But I think you're confused about what you want, and we'd be taking a tremendous risk by hiring you."

"I'm not confused. I know exactly what I want. I'm filing for divorce. I met with the attorney this morning." As the words left her mouth, a sharp pain ripped through Lizbet's body, and the glass slipped out of her hand, crashing to the hardwood floor. When a more intense pain followed, she screamed and slid out of the chair to her knees. She crawled across the floor through the tea and broken glass to the trash can where she vomited up the contents of her stomach.

Annie rushed to her side. "Lizbet! What's wrong? Did you eat something? Do you have food poisoning?"

Lizbet hung her head into the trash can, explaining in a string of broken sentences, "Menstrual cramps. Endometriosis. Something's wrong. Get my phone. It's in my purse."

Annie collected the purse and handed her the phone. Lizbet tapped in her password and handed it back to her. "Call my gynecologist, Dr. Louise Carroll, at MUSC. Her contact is in there. She'll know what to do," Lizbet said, and threw up green liquid that alarmed everyone in the room.

"There's no time!" Heidi said. "We have to get her to the hospital. We need to call an ambulance."

Lizbet tried to argue, but no words came out. She collapsed onto the floor as another pain racked her body. Seconds later, everything went black.

When she woke again, she was in an ambulance, and Annie was sitting beside her, holding her hand and rubbing her forearm.

"We're on the way to the hospital. Heidi spoke to your doctor. She's going to meet us there. You're gonna be okay, Liz."

"No! I can't afford the hospital. I don't have health insurance."

Annie's confused expression was quickly replaced by recognition. "Yes, you do. Under Jamie's plan, remember? As his wife."

"He's no longer responsible for me. I can take care of myself," she said and projectile vomited the same green liquid all over Annie. "I'm so sorry. It hurts so bad."

"I know it does, sweetheart. Just hang on a little longer," Annie said, taking the towel the paramedic handed her.

Lizbet closed her eyes and prayed to whoever might be watching from above—God and her mother and father—begging them to put her out of her misery. Was she dying? What if she never again saw the sun rise over the ocean? What if she never again saw Jamie? Annie's words from earlier came back to her. *You and Jamie have something special, and I hate to see you throw it away. I believe your love is strong enough to work through anything.*

What a fool she'd been for shutting Jamie out of her life when she needed him the most? He was right. Marriage was about *we*, not *me*. She'd never actually believed he was having an affair with Kirstin Bowman. She'd needed to blame him for something to make herself feel better. But none of this was his fault.

She envisioned the tombstone on her grave next to her parents in Magnolia Cemetery. Lizbet Horne Sweeney, dead at age 28. She'd only just begun to live. She hadn't had time to leave her mark on the world. Life was precious, and she had squandered so much time these past months. She prayed to God, asking for another chance and promising not to screw it up this time.

jamie

The sky was darkening with an approaching storm by the time Jamie arrived at his house. He pulled into the driveway and then backed out again. He couldn't bear to be in the house he shared with his wife, knowing she would never come home again.

He drove to the marina and hurried up the stairs to The Lighthouse. At five o'clock, the restaurant was nearly empty with only an elderly couple seated at a table by the window and a handful of hardened drinkers at the bar.

He slid onto a stool at the end of the bar nearest the window. "Where's Sean?" he asked Randy.

"He went home to check on the kid and exercise the puppy."

The lines on Jamie's forehead deepened. "What puppy?"

"He and Cooper got red labs from the same litter. She's a cute little thing named Emmie." Randy tossed a napkin in front of him. "What can I get you?"

"Tequila. Neat," Jamie said.

Randy reached for the tequila bottle and poured two fingers of clear liquid in a glass. "I've never known you to hit the hard stuff. You must be having a rough day."

"I've had better," Jamie said, downing the shot. The liquor burned his throat, and he coughed into his fist. "Hit me again."

Randy poured two more fingers. "Easy there, pal. This stuff will go to your head fast. Especially for a rookie drinker like you."

"That's the point." Jamie kicked back the liquor and slammed the glass on the bar.

Randy held up the bottle, as if to ask if he wanted another. "One more. Then I'm cutting you off."

Jamie shook his head. "I'm good."

He set his phone on the bar, screen side up so he could see the screensaver picture of Lizbet taken on their wedding day. He longed to call her, to beg for another chance. He clicked on Kirstin's contact information instead. "Where are you?" he blurted when she answered.

"At my office. Getting ready to head home. Why? Where are *you?*"

"At The Lighthouse. I could use a friend."

"I'm on my way."

Jamie swiveled his barstool to face the window. The tequila took the edge off his distress, and a sense of calm overcame him as he stared out over his marina. *His marina.* He mumbled the words to himself. He'd accomplished a lot in the months since Lizbet left. Truth be told, he'd already survived the worst, the lonely nights, eating dinner in front of the television and sleeping in an empty bed. He was used to being on his own. The only thing that would change was his marital status.

The guy sitting next to Jamie whistled when Kirstin entered The Lighthouse wearing a slim-fitting black sleeveless dress that revealed an inappropriate amount of cleavage.

Kirstin eased onto the seat next to him and signaled for Randy to bring her a glass of wine. She eyed Jamie's empty glass. "Do you need a drink?"

Jamie shook his head. "I'm good. Two shots of tequila is enough for a lightweight like me."

She squinted as she looked more closely at him. "Are you drunk?"

"Let's just say I'm pleasantly numb. I've had a rough day. My marriage is officially over. I'm getting a divorce." He fell back in his chair. "There. I said it and lived to tell about it."

"Oh, Jamie. I'm so sorry. I know this is an enormous disappointment for you."

"I'm actually relieved. The uncertainty is over." He punched the air. "I'm a free man."

"Wow. You're much better than you sounded on the phone."

"While I was waiting for you, I realized how much better off I am than I thought. Lizbet and I have been separated for seven months. I've already been through the stages of grief most people experience after a divorce." He ran a finger down Kirstin's arm. "I've been feeling guilty for being attracted to you. When actually, it's a sign I'm ready to move on with my life."

"Or a sign you've had too much tequila," Kirstin said with a chuckle.

Jamie twirled a strand of her hair around his finger. "Are you saying you're not attracted to me?"

"You know I am." Her pink lips parted, and she ran her tongue seductively around the rim of her wineglass.

Desire stirred inside of him, and he shifted in his seat to hide his excitement. "Let's get outta here."

"We can go to the houseboat." Kirstin slid off the barstool, pulling him with her.

Jamie called out to the bartender. "I'm leaving, Randy! Please close out my tab."

Randy gave him a thumbs-up.

Outside, the rain was coming down in sheets. Kirstin took off her sandals and stuffed them in her bag. "I should've brought a raincoat to work this morning."

"Come on," Jamie said, taking her by the hand. "We'll make a run for it."

Their clothes were soaked through by the time they got to the boat. Inside the main cabin, Kirstin peeled off her wet clothes and stood before him in a nude-colored strapless bra and thong. She was so damn beautiful, and Jamie couldn't stop himself. His hands roamed her body as his mouth clamped down over hers. She pulled his saturated shirt over his head and led him up the stairs to her bedroom.

He kissed her again, his body pressed hard against hers. "Lizbet, baby," he said in a breathy voice.

Kirstin pushed him off of her. "I'm not Lizbet, you jackass. I knew this was a bad idea. You are so *not* over your wife."

Jamie sank down to the bed with his face in his hands. "Oh god. I'm so sorry, Kirstin."

Kirstin sat down beside him with a hand resting on his back. "I'm the one who's sorry. I should never have taken advantage of a drunk man. Despite your attraction to me, you're still in love with your wife. I don't want to lose you as a friend, Jamie. I promise this won't happen again."

She left the bed and disappeared into the bathroom. When she returned, she was wearing a white fluffy robe. She draped a towel around his bare shoulders and helped him to his feet. "Come on. I'll make you some eggs, and we'll figure out how to get your wife back."

"What's the point? Lizbet made it clear she doesn't want me back. What I need is help in figuring out how to get over her."

Jamie was toying with his scrambled eggs, and Kirstin was sitting across from him sipping wine when Annie called. He snatched up the phone. "What's up?"

"Lizbet's sick. We're at the hospital. You should come."

The panic in Annie's tone got Jamie's attention, and he

dropped his fork onto his plate with a clatter. "*The hospital?* What's wrong with her?"

"I don't know, Jamie. The doctor's in with her now. We were meeting in my office about a job. She just fell out of her chair onto the floor and started puking everywhere. She was too sick for us to move her. We had to call an ambulance."

"An ambulance? Do you think it's her appendix?"

"No," Annie said. "I think it's probably female related."

"That makes sense," Jamie said. "I saw her earlier in Charleston. She was clearly in pain, and she told me she was having a bad period. What hospital?"

"MUSC. I'll drop you a pin."

"Great. I'm on my way. Call me if you get an update." Jamie ended the call and looked across the table at Kirstin. "I assume you heard all that. I need to get on the road," he said, getting up from the table.

Kirstin slid off the banquet bench to her feet. "Are you sober enough to drive?"

"I only had two tequila shots. I'm fine."

"You weren't fine a few minutes ago when you mistakenly called me Lizbet while we were making out."

"Well, I'm fine now," he snapped, picking his wet shirt off the floor and ringing it out in the sink.

Kirstin snatched the shirt from him. "You can't wear that. I have a marina logo shirt around here somewhere. It's way too big for me. I'll find it and make you some coffee for the road while you take a cold shower." Taking him by the arm, she walked him to the bathroom. "The towel on the rack is clean."

The cold water revived Jamie, and the marina shirt fit fine, even though hot pink wasn't his color.

Kirstin handed him a large cup of coffee and walked him to the door. "Drive carefully."

He kissed her cheek. "I'm sorry about tonight. Are we still friends?"

"You're a great guy, Jamie Sweeney. I'm honored to be your friend." She patted his cheek. "Go! Be with your wife. I'll be praying for her."

The rain had slowed to a drizzle as he hurried to his truck. The traffic was light because of the storm, and he made it to Charleston in record time.

In the emergency room, Annie and Heidi were seated side by side with dazed expressions and hands clasped while Brooke gnawed at her fingernails and paced the floor.

Jamie embraced Brooke's petite frame. "Any word about her condition?"

"Not yet." Brooke buried her face in his chest. "I'm scared to death, Jamie," she cried. "I've lost both my parents. I can't lose my sister too."

"Shh!" He tightened his grip on her. "We're not gonna lose her. She's strong. She'll pull through."

An attractive redhead in blue scrubs and a white doctor's coat called for the Horne family. Brooke separated from Jamie and ran toward her, calling, "Over here!"

"Why did you give them her maiden name?" Jamie asked Annie as they walked toward the doctor.

Annie shrugged. "Lizbet did that. She was worried about medical insurance. I'm not sure what she was thinking. She was out of her mind in pain."

Jamie extended his hand to the doctor. "I'm Jamie Sweeney, Lizbet's husband. What can you tell us about my wife?"

The doctor shook his hand. "It's nice to finally meet you, Jamie. I'm Louise Carroll, Lizbet's gynecologist. She's been under my care for the past several months. I'm sure you have a lot of questions, and I'll be happy to answer them all later, but for now, I'm pressed for time. The endometriosis has worsened since I last saw her a month ago. In addition, she has a ruptured ovarian cyst, which has resulted in an ovarian torsion, meaning the ovary has twisted."

Jamie's knees went weak. "Is that serious?"

"In your wife's case, it's not only serious, it's dangerous. Lizbet is being prepped for an emergency hysterectomy. We'll be able to perform the procedure laparoscopically, which will allow for a much easier recovery."

When Jamie and Brooke bombarded the doctor with questions, she held up her hand to silence them. "Your questions will have to wait. Time is of the essence," she said and hurried away down the hall.

"I wonder what *time is of the essence* means," Annie whispered to Jamie.

Jamie gave his head a grave shake. "I don't want to think about it." He sniffed. "What's that smell?" He looked down at the blue scrub top she was wearing. "And why are you dressed like a nurse?"

"Lizbet projectile vomited all over me. A kind nurse took pity on me and found this in the supply room. I threw my blouse in the trash can."

He lifted a stiff strand of her hair. "I think there's puke in your hair."

"Whatever. That's the least of our worries."

A nurse with dark hair pulled back in a ponytail approached them. "Dr. Carroll asked me to direct you to the surgical waiting room on the second floor. You'll be more comfortable there while you wait." She pointed to a bank of elevators behind them. "Take the elevator to the second floor. Go right off the elevator and the waiting room is on the left. You can't miss it."

"Thank you," Jamie said to the nurse's back as she walked away.

"I'll go to the cafeteria for coffee." Heidi volunteered. "I'll meet y'all upstairs in a few."

Jamie, Annie, and Brooke migrated to the empty waiting room on the second floor and sat down on a sofa with Jamie in the middle.

Brooke dabbed at her wet eyes with a tissue. "Poor Lizbet, going through all this alone. I wish she'd told me sooner."

Jamie's head jerked back in surprise. "You mean you didn't know?"

Brooke shook her head. "Not until a couple of weeks ago. You know how private she is about everything."

Jamie turned to Annie. "Did Liz mention anything about her problem to you?"

"She told me she was having some health issues, but when I pressed her, she refused to talk about it."

Brooke sniffled into a wadded tissue. "She also internalizes everything. She blamed herself for being infertile and tried to fix the problem herself."

Jamie experienced a pang of guilt. He'd accused his wife of always thinking about *me* and not *we*. By nature, Lizbet wasn't a team player. But that didn't make her a bad person. It made her independent, strong, and determined—the qualities he wanted in a life partner. With his help, she could work on being a team player. If she would only give him another chance.

"She's filing for divorce," Jamie blurted.

Annie didn't appear surprised, but Brooke came off the sofa. "You've gotta be kidding me? When did she decide that?"

"She met with an attorney this morning." He nudged Annie's arm. "So you knew?"

Annie nodded. "She blurted it right before she collapsed onto the floor. She was trying to convince us she was staying in Charleston, so we'd hire her full-time."

Brooke sat back down beside him. "Lizbet's confused about a lot of things right now, Jamie. Losing Dad didn't help."

Jamie hung his head. "I should've tried harder to get through to her."

The threesome sat in silence until Heidi returned with two thermoses of coffee and a picnic basket filled with food—warm ham biscuits, fried chicken drumettes, and single-serve-size containers of potato salad.

"Did you get all this from the cafeteria?" Jamie teased, knowing full well no hospital cafeteria provided such delicious offerings.

Heidi's cheeks flushed pink. "The cafeteria was closed, and I refuse to drink coffee from a vending machine, so I ran back to the shop. Besides, it's dinnertime, and we might be here for a while."

"Well, thank you for your trouble," Jamie said, popping a whole ham biscuit into his mouth.

Several hours passed before Dr. Carroll returned. "Everything went well. They are taking Lizbet to recovery now," she said, pulling up a chair.

"Was this avoidable, Doctor?" Jamie asked.

"If you're asking if we could've avoided a hysterectomy, the answer is unequivocally *no*. Your wife's endometriosis was too severe. The pain she's been suffering these past few months is unimaginable."

"Really?" Brooke moved to the edge of her seat. "And she never once complained. No wonder she spent so much time in her room."

The doctor gave a knowing nod. "I've gotten to know Lizbet pretty well over the past few months. You might say, I took a special interest in her. She's an unusual young woman, and I've grown quite fond of her."

"Do you know why my wife has been using her maiden name when her medical insurance is under my name?" Jamie asked.

"She refused to use your medical insurance. I'm not entirely sure why. She seemed determined to figure out her problem on her own. She insisted on paying for everything out of pocket, including the procedure to retrieve her eggs."

Jamie's mouth fell open. "The procedure to do what?"

"I convinced her to freeze some eggs in the event she decided to use a surrogate to carry her baby down the road." Dr. Carroll smiled softly. "She's not a fan of that idea. She's worried the surrogate will become too attached to the baby. I have a hunch she'll come around once she realizes the law is on her side."

Hope stirred inside of Jamie. Maybe he and Lizbet would get their biological child after all. "She is technically still my wife. The expenses from today, including the ambulance and surgery, should be filed with my insurance company."

"I agree, and I'll have someone talk to you about that." The doctor stood to go. "We'll keep her overnight for observation. She should be able to go home in the morning, provided she's feeling okay."

"Can I see her now?" Jamie asked.

"A nurse will be out to get you soon." She wagged a finger at Jamie. "But don't upset her. She's been through quite an ordeal today."

"You have my word. Thank you, Dr. Carroll, for taking such good care of her."

When he offered his hand, the doctor pulled him in for a hug and whispered in his ear, "Don't give up on her. Anyone can see how much she loves you. You just need to get her head to listen to her heart."

Jamie nodded, not trusting his voice.

After the doctor left the room, the women all began talking at once, discussing how they could help Lizbet through her recovery. If Jamie had his way about it, he would be the one nursing her back to health.

A tsunami of relief overcame him when a nurse summoned him to the recovery room. "Your wife is asking for you," she said and showed him the way.

Lizbet was so frail looking in the big hospital bed with tubes and monitors everywhere. But she was smiling at him like she hadn't smiled at him in a very long time.

Jamie eased into bed beside Lizbet. "Am I hurting you?"

She shook her head. "I'm so sorry, Jamie. I was so wrong about so many things." Tears streamed down her face. "Earlier, when they rushed me to the hospital in an ambulance, I was sure I was dying. I thought I might never see you again, and I realized how foolish I've been. I don't want a divorce. I don't wanna go through life without you. I wanna be *we* not *me*. Can we please try again? I promise not to blow it this time."

"I'm equally to blame, sweetheart. I suspected something was wrong, and yet I let you walk out of our house during a hurricane. My wounded pride clouded my judgment. If only I'd tried harder, we could've worked things out sooner."

"I was being stubborn. I had to learn things the hard way." She touched her finger to his lips. "There will be plenty of time for talking later. For now, just hold me. Will you stay with me tonight?"

Gingerly, he took her into his arms. "Are you kidding me? I'm never letting you out of my sight again."

twenty-eight
sean

The puppy cried all throughout the hectic lunch rush on Thursday. Sean let Emmie out of the kennel several times, but he couldn't get her to calm down no matter what he tried. Around two o'clock, when the whining intensified into full-on howling, Carla demanded, "Do something with that dog! I can't take the noise anymore!"

"Fine." Removing the puppy from the crate, Sean put on her leash and took her for a long walk on the wooded trails beside the marina. He stopped in to speak to Winnie on his way back up to the restaurant.

She came out from behind the counter and knelt down to pet Emmie. "Come here, Emmie girl." The puppy bounded over to her, and when Emmie leaped into her lap, Winnie fell backward onto her bottom. "What're you two up to?" she asked as the puppy covered her face in licks.

"Emmie is a handful today. She's turning out to be high maintenance. What was I thinking? I should've picked the chill dog." Sean heard a whimper and glanced over the counter to see Willa in her crate on the floor. "What's Willa doing here?"

"I'm keeping her for Cooper while he paints."

Hiding his irritation at his brother's blossoming romance with Winnie was getting more difficult by the day. "That was nice of you. I'm sure Cooper appreciates it."

"I'm happy to do the same for you anytime." She went behind the counter and let Willa out of the crate. The two dogs began chasing each other around the store. "Why don't you leave Emmie here now? The two can wear each other out."

"That would be awesome. They certainly seem happy. But are you sure?"

"Positive. We've been slow today. If business picks up, I'll throw them back in the crate."

Sean glanced at the wall clock. "It hardly seems worth the trouble when you get off in thirty minutes."

"I'm staying overtime to help Lester out. He has a dentist appointment. I'll be here until at least five o'clock."

"That's perfect. I'm going home around four thirty to spend some time with Josh. I can take both dogs with me then." Sean smiled at her. "I really appreciate this, Winnie. Carla can't stand the whining. She's about to go postal on me."

Winnie rolled her eyes. "What's her problem?"

Sean shrugged. "She's a cat person, I guess."

Carla didn't appear to notice when he returned to the restaurant without the puppy. Sean had never met anyone so self-absorbed. She'd hardly paid any attention to her son all week. Sean had been driving him to his new summer program in the morning and to swimming lessons in the afternoons. Macy had offered, but Sean didn't mind. Josh needed as many adults in his life as he could get, and the kid seemed to appreciate their special one-on-one time.

Sean was unprepared for the scene he encountered when he returned to the marina store to pick up the dogs at four. Winnie and a scraggly deadbeat had pistols aimed at each other. The deadbeat's friend bounced from foot to foot, looking nervously at the door as though planning his escape.

"Come on, Roscoe," the friend said. "Let's get outta here! I told you this was a bad idea."

"Shut up, Buck! We'll leave as soon as this little bitch gives us all the money in her cash drawer."

Sean's eyes darted around, locating Emmie first in the crate behind the counter and then Cooper clinging to his puppy while cowering in the far corner of the store.

"Call the police, Sean," Winnie ordered with her eyes and gun trained on Roscoe.

"Don't you dare," warned Roscoe. "Or I'll put a bullet in her pretty little head."

"Do it, Sean!" Winnie said in a tone that told him she meant business.

Sean pulled his phone out of his pocket and tapped in 9-1-1. "I'd like to report an armed robbery at the Inlet View Marina store. Please! Send help quick!"

Winnie shifted her body slightly to the right and fired her weapon. When Roscoe recoiled from the bullet whizzing past his head, he lost control of his gun and it clattered to the ground. Sean dove on top of the gun and rolled onto his back with the gun pointed up at Roscoe. "Move, and you're a dead man!"

At the sound of approaching sirens, Winnie said, "I've got this, Sean. You go let the police in."

Sean, with his gun still aimed at Roscoe, got to his feet and walked backward to the front of the store. He opened the door and hollered to the police. "In here! Hurry!"

A small army of armed police officers filed into the store and handcuffed Roscoe and Buck.

Sean rushed to his brother's side. Cooper's face was slick with perspiration and his body trembled as though in shock. "Are you okay, bro? You don't look good."

"No, I'm not okay. Take this dog. I don't want her." Cooper shoved the dog at Sean and bolted for the door.

Sean tried to go after him, but a police officer grabbed him by the arm, preventing him from exiting the store. "Not so fast, buddy."

"Dude! I'll come right back. I just need to check on my brother."

"Sorry," the officer said. "I can't let you go until you've given your statement. Was your brother involved in this incident?"

Winnie shook her head. "No! Leave him alone. He was an innocent bystander."

"Fine," the officer conceded. "But we may need to talk to him later."

Sean and Winnie gave their statements to the police and answered a barrage of questions. He was a nervous wreck, ready to jump out of his skin by the time the police finished with them thirty minutes later.

Sean turned to Winnie and said, "Where's Jamie? He should be here."

"He's in Charleston with his wife. She had a medical emergency of some sort."

Sean frowned. "I hope she's okay."

"She will be. According to Jamie, the two are getting back together."

Sean punched the air. "That's the first good news I've heard all day."

Winnie walked him to the door. "Go! You need to check on Cooper."

"But I'm worried about you. Are you sure you're okay?"

"I'm fine. I'll keep the dogs with me. When Lester gets here at five, I'll bring them out to Moss Creek."

"You're the best." As he kissed her cheek, Sean got a whiff of her shampoo. Despite the drama she'd just been through, she still smelled fresh, like an early June day at the beach.

Sean raced out to Moss Creek where he found Cooper wrapped in heavy blankets on the sofa in the guesthouse. Despite the perspiration covering his face, he was shivering so hard his teeth chattered.

"Cooper! Bro! You're a mess. I think you're having a nervous breakdown. Come on. I'm driving you to the hospital." Sean tried to pull him off the sofa, but Cooper shoved him away.

"Leave me alone, Sean."

"Not happening." He removed his phone from his pocket. "If you won't come willingly, I'm calling an ambulance."

Cooper rubbed at his eyes. "I'm not a mental case. I'm just dealing with some stuff."

Sean sat down next to him on the sofa. "What *stuff*? This has gone on long enough. Either talk to me, or I'm calling Mom and Dad."

"No! Don't call them. Please!"

"Then tell me why you want to give your puppy back. I thought you loved Willa."

"I do love Willa," Cooper cried. "I freaked out at the marina store. I was terrified she'd get shot. And I couldn't stand to lose someone else I love."

Now we're getting somewhere, Sean thought. "Who have you lost, Cooper?"

Cooper's face contorted in pain. "My roommate. The only best friend I've ever had, other than you."

Goose bumps broke out on Sean's skin. "What happened to Charles?"

His brother fell back against the cushions, pulling the blankets tighter around him. "I was seeing this girl. Her name was Maggie. She was seriously hot, and we really connected. At least I thought we did."

His brother's use of past tense made Sean's blood run cold. Did Maggie die too? "You never mentioned her."

"It was too soon. We hadn't been dating that long." Cooper picked at a loose thread on the blanket. "I came home one night from playing pickup basketball to find them both dead in my apartment, Maggie with her face in a pile of cocaine and Charles with a gunshot wound to his head."

"Oh my god," Sean said, clamping his hand over his mouth. "What happened to them?"

"She died from fentanyl poisoning. The police think Charles felt guilty for giving her the drugs and took his own life. Charles knew I didn't approve of him using drugs. I didn't think Maggie was into that kind of thing."

"Do you think Charles and Maggie were hooking up behind your back?"

Cooper shook his head. "Charles is the one who introduced me to Maggie. They were childhood friends. I didn't know what to do, Sean. I should've stayed, should've flown to Nashville, where they're from, for their funerals. But I couldn't stay in that apartment, so I drove home the next day."

"In the middle of a hurricane." Sean sat back on the sofa, shoulder to shoulder with his brother. "Everything makes sense now. This explains your sudden interest in art."

"Painting is the only thing that makes me feel anything except sorrow and rage."

"I'm so sorry. I wish you'd told me sooner. You've been through some serious stuff, man. You need someone to help you cope with it all. You need Big Mo."

"I realized that today. I'm so ashamed of what happened earlier at the store. The sight of those guns rendered me completely useless. That guy could've killed Winnie, and I did nothing to try to stop him."

"I think you're suffering from PTSD," Sean said.

Cooper shrugged. "Maybe. You know me, Sean. The old me would've gone after him. I've never been afraid of anyone in my life. I'm the one who fought our fights when we were growing up. But I froze when Winnie asked me to call the police. I couldn't even do that."

Sean squeezed his shoulder. "Tell Winnie what happened.

She'll understand. You'll jeopardize your relationship if you keep something like this from her."

Cooper's head shot up. "What relationship?"

"Aren't you and Winnie together?"

Cooper looked at Sean as though he'd lost his mind. "Um, no. I'm too much of a mess right now to even think about women. Besides, you're the one she likes."

Sean's heart skipped a beat. "Me? Are you sure about that?"

"Duh. You have to be blind not to see how she looks at you."

Sean heard a car door outside, and he got up to go to the window. "She's here now with the dogs. Please tell me you're not giving your puppy back."

"No way! I love her too much. Aside from you, Willa and Josh are the only bright spots in my day. Although, I would definitely be on board with getting rid of Carla. She's turned our home into a hostile environment."

"I admit, Cooper, I totally misjudged Carla. But you and I have made a positive impact on Josh. He's not the angry little boy he was when they moved here a few weeks ago. If I kick her out, he'll be the one who suffers."

"I get that. For the kid's sake, I can tolerate Carla a little while longer." Cooper, with his blankets wrapped around him like robes, joined him at the window, and they watched Winnie chase the puppies around. "She's been through an ordeal today. She needs your strong shoulder to cry on."

"Ha. Winnie doesn't strike me as the type who cries."

"She's truly amazing."

Sean chuckled. "Can you believe she fired a shot at that deadbeat like that? I was sure she'd killed him. Jamie told me she's an excellent shot, but I didn't believe him." He felt his brother's eyes on him. "What?"

"You should see your face right now. You've got it bad for her too." Cooper nudged him. "Go talk to her."

Sean turned to face his brother. "I will. After we work out a plan to get you some help. I'm here for you, Coop, but you need professional help too."

"I've already texted Big Mo. I'm meeting with him first thing in the morning."

"Way to go!" Sean offered him a high five. "Will you promise to talk to me from now on? Keeping your feelings inside isn't healthy."

"I promise." Cooper pulled Sean in for a hug, blankets and all.

They stood together at the window a minute longer, each lost in his own thought. They'd made an enormous breakthrough today. Sean suspected his brother had a long recovery ahead of him, but if anyone could get through to Cooper, it was Big Mo.

Sean exited the guesthouse and crossed the driveway to the yard. Winnie was sitting in the grass while Emmie and Willa crawled all over her legs. She looked up at him, her face wet with tears. "I'm sorry. I'm having a delayed reaction."

"And understandably so." Taking her by the hands, he pulled Winnie to her feet and into his arms. "What you did today takes real guts. I can honestly say you're the most intriguing woman I've ever met."

twenty-nine
lizbet

Lizbet woke on Friday morning to find Jamie propped on one elbow staring at her. She smiled up at him. "What're you thinking about?"

"What a beautiful life we're going to have together."

She ran a thumb over his lips. "*We*. I love the sound of our new favorite word on your lips."

"I can't wait to get you home to our bed."

"I want that too. But I'm worried about Brooke. I'm partially responsible for her breakup with Sawyer. I hate to leave her here alone, especially now that Dad is gone."

"It will be an adjustment for both of you." He fingered a lock of hair off her forehead. "Are you hungry? I can fix you whatever you would like and bring it to you on a tray. Can I tempt you with an omelet or waffles? How about blueberry pancakes?"

"Scrambled eggs will be fine. But I can't stay in this bed another minute." She eased out from beneath the covers, letting her legs fall over the side of the bed. "We'll have breakfast together in the kitchen and then go for a short walk in the neighborhood. Maybe I can make it down to the seawall."

Jamie sat up in bed. "Isn't it too soon for you to exercise?"

"Nope. Dr. Carroll says I can do whatever I want, within reason, as long as I listen to my body. And my body is telling me to go outside and get some fresh air." Lizbet slowly stood up and slipped on her robe. "We'll stroll. We won't walk fast."

"If you say so," Jamie said, pulling on a pair of running shorts over his boxers.

Downstairs in the kitchen, they found Brooke hunched over her computer, an untouched cup of coffee on the table beside her. She slammed the computer shut and looked up at them with a guilty smile on her lips.

"What're you up to?" Lizbet asked in a suspicious tone.

"Oh, nothing. Just checking my emails." Brooke sipped her coffee, made a funny face, and got up to reheat it in the microwave. "So when are you moving back to Prospect?"

"Why? Are you trying to get rid of me?"

"Not at all. I love having you here. But it's the obvious next step." The microwave dinged, and she removed her coffee. "I'm thinking about getting a roommate."

Lizbet raised an eyebrow. "A new love interest so soon?"

"Not hardly." Brooke leaned back against the counter. "Polly is moving back to town."

"Polly Buckingham, your best friend from high school?"

Brooke nodded as she sipped her coffee. "She's the only Polly I know."

"Is she gay?"

"No. She has a boyfriend in Charleston. She met him when she was here over Christmas. She does something in finance in New York. She's moving back to be near him."

"Good for Polly." Lizbet gripped the table as she lowered herself into a chair. "You won't give Polly my room, will you?"

"Of course not. She can have the guest room. Your room will always be here for when you come to visit." Brooke grinned, mischief tugging at her lips. "Maybe next time, don't stay for seven months."

Jamie chuckled. "Please, no!" He opened the refrigerator and removed a carton of eggs. "Would you like some breakfast, Brooke?"

"No thanks. I just ate some yogurt." Brooke returned to the table. "But I have something important I want to talk to you both about." She ran a hand across her computer. "I've been doing some research, and if you decide to have a baby, I'd very much like to be your surrogate."

Jamie spun around with an egg in one hand. "Are you serious?"

Lizbet stared at her with mouth wide open. "Do you have any idea what you're offering?"

"Yes, and yes." Opening her laptop, Brooke clicked the tabs on her internet browser, revealing a dozen websites about surrogacy. "I've thought of little else since Dr. Carroll mentioned it the other night. I'm all in. But I'd like to have my own child soon, so let's get on with the process."

"Heck, yeah!" Jamie said and cracked the egg into a bowl.

With tears in her eyes, Lizbet reached for her sister's hand. "I don't know how to thank you. This is the greatest gift you could ever give us."

Brooke got up from the table and hooked an arm around her sister's neck with her mouth close to her ear. "I will be honored to carry your baby inside of me." She straightened. "Now, I need to get to work. I'll see you tonight." She grabbed her computer and purse and headed out the back door.

Lizbet could hardly believe this turn of events. She'd previously refused to consider surrogacy as an option. The risk of the surrogate refusing to give up her baby after birth seemed too risky. Asking Brooke to make such a sacrifice never entered her mind. That her sister would undergo this physically and emotionally exhausting process touched her deeply.

Finishing at the stove, Jamie joined her at the table with two plates of eggs and sausage. "Brooke's offer is incredibly generous.

Not many women would go through nine months of pregnancy to carry someone else's baby."

"I was just thinking that. But we're sisters. I would do the same for her." As the words left her mouth, Lizbet realized they were true. If the situation were reversed, she would have Brooke's baby in a heartbeat.

Jamie dug into his eggs. "I don't wanna wait, do you?"

"No." Lizbet giggled. "Brooke might change her mind."

While they ate, they talked excitedly about the possibility of having their own child. "The sooner we get you home and settled, the sooner we can make plans for the baby," Jamie said.

"There's something I need to talk to you about first." Her phone vibrated the table with the call she'd been waiting for, and she snatched it up before Jamie could identify the caller.

"Hello," she said, and went into the family room to speak with Chef Weber in private.

She was flattered when Weber offered her the job with a higher than previously mentioned salary. "You're overqualified, but with your lack of experience in a work environment such as ours, in the long run, I feel you'll benefit from starting out as line chef."

"Thank you for the opportunity, Chef Weber. If you don't mind, I'd like a couple of days to consider your offer. I encountered a medical crisis since we last spoke. Everything is fine, but I'd like to clear my head before making this commitment."

Weber hesitated, and she feared he would rescind his offer. She was relieved when he said, "Of course. I'm glad it wasn't anything too serious. Get some rest and call me on Monday."

Her mind raced as she ended the call. She imagined commuting from Prospect to Charleston for work. Thirty minutes each way of driving time, plus traffic, would take a considerable chunk out of her day. And being on the road alone late at night would get old fast. She could do it for a while, but certainly not after the baby came.

She returned to the kitchen and sat down across from her husband.

"Who was that?" Jamie asked, with a hint of suspicion in his voice.

"The head chef at Husk. He offered me a job as a line cook. That's what I was getting ready to talk to you about. Working in an upscale restaurant has always been my dream. I lost sight of that when I married you and moved to Prospect." She held up her hands, palms facing him. "No regrets. But I need this challenge. I won't be satisfied if I don't pursue my career."

Jamie frowned. "Are you considering taking the Husk job?"

"I did. For about a second. I quickly realized the commute would put a damper on my quality of life."

"What about your dream of opening your own restaurant? I'm sure Kirstin still has space. Maybe even the primo location at the tip of the complex nearest the marina."

Lizbet reached for a paper napkin and began tearing it into pieces. "I don't have any money, Jamie. I spent all my savings on fertility specialists. Dad was basically broke. We inherited this house and his condo. But I can't ask Brooke to sell her home. We'll get rid of the condo once it goes through probate, but I don't know when that will be, and if that will be enough to start a restaurant."

Jamie placed his hand over hers, stopping her from shredding the napkin. "Don't worry about the money, sweetheart. We'll figure it out. My business ventures are doing extremely well."

"What will I do in the meantime, while Creekside Village is being built?"

"Mom will hire you at Sam Sweeney's. The wine shop is thriving, and she's crazy busy."

Lizbet shook her head. "That's more of the same as what I've been doing. And it won't give me the experience I need to run my own restaurant. Maybe Sean would let me work as a line cook at his new restaurant."

"I'm sure he would." Jamie's phone rang. He answered and said to the person on the other end of the line, "I'll call you right back."

A chill crawled across Lizbet's skin. "Was that Kirstin?"

Jamie's cheeks turned pink. "I told you there's nothing going on between Kirstin and me," he said, even though that was not what she asked.

If something happened between Jamie and Kirstin, Lizbet didn't want to know about it. She had only herself to blame for running away from her marriage. "Then who was it?"

"Sean. He and I were planning a cookout for our moms' birthdays tomorrow. I didn't know what to tell him, and I wanted to talk to you first. I don't want to leave you alone in Charleston, and I doubt you'll feel up to going to a party."

"You can't bail on your mom's birthday. And Sean is counting on you. I'll be fine here. It'll give Brooke and me some time alone. Our last night together. You can come pick me up on Sunday and take me home."

Jamie appeared surprised. "Do you think you'll be ready so soon?"

"It's not soon enough. I can hardly wait to get back to our lives." Lizbet got to her feet and offered her hand. "Now, how about that stroll? I could use some fresh air. And we have a future to plan."

thirty
sean

Saturday dawned with clear blue skies, warm temperatures, and relatively low humidity. On the way out in the boat, Cooper drove while Winnie, Josh, and Sean sat in the front with the puppies.

"Why do they call it Ghost Island?" Josh asked Sean. "Is it haunted?"

"Maybe," Sean said with a mischievous glint in his blue eyes. "There's a rundown shack on the island. When Cooper and I were little, we were convinced a ghost lived in the shack."

Concern crossed Josh's face. "I'm afraid of ghosts."

Sean mussed the boy's curls. "Don't worry. I doubt seriously a ghost lives on the island. But if there is one, I'm certain it's a friendly ghost."

"Okay," Josh said, placated.

Winnie smiled at Sean over the top of the boy's head, and he winked back at her. Sean had yet to kiss her, but their attraction was strong, and it was only a matter of time.

When they reached the island, they anchored the boat and took the puppies over to the beach. Emmie and Willa had a big time, chasing each other around and digging deep holes in the sand. When Cooper waded into the water, the puppies followed and took off swimming.

"Isn't their natural love of the water and innate ability to swim amazing?" Winnie said, watching from the shore.

Josh scrunched up his nose. "What does *innate* mean?"

"It means they automatically know how to do it without being taught," Winnie explained.

Josh pouted. "I wish I was born knowing how to swim."

Sean nudged him. "Hey! Your instructor says your swimming has improved this week." He felt sorry for the kid. Swimming hadn't come easy for him, but he was slowly getting the hang of it.

His chin quivered. "But I'll never be as good as the other kids."

Winnie bent down to look him in the eye. "That's all right, kiddo. You may be better than they are at something else. Like fishing or playing ball. When it comes to swimming, safety is the most important thing. You only need to swim well enough, so you won't drown if you fall in."

"I can already do that. Watch!" he said and sprinted into the water.

Winnie and Sean joined them, and the foursome floated and paddled around until the puppies tired out.

"I don't wanna go home yet," Josh whined on the way back to the house. He was seated beside Cooper, helping him steer the boat.

"I know, buddy," Cooper said in a sympathetic tone. "But we're having a party tonight, and Sean and I need to get ready."

"Can I come to the party?" Josh asked in a hopeful voice.

"I'm afraid not. This party's just for grown-ups. You'd be bored."

"No, I won't. Puh-lease!"

Sean turned in his seat so he could see Josh. "How about if you come down after dinner for cake?"

Josh thought about it a minute. "I guess that'd be all right."

Sean leaned into Winnie. "You're a grown-up. Would you like to come to the cookout tonight?"

Winnie nonchalantly hunched a shoulder. "Depends. What's the occasion?"

"Our mom and her two sisters all have birthdays this week. We celebrate together whenever we can. It's been a few years since we've had a party."

"I appreciate the invitation, but I don't want to intrude on your family's event."

"Puh-lease," Sean said, giving her his best puppy-dog expression. "My parents don't get down here very often, and I'd really like for them to meet you."

She peered at him over the top of her sunglasses. "Aren't you getting a little head of yourself? You haven't even kissed me yet. What if there's no chemistry?"

Sean puffed out his chest. "We have chemistry. Powerful chemistry. My goal is to kiss you before the day is over. I would prefer to wait until later tonight in the moonlight at the end of the dock. But if you refuse to come to the party, I'll have to kiss you now with Cooper and Josh watching us."

Winnie smiled. "Fine. I'll come to the party as the dog sitter. That way, if we don't have chemistry, you'll be off the hook with your parents."

———

Winnie volunteered to return early to help get ready for the party. While Cooper and Sean cleaned the soft-shell crabs and prepared the beef tenderloin for the grill, Winnie set the serving table under the carport and the dining table on the patio with linens and flowers.

All the parents arrived at once, the moms leading the parade down the driveway and their spouses following dutifully behind, their arms ladened with birthday gifts and food items. Bitsy brought up the rear, strolling along while texting on her phone.

When Sean introduced Winnie to his family, they welcomed her with warm hugs and kisses.

As predicted, Sean's mom turned up her nose at the puppies. "Where did they come from? You better not let them pee in my house."

Sean laughed. "It's not your house anymore, remember? Or did you have a change of heart about giving it to Cooper and me?"

Jackie kissed the air beside his cheek. "No change of heart. Regardless, do not let those little buggers pee on the rugs."

His father's face lit up when he saw the puppies. "Finally! We have dogs in the family again," he said, dropping his armload on the table and going to visit with Emmie and Willa.

Sean whispered to Winnie, "You can tell who the dog lover in the family is?"

"Is she a cat person?" Winnie asked.

"She doesn't like animals of any kind. She especially hated the pet snake Cooper brought home in the sixth grade. Fortunately for us, Dad always took our side."

After everyone had settled in with a cold beverage, the cousins busied themselves with preparing dinner. Cooper tended the grill while Jamie helped Sean fry soft-shell crabs in the outdoor kitchen.

"Tell me about Lizbet," Sean said as they coated the first batch of crabs in flour. "I heard she had a medical crisis."

"She had an emergency hysterectomy on Wednesday. Poor thing, her female organs were all messed up."

Sean shook his head. "I'm sorry, man. That's a bummer. Isn't she young for something like that to happen?"

"It's not unheard of. She had endometriosis. Usually, it's curable. In Lizbet's case, it wasn't. She moved back to Charleston because she was afraid to tell me the truth. She got it in her stubborn head to try to fix her problem herself."

Sean dropped two crabs into the sizzling grease. "Does this mean you can't have children?"

"Not in the conventional way. But Lizbet had the foresight to freeze some of her eggs, and her sister, Brooke, has offered to be our surrogate."

"That's awesome, Jamie. Congratulations." When the crabs were golden brown, Sean removed them from the grease and placed them on a cooling rack to drain. "I have to admit, I was skeptical. I thought for sure your marriage was over. Did anything happen between you and Kirstin? It's none of my business. You don't have to tell me if you don't want to."

"I don't mind telling you. I trust you not to say anything. The truth is, I came close to sleeping with her." Jamie wiped imaginary sweat off his forehead with the back of his hand. "In my defense, I was in a bad place, and Kirstin came on to me pretty hard. Still, I should've tried harder to resist her."

Sean dropped two more crabs into the grease. "Are you going to tell Lizbet about Kirstin?"

"That's a good question, and I've thought about it long and hard. But what's the point of upsetting her when nothing happened? I love my wife, and I'm thrilled we're back together."

"You don't think Kirstin would ever spill the beans to Lizbet, do you?" Sean asked. "After all, they're gonna be living in the same town."

Jamie shook his head. "Kirstin's not like that. She's a good person, and she's been a sympathetic friend to me throughout all this. One day, she's gonna make some guy damn lucky."

"Has Lizbet moved back in with you yet?" Sean asked, dropping the last two crabs into the grease.

"I'm going to Charleston to get her tomorrow. She's always dreamed of having her own restaurant. She's hoping for a spot at Creekside Village. In the meantime, she's looking for a job, if you have any openings for line cooks."

Sean looked over at his cousin. "A line cook? She's too quali-
fied for that."

"Not really. She lacks experience in a fast-paced environment."

"If she's looking for experience, I can certainly accommodate
her. I'd be thrilled to have someone with her talent in my kitchen.
Tell her to come talk to me when she's feeling better," Sean said,
adding the last crabs to the platter and sliding them into the oven
to keep warm.

After Jamie sliced the tenderloin, the husbands brought out
their side dishes and called the women to dinner. They migrated
to the dining table on the patio, sitting with the younger genera-
tion at one end of the table and their parents at the other. They'd
no sooner said the blessing when Carla drove up.

She got out of her car and sauntered over to the table. "Hello,
everyone! I'm Carla. Happy birthday, ladies. Please, don't stop
eating on my account. I'm sorry I'm late. I got held up at work.
Let me run inside and change. I'll be right back."

"Who is that woman? And why is she living in my house?"
Jackie asked, her gaze shifting from Sean to Cooper and back to
Sean.

Sean was too stunned to speak. *What was Carla doing here? And
who was running his restaurant?*

Sitting next to him, Cooper dug his elbow into Sean's side.
"You gave us the house, Mom. I assume that means we can ask
whomever we want to live here."

"That's very true, Cooper. But I didn't mean for you to turn
the place into a brothel."

Sean found his voice. "Carla is my chef, Mom. She got kicked
out of her apartment, and I invited her to live here until she
straightens out her life."

The back door banged open and Josh ran out. "Mama says I
can come to the party."

Winnie got up from the table and chased after the boy,
scooping him up before he could wake the sleeping puppies.

Jackie's hazel eyes flashed with anger. "Mama? Is that child living here too? What on earth is going on, Sean?"

Faith set down her fork and wiped her mouth. "You should be proud of your son, Jackie. The woman fell on hard times, and Sean has been helping her work through her problems." Faith looked from Jackie to Sean. "Macy tells me you and Cooper have been spending a lot of time with Josh. She gives you two credit for his improved behavior."

Jackie pressed her lips thin as she turned toward her sister. "I'm so confused. Who is Macy? And how do you know about this Carla person and her problems?"

"Macy is one of my residents," Faith explained. "She's now the boy's live-in nanny."

Jackie nearly came out of her chair. "So you have *three* strangers living in my house?"

Sean shot daggers at his mom. "I didn't realize *your* house came with strings attached."

Sean's dad placed a hand on Jackie's arm. "Calm down, sweetheart. We gave the boys the house. They can do with it as they please."

Carla emerged from inside wearing a seductive black cocktail dress that was completely inappropriate for the occasion. Grabbing a plate, she began helping herself to the food on the serving table.

Sean jumped up and marched across the patio. Snatching the plate from her, he said, "What do you think you're doing? And who is in charge at the restaurant?"

Carla waved away his concern. "Don't worry about it, Sean. Everything is fine."

He ignored the eyes, watching them from the table. "Everything is *not* fine. It's Saturday night. Last time I checked our reservation status, we were sold out."

"Not anymore," Carla said with a maniacal laugh that sent a chill down Sean's spine.

Josh ran up to them, shoving Sean out of the way to get to his mom. "I want cake, Mama! Cut me some cake," he said in the demanding voice Sean hadn't heard from him in weeks.

"It's not time to cut the cake, Josh," Sean said, his tone firm. "We haven't sung happy birthday yet."

Josh stomped his foot. "Give me cake now!"

Carla picked up a knife and sunk it into the cake, cutting a wedge big enough for three little boys and dumping it onto a plate.

Macy appeared on the scene, taking the plate away from her. "I'm sorry, Miss Carla, but he can't have that much sugar this time of night."

Carla looked from the knife in her hand to the nanny with an evil glint in her eyes that made Sean worried she might stab Macy. Sean was grateful when Eli and Faith rushed to his aid.

"May I have the knife, please?" Eli asked, his hand extended to Carla.

Carla tightened her grip on the knife. "Why? Are you going to arrest me for cutting the cake?"

Faith gently pried the knife from Carla's hand. "What's wrong, Carla? You don't seem like yourself tonight," she said, displaying a compassionate manner and tone of voice that came from all her years of experience with emotionally disturbed residents.

"I'll tell you what's wrong," Carla said, her chin set in defiance. "I asked for tonight off to spend with my son. And Sean refused to give it to me."

Sean's temple throbbed as his blood pressure rose. "Because I'd already planned this party. I gave you yesterday off. But you didn't spend any time with your son, did you? You slept all day instead."

Faith shot Sean a warning look. "Your anger isn't helping anything."

Jamie tapped Sean on the shoulder. "I hate to interrupt, but

Randy just called me. He's trying to get in touch with you. He says it's urgent."

Removing his phone from his back pocket, Sean saw he had ten missed calls from Randy. He scrolled down the string of texts from his head bartender. "I can't believe this," he said, waving the phone at Carla. "Why would you close the restaurant when we had a packed house?"

Carla folded her arms over her chest. "That's what you get for not giving me the night off."

"You're fired, Carla. And I want you out of my house right now," Sean shouted, his face crimson red.

"No! I like it here! You can't make us leave, you big bully," Josh screamed, kicking Sean hard in the shin.

Eli grabbed the kid with both hands and lifted him off the ground. "Easy there, buddy. We don't solve our problems by hitting and kicking."

Josh squirmed and kicked some more, but he couldn't free himself from Eli's grip.

Eli held the boy higher, so he could look him in the eye. "I'll let you down, as long as you promise to behave. Can you do that?"

Josh bobbed his head. "Yes, sir."

"Thatta boy," Eli said and lowered the kid to the ground.

Josh ran over to his mother, hiding behind her and wrapping his arms around her legs.

"Let's see if we can work this situation out," Eli said. "Anybody have any ideas?"

Macy's hand shot up. "I do. But I'd like to discuss it with Faith first."

"By all means," Eli said with a nod of approval.

Macy pulled Faith away, and the two women talked in hushed tones with their heads pressed together.

Sensing a presence behind him, Sean turned to see Winnie standing nearby. Placing a hand on his back, she offered him a smile of encouragement. He smiled back, pulling her into a half hug.

Faith and Macy rejoined the group. "Carla, I'd like for you and Josh to stay with us at Lovie's until you get your feet back on the ground. I rarely allow children at the home, but in this case, I'm willing to make an exception."

Carla gave her head a vigorous shake. "No way. I'm not going to that nuthouse."

"Do you have a better solution?" Eli asked.

Carla's chin fell to her chest. "No."

Faith placed a hand on Carla's shoulder. "Lovie's is not a nuthouse, although we've had our share of emotionally unbalanced residents over the years. We help people with all kinds of issues. Ones who've been abused or have addictions or have no place to live. I believe you currently fall into the latter category."

Carla looked up with pleading in her emerald eyes. "Sean? Will you please give me another chance?"

His heart went out to her, but she was on a collision course with disaster, and he refused to let her take his restaurant down with her. "I'm sorry, Carla. You and I have reached the end of our journey. The Humphrey Estate where Lovie's Home is located is amazing. There's so much for Josh to do there. Give it a chance. If you don't like it, you can figure something else out."

Macy opened the back door. "Come on, Carla. I'll help you pack."

Carla and Josh, their faces long, trailed behind her.

Sean hugged his aunt. "Thank you, Faith. She desperately needs your help."

"I agree. That young woman has emotional problems. But don't worry. I'll get to the bottom of it." She turned toward the house. "I'll go help them pack."

Sean offered Eli a fist bump. "Thanks for defusing the situation."

Eli smiled. "I'm just glad I was here," he said and reclaimed his seat at the table beside Sam.

Jamie gave Sean's shoulder a squeeze. "If you wanna reopen the restaurant tonight, I'm happy to give you a hand."

"I thought about it. But there's no way I can get my employees to come back this late." Sean scrolled back through the text messages from Randy. "Apparently, Carla used a plumbing problem as an excuse to close early. At least she came up with a legitimate reason, even if it was fabricated. Randy put a sign on the restaurant's door, explaining the situation and stating that we will reopen at the usual time on Sunday morning." Sean stuffed his phone into his pocket. "I have a bigger problem. How will I survive without a chef?"

"I know a chef looking for work."

Sean palmed his forehead. "Lizbet! Of course! She'd be perfect. Do you think she'll be interested?"

Jamie beamed. "I'm certain of it."

"There is a bright spot in all this. Now, let's see what we can do about salvaging this party," Sean said, and returned with the others to the table.

Sean was disappointed things ended this way for Carla. She was so young, and he hoped she would get the help she needed. But he was relieved to have her out of this house. And his restaurant.

After dinner, everyone pitched in to clean up. They were doing dishes when Carla came down the stairs, a suitcase in one hand and dragging a crying Josh with the other.

When Josh saw Winnie, he jerked his hand free and ran over to her. She picked him up. "Wanna help cut the cake for real this time?"

With top teeth clamped on bottom lip, Josh bobbed his head.

"We brought the cake inside. It's right over here on the table," Winnie said and walked Josh over to the cake.

Sean lit the candles, and for the sake of the child, the others sang "Happy Birthday" to the three Sweeney sisters.

When it was time to go, the men helped Carla load her things in her car.

Sean gave Josh a hug goodbye. "You're gonna enjoy living at Lovie's Home. And it's not far from here. You can come fishing with me, and I'll bring the dogs to see you."

Josh squeezed his arms tight around Sean's neck. "But I'm gonna miss you."

"And I'm gonna miss you too, buddy." Sean buckled Josh into his car seat and closed the door.

Jackie pulled Sean aside. "I owe you an apology for what I said earlier. I'm proud of you for helping that young woman and her son."

Sean watched Carla's taillights retreat down the driveway. "What she lacks in parenting skills she makes up for in culinary talent. I hope Faith has better luck than me getting through to her."

Jackie looked over at Cooper, who was in the backyard with Winnie and the puppies. "Despite everything that happened tonight, Cooper seems better."

Sean nodded. "Poor guy finally came clean about what's been bothering him. His roommate, Charles, and the girl Cooper had been seeing both died a pretty gruesome death."

His mom appeared horrified. "What on earth?"

"Cooper should be the one to tell you when he's ready. At least he's getting help. He had his first session with Big Mo yesterday."

"You're a wonderful son and brother, Sean Hart." Jackie pinched his chin. "And Winnie is precious. Which one of you is dating her?"

"Neither of us. Although I hope to be soon," Sean said with a sheepish grin.

Sean stood with Cooper and Winnie in the driveway, waving as the parents drove away.

"Well, that was some shindig," Cooper said. "Next year, I suggest we let them throw the party for themselves."

"Everything would've been fine if not for Carla."

"I'll miss the kid, but I'm grateful she's out of our lives." Cooper scooped up both puppies and started toward the guesthouse with one under each arm.

"Hey! Where are you going?" Sean called out to his twin.

"To bed," Cooper said over his shoulder. "Willa and Emmie are having a sleepover. Emmie's daddy needs a night off."

After Cooper had gone inside, Winnie gestured at the sky. "Look! The moon is out. It's only a half moon, but it's plenty bright."

Sean offered her an arm. "Fancy a stroll on the dock."

"I thought you'd never ask." Winnie took his arm, and as they walked across the lawn, she said, "You'll be busy these next few weeks, working as both manager and head chef. I'm happy to share puppy duties with you."

He smiled over at her. "I accept. That's awfully generous of you."

"I have an ulterior motive. It gives me a chance to see Emmie's daddy."

"You never need an excuse to see me." When they reached the end of the dock, Sean turned toward her. "You're full of surprises, Winnie Randolph."

"Good surprises, I hope."

"The best." He brushed a lock of white-blonde hair out of her face. "I've wanted to kiss you for a very long time."

She smiled up at him. "Then what're you waiting for?"

He placed his hands on her hips and pulled her toward him. When their lips met, a sense of peace, unlike anything he'd experienced with his twin, overcame him. This was a feeling of belonging. Winnie was his person and the Lowcountry was their place.

I hope you've enjoyed *After the Storm*. Please consider leaving an honest review at your favorite online retailers and book-related social media platforms. Recommendations from like-minded readers helps other readers discover new authors and titles. If you're looking for more action-packed Southern family drama, you might consider my latest stand alone novel, *Scent of Magnolia* or my newest series. Virginia Vineyards is a family saga featuring the Love family with characters you'll love and those you'll love to hate.

also by ashley farley

Only One Life

Home for Wounded Hearts

Nell and Lady

Sweet Tea Tuesdays

Saving Ben

Sweeney Sisters Series

Saturdays at Sweeney's

Tangle of Strings

Boots and Bedlam

Lowcountry Stranger

Her Sister's Shoes

Magnolia Series

Beyond the Garden

Magnolia Nights

Scottie's Adventures

Breaking the Story

Merry Mary

acknowledgments

I'm forgiver indebted to the many people who help bring a project to fruition. My editor, Pat Peters. My cover designer, the hardworking folks at Damonza.com. My beta readers: Alison Fauls, Anne Wolters, Laura Glenn, Jan Klein, Lisa Hudson, Lori Walton, Kathy Sinclair, Jenelle Rodenbaugh, Rachel Story, Jennie Trovinger, and Amy Connolley. Last, but certainly not list, are my select group of advanced readers who are diligent about sharing their advanced reviews prior to releases.

I'm blessed to have many supportive people in my life who offer the encouragement I need to continue my pursuit of writing. Love and thanks to my family—my mother, Joanne; my husband, Ted; and my amazing children, Cameron and Ned.

Most of all, I'm grateful to my wonderful readers for their love of women's fiction. I love hearing from you. Feel free to shoot me an email at ashleyhfarley@gmail.com or stop by my website at ashleyfarley.com for more information about my characters and upcoming releases. Don't forget to sign up for my newsletter. Your subscription will grant you exclusive content, sneak previews, and special giveaways.

about the author

Ashley Farley writes books about women for women. Her characters are mothers, daughters, sisters, and wives facing real-life issues. Her bestselling Sweeney Sisters series has touched the lives of many.

Ashley is a wife and mother of two young adult children. While she's lived in Richmond, Virginia, for the past twenty-one years, a piece of her heart remains in the salty marshes of the South Carolina Lowcountry, where she still calls home. Through the eyes of her characters, she captures the moss-draped trees, delectable cuisine, and kindhearted folk with lazy drawls that make the area so unique.

Ashley loves to hear from her readers. Visit Ashley's website @ ashleyfarley.com

Get free exclusive content by signing up for her newsletter @ ashleyfarley.com/newsletter-signup/

Made in the USA
Middletown, DE
24 September 2023

39132948R20146